A face in the snow?

There was nobody there.

Yet she sat up. She let the duvet fall back and climbed out of bed again. She stood there in the darkness, staring toward the window. Again, she had the sense of someone watching her. Again logic screamed at her: no one could be hiding behind the curtains and no one could be outside the windowpane.

She took a step toward the window. She had to sort this out once and for all. She'd check the window and reassure herself, and then she'd go back to bed and sleep. She wouldn't even bother putting the light on again. There was nothing to be afraid of. She'd just check the window and go to sleep.

She walked toward it. The curtains were still. No draft was pushing through. She reminded herself that the window was closed—another good reason for her to be reassured. No one could have climbed in from outside. All was well.

She drew closer to the curtains. For some reason they seemed brighter than usual. It had to be the brightness of the snow pushing through from outside. She could think of no other cause.

She stared at the strange, almost glowing curtains. Before her eyes they were burning with a chilly fire. Even as she watched, shivering in the night, a snowy blaze was moving up them like an icy conflagration. She reached out a hand and touched them. The warmth of the velvet was still there. She relaxed and pulled back the curtains—and saw to her horror a face staring in at her.

OTHER BOOKS YOU MAY ENJOY

Dreamland	Sarah Dessen
The Ghost Belonged to Me	Richard Peck
Jerk, California	Jonathan Friesen
Just Listen	Sarah Dessen
Love Sick	Jake Coburn
Things Not Seen	Andrew Clements
Wait for Me	An Na
Walk of the Spirits	Richie Tankersley Cusick
Where I Want to Be	Adele Griffin

FROZEN FIRE

TIM BOWLER

speak

An Imprint of Penguin Group (USA) Inc.

SPEAK
Published by the Penguin Group
Penguin Group (USA) Inc., 345 Hudson Street, New York, New York 10014, U.S.A.
Penguin Group (Canada), 90 Eglinton Avenue East, Suite 700, Toronto, Ontario, Canada M4P 2Y3
(a division of Pearson Penguin Canada Inc.)
Penguin Books Ltd, 80 Strand, London WC2R 0RL, England
Penguin Ireland, 25 St Stephen's Green, Dublin 2, Ireland (a division of Penguin Books Ltd)
Penguin Group (Australia), 250 Camberwell Road, Camberwell, Victoria 3124, Australia
(a division of Pearson Australia Group Pty Ltd)
Penguin Books India Pvt Ltd, 11 Community Centre, Panchsheel Park, New Delhi - 110 017, India
Penguin Group (NZ), 67 Apollo Drive, Rosedale, North Shore 0632, New Zealand
(a division of Pearson New Zealand Ltd)
Penguin Books (South Africa) (Pty) Ltd, 24 Sturdee Avenue, Rosebank, Johannesburg 2196, South Africa

Registered Offices: Penguin Books Ltd, 80 Strand, London WC2R 0RL, England

Originally published in the United Kingdom by Oxford University Press.
First published in the United States of America by Philomel Books,
a division of Penguin Young Readers Group, 2008
Published by Speak, an imprint of Penguin Group (USA) Inc., 2010

1 3 5 7 9 10 8 6 4 2

Copyright © Tim Bowler, 2006
All rights reserved

THE LIBRARY OF CONGRESS HAS CATALOGED THE PHILOMEL BOOKS EDITION AS FOLLOWS:
Bowler, Tim.
Frozen fire / Tim Bowler.
p. cm.
Summary: Fifteen-year-old Dusty gets a mysterious call from a boy who says he is going to kill himself,
and while he claims to have called her randomly, he seems to know her intimately.
ISBN 978-0-399-25053-8 (hc)
[1. Supernatural—Fiction.]
I. Title
PZ7.B6786Fr 2008
[Fic]—dc22 2007043880

Speak ISBN 978-0-14-241465-1

Printed in the United States of America

Designed by Richard Amari.
Text set in Adobe Jenson.

Except in the United States of America, this book is sold subject to the condition that
it shall not, by way of trade or otherwise, be lent, re-sold, hired out, or otherwise
circulated without the publisher's prior consent in any form of binding or cover
other than that in which it is published and without a similar condition
including this condition being imposed on the subsequent purchaser.

The publisher does not have any control over and does not assume
any responsibility for author or third-party Web sites or their content.

For Rachel with love

FROZEN FIRE

1

I'M DYING," said the voice. Dusty clutched the phone. She had no idea who this was. A boy about her age, by the sound of him—fifteen, sixteen, maybe a bit older.

"Is anyone there?" he muttered.

His voice was slurred and angry. She glanced at the clock. Twenty minutes to midnight. She'd answered the phone at once, thinking it would be Dad ringing to say he'd been held up by the snow but was on his way back. The last thing she needed was this boy.

"Is anyone there?" he said.

"Who are you?"

The only answer was a cough.

"And how did you get this number?" she said. "We're unlisted."

Another cough but this time the boy answered.

"I just made up a number and dialed it."

She frowned. This had to be a prank. Friday night, New Year's Day. Some boy messing around with his mates. If she listened hard enough, she'd probably catch the sound of them sniggering in the background. But all she heard was the labored breathing of the boy at the other end of the line.

She thought of Dad out in Beckdale on his date. She'd been enjoying having the house to herself for the first time in weeks, especially after all the trouble it had taken her to get him to go, but now she wished he'd hurry back.

"Didn't you hear me?" mumbled the boy. "I said I'm dying."

She knew that wasn't true. If the boy was really in danger, he'd hardly make up a number and ring it. He'd dial 911.

"You need to ring the police," she said.

"I don't want the police."

"An ambulance, then."

"I don't want an ambulance."

"But you said you're dying."

"I am dying."

"Then you need to ring—"

"I don't need to ring anyone. I said I'm dying. I didn't say I wanted to live."

There was a silence between them that she didn't like.

"I've taken an overdose," he said.

She bit her lip, unsure what to believe and reluctant to be drawn any further into this boy's world. Maybe he was telling the truth, maybe he wasn't, but whatever his problem was, it was for other people to sort out.

"I can't help you," she said.

"You can. I just want a friendly voice. Someone to talk to as I slip away."

"You need the Samaritans, not me. I'll get you their number."

"I don't need the Samaritans," said the boy. "I need you."

This was getting a little creepy. All her instincts told her to put the phone down. But before she could do so, he spoke again.

"How old are you?"

"None of your business."

"You sound about fifteen."

She said nothing. His guess was spot on and probably a fluke but it was still disconcerting.

"What's your name?" he said.

"That's none of your business either."

"Why won't you tell me?"

"Because it's none of your business."

"My name's Josh."

She squeezed the phone tight. Josh—of all the names to choose. The boy spoke again.

"I said my name's Josh."

"No, it's not," she said.

She prayed she was right. She didn't want this boy to be called Josh. She didn't want anyone to be called Josh. There was a silence, then the boy said, "You're right. It's not. But you can call me Josh if you want to. I mean, just to give me a name."

"I'm not interested in giving you a name."

"Suit yourself." The boy paused. "What about you?"

"What about me?"

"Give me a name I can call you. Any name you like."

Again her instincts screamed at her to put down the phone. This stuff about names made her feel vulnerable, especially all the talk about Josh. She started to wonder about this boy. He was a complete stranger to her, yet he had picked out the one name that mattered most to her. Maybe it was coincidence. Or maybe he knew who she was and where she lived and was watching the house right now.

She ran her eye over the living room. It was the only room in the house with the light on at the moment, and if he was watching from the lane, he'd almost certainly be staring at this very window. She was glad that the curtains were drawn across.

But it didn't make her feel safer. Thorn Cottage was a lonely house all on its own. With the outskirts of Beckdale some miles to the right and nothing to the left save Stonewell Park and Kilbury Moor, and beyond that the lake and fells, there was little protection here.

"I'm not watching the window," said the boy suddenly. "I don't know who you are and I don't know where you live."

She shivered. It didn't seem possible that he could speak the very fears that were running through her mind. But the next thing he said only deepened her unease.

"Daisy?"

She stiffened.

"What did you say?"

"Daisy. I'm trying to guess your name. It's something like Daisy."

She swallowed hard and again found herself glancing toward the curtains.

"I told you," said the boy. "I'm not watching the window."

She was scared now, really scared. This boy seemed to know everything she was doing and thinking. She tried to be rational. Maybe it wasn't so difficult for him. He must know a young girl would be frightened in a situation like this, must realize she'd be wondering where he was and probably glancing at the window. But the name Josh, and then . . . Daisy. It wasn't right but it was close.

"I'm not called Daisy," she said slowly.

"I didn't think you were," said the boy. "But it's something like that, isn't it?"

She didn't answer.

"What about . . . Tomboy?" he said. "Can I call you that? I know it's kind of weird but you sound like a bit of a tomboy."

She gasped. Now it was serious. Only one person in the world had ever called her Tomboy. It was his own pet name for her, and too unusual to guess. This boy knew who she was—and much more.

"Where's Josh?" she said coldly.

"I don't know anyone called Josh."

"Where is he? Tell me."

"I don't know anyone called Josh."

"You said the name Josh a moment ago."

"I made it up. Like I made up your phone number. And the name Daisy."

"And Tomboy."

"Yes. Why? Has someone else called you that?"

She didn't answer, didn't want to answer. Suspicions were now racing through her. This boy knew far more than he was admitting. She had to find out what she could. A face drifted into her mind: a face she hadn't seen for two years but that haunted her every day, sometimes every hour, sometimes—it seemed—every moment of her life.

"Where's Josh?" she said again.

"I told you. I don't know anyone called Josh."

"You do."

"I don't."

"But you just said—"

"I don't care what I just said." The boy sounded tetchy now. "I don't have any control over that, OK? I just say what I say. I don't know where it comes from."

She tried to calm herself. She knew she had to be careful. She had to probe this boy, but if she pushed him too hard, he'd hang up.

"Tell me why you chose those names," she said.

But the boy didn't answer. Instead she heard him retching at the other end of the line. She listened, her mind riddled with confusion. If this was acting, it was pretty convincing. The retching went on for what seemed a long time, then suddenly stopped.

"Are you all right?" she said.

No response, just another sound, which she recognized at once.

"You're drinking something," she said. "What is it?"

"Cheap plonk," came the answer. "Tastes like crap."

She heard a rattling noise.

"What's that?" she said.

"What's what?"

"That sound."

"This?"

And she heard the rattling sound again.

"Yeah."

"Bottle of pills," said the boy. "Think I might have gobbed up the last lot. So I'm taking some more. If I can get the top off the bloody thing."

"Listen—" she started.

But the boy wasn't listening. He seemed to have put the phone down and was struggling to open the bottle of pills. She could hear him swearing to himself as he wrenched at the top. Then she heard a grunt of satisfaction, followed by more silence.

"Are you there?" she said.

No answer.

She tried to think. She was convinced now that the boy had taken an overdose and was even at this moment swallowing more pills. But she was also convinced that he knew something about Josh. She had to glean what she could from him. But first she had to save his life, and that meant finding out where he was. With any luck he'd tell her. It was just possible this wasn't a genuine suicide attempt but a cry for help.

"Are you there?" she said again.

Still no answer. She took the phone over to the window and peeped around the side of the curtain. Everything glistened with snow. The latest fall had deepened the previous layer by several inches and it was now a thick blanket, still virgin by the look of it.

She glanced to the right. No sign of Dad coming back from Beckdale, just the deserted lane stretching away into the night. She looked to the left and followed the same lane past the broad turning area outside the house and on to where it narrowed again and finally ended at the gate into Stonewell Park. No one there either, just whiteness, stillness, emptiness. Suddenly she heard the boy's voice again.

"Daisy?"

"Don't call me Daisy," she said. "It's not my name, OK? Now listen—"

"No, you listen." The boy's voice had changed again. It was more drowsy, yet somehow more forceful too. "Listen ... I haven't got much time ... and there's something I want to say. I ... I'm sorry if I scared you."

"You didn't scare me."

"I did." The boy's breathing sounded heavier. "I did scare you. I know I did. And I know I'm ... I'm still scaring you."

She said nothing, but she knew he was right.

"So I'm sorry," he said. "That's all I wanted to say. I'm really sorry ... whoever you are ..."

"My name's Dusty."

She hated telling him. It made her feel more vulnerable than ever. But she knew she had to take the risk. She had to bond with this boy somehow if she was to find out where he was.

"It's a nice name," he said.

"What's yours?"

"Doesn't matter."

"You must have a name."

"I've got lots of names."

"So give me one of them. I've given you mine."

"Too late for names now."

There was a finality in the boy's voice that chilled her.

"Dusty?" he said.

"Yes?"

"Thanks for not putting the phone down."

"Tell me where Josh is."

"I don't know anyone called Josh."

"You do. I know you do."

The boy didn't answer.

"Where is he?" she said.

The boy spoke, but not to answer her question.

"These trees," he murmured. "They're so beautiful."

"Tell me about Josh. Please tell me about Josh."

"So beautiful . . ." The boy's voice was fading. "I'm glad I'm dying near trees."

"Where are you?"

"Doesn't matter."

"Why won't you tell me?"

"Because you'll send an ambulance and they might save my life."

She shuddered. This was no cry for help. This was a farewell.

"Tell me where you are," she urged him.

"Don't want to."

"Please."

"Don't want to."

"But you'll die."

"Want to die. Must die."

"But why?"

"Too much pain. Just want it to go away."

Dusty's mind was racing. There had to be some way of working out where the boy was. He'd talked about trees, but that didn't help much. There were loads of places with trees around here, and there was no guarantee the boy was even phoning from the Beckdale area. He hadn't said he was. He could be anywhere in the country, even abroad. Suddenly she caught a new sound at the other end of the phone.

Something metallic, a kind of groan, like some heavy object moving on a hinge, maybe a pub sign swinging in the wind or an iron gate opening. She listened. There was something familiar about it. It was a sound she'd heard recently. She was sure of it.

The sound ceased. She listened for it again, her thoughts running fast. The boy was somewhere near. She sensed it. If she could just hear the sound again, she might be able to place it. But instead she heard the boy's voice—distant, detached, as though speaking to himself. Yet his words were for her and they shook her to the core.

"I'm sorry, little Dusty. Good-bye, little Dusty."

She trembled. It wasn't possible. Not those very words. She remembered the last time she had heard them. She remembered gripping the phone with all her might, just as she was doing now. She remembered standing by her bedroom window watching the sun setting over Kilbury Moor. She remembered the feeling of a day dissolving and a life dissolving with it. She remembered the small words in her ear, the last her brother had ever spoken to her.

"Good-bye, little Dusty," said the boy.

"Josh!" she screamed.

No answer came back. All she heard before the line went dead was the strange metallic groan again. But this time recollection came flooding with it. Stonewell Park . . . the trees . . . the children's playground . . . the swing! She'd sat on it only yesterday when she went walking in the park with Dad. She'd even swung on it—and heard that very noise. If she was right, the boy was barely two hundred yards away.

She threw down the phone, rushed into the hall and pulled on her coat and boots. Then she picked up her mobile, switched it on and scribbled a note to Dad on the pad.

Gone out. Mobile on. Back soon. Dusty x

She prayed she'd be back before he read it. He'd be apoplectic if he saw this. But there was nothing she could do about it now. She had to find this boy, and quickly. She stepped out of the house, slammed the front door behind her and raced off into the night.

2

THE COLD AIR POUNDED her face as she ran. She breathed hard. She was still trembling but she knew she had to go through with this. If the boy had overdosed—and she was sure he had—then he shouldn't be dangerous, and even if he was, she had to take the risk.

Josh would. He wouldn't hesitate, no matter what the danger. She'd always admired him for that, and now that there was a chance to find out what had happened to him, she owed it to him to show the same courage. Suddenly she noticed something she had missed from the window.

She stopped and looked down. The snow in the lane was not virgin after all. A single trail of footprints stretched away toward the gate into Stonewell Park. She glanced to the right and saw that they came from far down the lane. Someone had walked this way from Beckdale since the last snowfall.

There was no certainty that these were the boy's prints but she was sure he was near and she didn't imagine anyone else would be out in this remote spot on such a night. She forced herself to run on down the lane toward the park, tracking the other prints as she did so; and as she ran, she heard Dad's voice inside her head, screaming at her to stop, go back to the house, ring the police, ring him.

But she pushed these thoughts aside. This was about Josh. It wasn't a matter for the police, not yet anyway. It was a matter for the family. Dad wasn't here, and even if she rang his mobile, he wouldn't be able to get to the boy as quickly as she could. So it was up to her and probably that was best. Whatever he might insist to the contrary, he was hardly the man for a crisis.

The gate into Stonewell Park was locked as she expected. She stared down at the prints to see whether the other person had climbed over the gate or used the gap in the fence.

The gap in the fence: no surprise. She squeezed through as well and ran on after the footprints. They led down the slope toward the little wood at the bottom of the park. There was no sign of anyone here but something about the stillness of the place made her slow down.

Something felt wrong and it wasn't just the silence. The very light seemed strange. Maybe it was the combination of darkness and snow but there was a cold, unearthly brightness hanging in the air. The trees below her glistened with what seemed an unnatural brilliance and far away in the distance the peak of Raven's Fell glowed in the night.

She put on speed, anxious to get this over with. At least she should be alone here, apart from the boy. There wouldn't be any druggies or tramps using the park in weather like this. She caught the sound of an engine back in the lane and stopped.

It wasn't Dad's.

She looked back toward the gate. There were only two reasons why someone would drive to the end of the lane: to visit Thorn Cottage or visit Stonewell Park. Neither was likely at this time of night. But there was an even eerier thing.

There were no headlights.

She was too low down to see the vehicle from here but she knew from long experience of driving home with Dad that a car would throw its beam well over the gate into the park.

There was no beam of any kind, nor was this a car. She could tell that from the sound of the engine. This was something bigger. She stared uneasily toward the gate, and as she did so, the sound of the engine ceased.

Silence fell once more.

She ran on down the slope toward the trees. She had to search for the boy, whatever was going on in the lane. Yet even as she tracked the other prints across the snow, she found herself glancing over her shoulder. She was feeling more and more vulnerable now: scared of what lay in front of her, scared of what lay behind.

She thought of Josh again. He would carry on. She knew he would.

She pushed on. Here were the trees before her. The path through the middle of the wood was buried under snow but she knew where it was from the sycamore to her right and the horse chestnut to her left. The footprints led straight through the wood along the invisible path. She checked over her shoulder again.

No figures at the gate but then, as she watched, a slight movement close to the gap in the fence—something dark, something low to the ground. She hurried into the trees. There was no decision to be made now. She couldn't go back. She had to go on, and there was no time to waste.

She started to run again, her eyes fixed on the footprints in the snow. Her fingers and toes were growing colder and a breeze was picking up. The lighter branches of the trees moved in the night. There was no sign of the boy but she didn't expect that. If she'd guessed right, he'd be on the other side of the wood, probably sprawled in the snow.

She ran on. The ground was more slippery here. The trees had kept some of the snow out but it was still deep enough for her to see the footprints stretching ahead of her. She hurried on, her mind on the boy, on Josh, on the person or the people behind her. She reached the clearing at the center of the wood and stopped by the old fountain.

No water gurgled from it now. It was thick with snow. She stared down at the ugly stone cherub and saw an empty wine bottle beside it; next to that, on its side, a small bottle of pills, also empty. Beyond the fountain the footprints continued through the wood. She set off after them, then caught a new sound in the night.

The growl of a dog.

It was some way behind her and coming from the direction of the lane. She heard another growl, then a bark: a harsh, savage bark that terrified her. More growls, more barks. She clenched her fists. There was more than one dog. She was certain of it.

She raced on through the wood, following the footprints as before. Still no sign of the boy. She could hear voices behind her now: a man's voice, rough and hard, then two more, both male but younger. She caught no words but didn't need to. Everything about those voices said danger.

She tore, slipping and stumbling, through the trees. She no longer knew what to do. She had to find the boy but she had to stay safe too. Part of her shrieked just to run. Forget the boy. She thought of the other gate out of the park, the one just down from the children's playground. She could climb over that and escape down the track to Knowle or maybe cut along the bridleway that ran around the edge of the moor. She could even cross onto the moor itself. But whatever she did, she'd have to be quick.

The growls and barks seemed closer now. She glanced over her shoulder but saw only trees and snow. She ran on through the wood and at last burst out the other side. The football and rugby fields stretched away in shimmering whiteness but here, close at hand, was the children's playground with its roundabout, sandpit, playhouse, and climbing frame, all brilliant with snow. The swing over to the right moved in the breeze with its dull, familiar squeak. The prints she had been following led straight to it.

She ran after them and saw, at the base of the swing, another wine bottle and a second bottle of pills, both empty. It looked as though the boy had sat on the swing as he drank the wine and swallowed the last lot of pills. He'd probably even swung a little and the sound had reached her that way. But he hadn't stayed here.

She could see more footprints heading from the swing toward the other gate. He appeared to have made his way out of the park and headed for the bridleway and moor. She bit her lip. At least the decision about what to do had been made for her. She had to climb over the gate just as the boy had done and run for her life. She pelted toward it, then suddenly stopped.

The prints ceased about ten feet from the gate and went nowhere. There was a flattened patch where he seemed to have lain down in the snow, then nothing. No footprints heading from the spot. The boy had simply disappeared.

But there was no time to ponder this further. She had to escape before those other people appeared, and she would have to climb this gate. There were no gaps in the fence to squeeze through. She heard the dogs barking again behind her. They were close to the edge of the trees now. She could tell from the sound.

She ran up to the gate and started to climb, her eyes darting back toward the wood. Still no sign of the people or their dogs. She reached the top of the gate and eased herself over. From inside the park came a cacophony of barks. Still clinging to the top of the gate, she stared back toward the trees.

Three figures were standing there. It was hard to see them clearly, even with the brightness of the night, but she saw enough. A stocky man with a ponytail and two powerful boys about eighteen or nineteen. The man had two fighting pit bulls on a double lead. He and the boys were staring toward the swing and didn't appear to have noticed her, but the dogs were tugging at their leads, straining toward her.

She slid down the other side of the gate, hoping no one would catch the movement. But the man gave a shout at once.

"There!"

And he pointed straight at her.

The next moment the dogs were racing toward her. They covered the ground in seconds and she was barely three feet back from the gate before they thrust their noses through the gaps in the ironwork, snapping as they struggled to reach her. Behind them she saw the man and the two boys charging across the snow toward her.

She hared off down the bridleway that cut around the edge of the moor. The gate soon disappeared from view around the bend in the path and she ran on, trying to make up her mind which way to go. The dogs wouldn't be able to squeeze through the gate or the fence and the man would probably have to stay with them but the boys could easily climb over and give chase.

She still wasn't sure which way to go. The moor was not the answer. It was a wild spot, and though she might be able to get away, it only led toward Raven's Fell and the bleak northern rim of Mirkwell Lake. She'd be heading away from home into frozen desolation.

The bridleway was little better. No one lived near it apart from old Silas, and he didn't count. The old man's hovel was half a mile down but it might as well be in Antarctica for all the help he'd ever give anyone. He'd be huddled by his stove, and if he wasn't already asleep, he'd pretend to be if she called for assistance.

Best to cut left down the track to Knowle. It was only a hamlet with three houses but somebody must be awake—if she could just get there. She ran on down the bridleway, breathing hard in the chilly air. Ahead of her she saw the start of the track. She glanced over her shoulder for signs of pursuit.

None yet. She ran on, keeping her eyes on the slippery ground. A fall now could be serious and the bridleway was treacherous. She turned left down the track to Knowle, then, as she'd expected, she heard the sounds she'd been dreading.

Panting breaths behind her. They sounded heavy in the night but she knew it was the boys, and they weren't far behind. She glanced over her shoulder.

No sign of them yet. She ran on down the track, her mind filling with panic. It had been a mistake coming this way. The track was as lonely as the bridleway. It eventually joined the Beckdale Road but the houses in Knowle wouldn't be for a mile yet, nor was there any concealment here. Stone walls on either side and fields beyond, and her prints in the snow to tell the boys exactly which way she was going.

She glanced again over her shoulder and this time, to her horror, saw two figures racing after her. They were barely fifty yards behind. She put on speed, desperate to shake them off. The snow was starting to fall again in light clear flakes. They blurred her eyes as she pushed herself on. She could hear the boys still breathing hard, but she was breathing harder now. She was tired and frightened and she knew from the sounds behind that they were steadily catching up.

She forced herself on, desperate to get away, her eyes peering through the falling snow for some sign of help, but all she saw was the empty track stretching away into the night. Somehow she kept ahead of the boys and for several minutes the distance between them stayed the same. Then, at last, just as she was starting to flag, she caught sight of headlamps ahead. She waved her arms and shouted as she ran toward them.

"Help! Help! Help!"

She looked quickly over her shoulder. The boys had drawn closer and were barely twenty yards behind, but they were slowing down, and now stopping altogether. They had obviously seen the car and were keeping back. The headlamps grew brighter. Now she could see the vehicle. It wasn't a car. It was a white van—and the engine sounded horribly familiar.

She stopped, fear flooding back.

The van pulled up a short way from her. The lights went off. The engine cut out. The man with the ponytail climbed out, walked to the back of the van and reappeared a moment later with the two pit bulls on the leash.

She stared in terror. He started to walk toward her with the dogs. She looked quickly around and saw the boys moving forward again. She thrust about in her pocket, searching for the mobile, then drew her hand out again. There was no time for that. They were too close. She had to escape and there was only one way left. She ran to the wall and started to scramble up it. As she did so, she heard a command from the man.

"Go!"

And saw the dogs tearing toward her.

3

SHE HEARD THE SNARLS as they raced forward. She twisted her
body in a desperate attempt to swing her legs clear of the ground
and scramble over the wall. But it was no use. She could see the
dark shapes shooting toward her and she knew she wouldn't make
it in time. She braced herself for the snapping teeth, then someone
caught her around the legs and pulled her back from the wall.

It was one of the boys. He was holding her to him and had turned
around with his back to the dogs. The other boy had run forward
too and was shouting at the man.

"Dad! Call 'em back! Call 'em back!"

The man gave a whistle.

To Dusty's relief, the animals ground to a halt, but with obvious
reluctance. They stood there, barely five feet away, growling.

"Sit!" shouted the boy holding her.

The dogs did not sit.

"Make 'em sit, Dad!"

"Sit!" bellowed the man.

And the two dogs sat.

"Let me go," said Dusty to the boy.

The boy simply dropped her to the ground. She rolled over in
the snow and stood up. Both dogs jumped up at once and started
toward her.

"Sit!" roared the man. "Stay!"

The dogs obeyed at once, but with the same reluctance. Dusty
started to edge away down the track.

"And you stay too!" shouted the man, watching her.

She stopped. There was no point trying to escape. The man would set the dogs on her at once. It was clear he was the only person who could control them. She cowered back against the wall, her eyes on the three figures closing around her.

The man was thickset and powerful with a black mustache and heavy features. His face housed an anger that she sensed was never far from the surface. The boys looked older than she'd thought before: probably about twenty or twenty-one. They were strong and athletic: one dark-haired and the spitting image of his father, the other—the one who had pulled her back from the wall—a fair-haired boy, taller, more slender, but clearly just as dangerous.

The man had reached the dogs and was standing between them. Keeping his eyes on her, he reached down and fastened the leads on them again. They bristled but did not try to break away. Their eyes too were on her. She tried to think, tried to stay calm. It wasn't clear what these people wanted. It might not be what she dreaded.

The man straightened up, his gaze still fixed on her. The snow was falling more thickly now. Dusty stared back at him. His eyes flickered toward the boys. She glanced quickly at them and saw an unspoken message pass between the three of them. What it was she didn't know but she didn't like it. The man spoke.

"Where is he?"

The voice was rough and deep, the accent not from around here. She couldn't place it. She answered as boldly as she could.

"Where's who?"

"Don't play games with me."

"I don't know who you mean."

Another exchange of glances between the man and his sons. She sensed the boys edging forward and glanced anxiously at the man. He gave a barely perceptible shake of the head and the boys stopped.

The snow continued to fall.

The man stepped closer. She eyed the dogs. They were yanking at the leash, straining toward her. The man's chunky fist was tight around the leads and she prayed he wouldn't let go. He stopped where the dogs were just out of range of her and spoke again.

"You walked with him down the lane to Stonewell Park. You stopped at the gate. You went through the gap in the fence with him. We could see both sets of prints in the snow, yours and his. They were child's play to read. You walked with him down the slope and into the trees and past the fountain to the playground. You even went over to the swing together. Then the two of you headed for the other gate."

She trembled. Only now did she understand how deeply she had implicated herself in this. The man went on.

"So what happened next? You climbed over the gate. Where did the boy go?"

She tried to organize her thoughts. Clearly they hadn't seen the boy's prints petering away into nothing. They'd seen her climbing the gate and had just rushed after her.

"You walked together to the gate," said the man, "and we saw you climbing over. So where did the boy go?"

"I don't know anything about any boy."

"Do you really expect us to believe that?" The man glanced down at the dogs, then back at her. "I think you need to find us a better answer."

She tried again to think. The simplest thing would be to tell her story exactly as it had happened. They might just believe it. But she doubted it, and even if they did, she felt a strange reluctance to tell them about the boy. Whatever he'd done, whatever he knew or didn't know about Josh, she trusted these people even less.

"I just followed the prints," she said. "I saw the tracks in the snow and followed them."

"You must think I'm an idiot."

"I don't. I—"

"You really must think I'm an idiot." The man's voice was hard and hostile. "You're a young girl and you're wandering in the park on your own around midnight and in the snow. That's stupid enough on its own. You see some footprints. You don't know whose they are. So you follow them out of curiosity. Are you expecting me to believe that?"

She said nothing.

"Are you?" he snapped.

"Yes, I—"

"Then you're insulting me as well as lying to me."

The man took another step closer. The dogs, seeing her almost within reach, jumped forward. She pressed herself against the wall but the man tugged the animals back and shortened the leash around his wrist. It kept them away but they were only inches from her now. The boys moved closer too.

"You wouldn't do that," said the man. His voice was chillingly low. "You look like a clever girl. You wouldn't go wandering in the park on your own. You wouldn't follow an unknown trail of footprints in the snow. You know why?"

She didn't answer.

"Because it's dangerous," he went on. "There are nasty people out late at night. You wouldn't want to get caught by any nasty people, now, would you?"

"Leave me alone."

"When you've told us the truth."

"I've told you the truth."

"So what were you following the prints for?"

"I just was."

She saw a look of scorn on the man's face.

"I thought you might have more sense," he said, "but I can see we're going to have to persuade you."

He glanced at the boys and nodded. They stepped toward her.

She screamed, though she knew it was a waste of time. Nobody would hear her on this snowy track. She screamed again, even so, then the fair-haired boy's hand clapped over her mouth.

She squirmed and tried to break free but his other hand locked over her stomach and thrust her against the wall. The other boy seized her shoulders and pinned her back. She struggled again to break free but their hands only tightened. She brought her knee up as hard as she could into the fair-haired boy's groin. He gave a cry of pain.

"Bitch!"

She saw his fist swing back, then whip forward. Somehow she ducked and it thudded into the wall. The boy groaned and stepped back, shaking his injured hand. She lashed out with both feet, striking at anything she could hit. One foot connected with the other boy's shin. He gave a yelp and stood back too, then both boys lunged at her again. She squirmed under their arms and ran off down the track.

But she didn't get far. She'd barely struggled five yards before hands gripped her shoulder and waist. She screamed again, then a fist struck her in the small of the back. She fell, moaning, in the snow. As the boys loomed over her, she heard her mobile ring in her pocket. She snatched it out, pressed the answer button and screamed into the mouthpiece.

"Help! Help! Track to Knowle!"

"Get the phone off her!" shouted the man.

"Track to Knowle!" she yelled. "Call the police!"

She saw hands reaching for the phone but went on screaming into it.

"Man! Two boys! Pit bulls!"

A hand closed around her wrist and fumbled for the phone. She tore it away somehow and screamed into it again.

"Black hair! Ponytail! White van! Registration number—"

The phone flew from her grasp. The fair-haired boy had kicked it from her. She stared up in dismay and saw both boys standing over her, and the man too. The dogs were still tight in his grasp but their jaws were only inches from her face. She waited for the next blow, but it didn't come. The man glanced at the boys.

"Wait in the van," he muttered.

They obeyed without a word. The man didn't watch them go. He ran his eye over Dusty, still lying at his feet in the snow, then glanced over at the mobile a few feet from them. He didn't bother going over to switch it off or smash it up. He stared back down at her, his black hair moist with snow, then spoke again in the same low voice.

"Seems I was right about you. You are a clever girl. Quick-witted."

She said nothing, her eyes on the dogs.

"But not much of a looker, are you?" said the man. "Bit of an ugly minx."

She scowled at him. His eyes radiated contempt. She hoped hers did the same.

"Which makes it all a bit of a mystery," he went on, "the boy hanging around with the likes of you. I mean, you're hardly a catch, are you? And we both know the kind of person he goes for."

He paused, as though waiting for her to speak. She wanted to. She wanted to scream at him. But only her mind screamed. The man sniffed.

"No, it's a bit of a mystery. You're just not his type. Too much of a tomboy."

There was that word again. It thumped into her like a fist.

"Now listen, girlie." The man narrowed his eyes. "Here's the bit you need to remember. I don't want the police involved or anybody else. You get my drift? Talk to the police or your family or your friends, and someone you care about's going to get hurt, and so are you. So think hard before you open that sparky little mouth of yours."

He leaned closer.

"This isn't over," he breathed.

And he turned back toward the van.

She curled into a ball and started to sob, the snow still falling upon her. She didn't look at the van. She couldn't bear to see it now. She heard the engine grumble into life, felt the glare of the headlamps fall upon her, then both the light and the sound receded as the van reversed. Sometime later she heard it turn in the wider section of the lane, then with a final roar of the engine, it headed off into the night, leaving silence and snow behind, and her still curled on the ground.

4

SHE WENT ON SOBBING. She couldn't stop herself. She was trembling too, and growing colder by the minute. She knew she had to move, yet she couldn't. All she wanted to do was curl up even more. She forced herself to sit up. She couldn't stay here. She had to get back and she had to compose herself. Somehow she had to compose herself.

She struggled over to the mobile and picked it up. It didn't seem to be broken. She was still trembling, still crying. She choked the tears back, dragged herself to the wall and slumped against it.

"Stop crying," she muttered. "Stop . . . bloody . . ."

But tears were still pouring from her, blocking vision, blocking thought.

"Don't lose it," she muttered.

She was losing it. She wanted to curl up again. She wanted to disappear, to die.

"Don't let them win."

She fumbled with the phone. Some part of her brain told her she had to find out who'd called, but the rest of her mind wasn't working. She was pressing buttons but nothing was happening,

"Calm down," she murmured. "You're pressing . . . you're pressing . . ."

She didn't know what she was pressing. She was just pressing all the buttons at once.

"Calm . . . bloody . . . down."

She forced herself to stop pressing buttons and slumped back against the wall, breathing hard. The snow was falling heavily now and settling more thickly over the track and the top of the stone walls, and over her. It was a strangely comforting sight, and freezing though she was, the cold touch of the flakes on her face and body seemed to clear her head for a moment. She took some slow breaths, then looked back at her mobile.

"Press cancel," she murmured. "Clear the screen."

She pressed cancel, and then again, and again, and finally found her way back to the main menu. She took some more slow breaths. She was still trembling and the snow had ceased to be comforting. She was soaked through and her teeth were chattering.

"Find out who called," she told herself.

Speaking aloud seemed to help. She checked the phone. It was Dad. He'd rung her from his own mobile. He hadn't left a message but he'd be worried sick after hearing her scream down the phone. She took a moment to collect herself, then rang his number. He answered at once.

"Dusty?"

He sounded tense. She tried to answer but found she could not. She knew her voice would betray the state she was in.

"Dusty?" he said again. "Are you all right?"

"Dad?" she managed.

She couldn't say more. Not yet. Just his name.

"Oh, you are there," he said, the relief clear in his voice. "Are you OK?"

"Yes."

"Sorry I'm not back yet. Helen's driven home but I'm stuck outside the pub, Bloody car won't start. But the breakdown people are on their way so I shouldn't be too long. I think the engine's damp or something."

She said nothing.

"I rang you a moment ago," he said.

"Yes."

"Only the signal must have gone funny or something. Did it ring your end?"

"Yes."

"Well, I didn't hear a thing. Did you answer it?"

Dusty let her hand fall to the side, the mobile clutched in it. He hadn't heard a word. She'd shouted into the phone for nothing. The police wouldn't be coming out. Nobody knew what had happened.

She gave a sigh. Perhaps it was just as well in light of the man's threat. Besides, she needed to think what to do and what, if anything, to say. One thing she was clear about: she wasn't going to tell Dad about this, not yet anyway. He'd never cope. He was still in a state over Josh and Mum and his jobless situation, not to mention this new woman he'd just met.

She wiped some of the tears and snow from her eyes. Down by the ground, in her other hand, the mobile was growing moist. She heard Dad's voice speaking through it, a soft, fragile sound in the still of the night.

"Dusty?" he was saying. "Did you answer it?"

She raised the phone to her ear again.

"Yes," she murmured. "I answered it."

"Why didn't you pick up the landline phone? I rang that first. Did you hear it?"

"I was in bed."

"Oh, sorry. Are you still in bed?"

"Yeah."

"Just as well you had your mobile on."

"Yeah."

"Anyway, sorry to ring you so late."

"That's OK."

"And sorry to have left you on your own this evening."

"That's OK."

"But I expect you quite liked it, didn't you? Bit of time to yourself without me getting all neurotic as usual."

She knew what she was meant to say. She was meant to reassure him. She was meant to ask him how it went tonight. She was meant to be everything she had always been to him since Josh and Mum left. But tonight was different. Tonight she didn't trust her voice, even at the risk of Dad misreading her silence, which he was bound to do.

"Dusty?" he said, on cue. "You're very quiet."

"Am I?"

"You're not angry with me for going out tonight, are you?"

"No."

"You sure? You sound a bit angry."

"I'm not."

"It was your idea, remember? About me going out."

"I'm fine about it. I'm all right."

"You don't sound all right."

"I'm not angry."

"A bit subdued maybe?"

"I'm fine."

"I so want things to be OK again."

"They will be."

She was desperate to put the phone down now. The more they spoke, the more he'd pick up her despair.

"I'm a bit tired, Dad," she said.

"Oh, sorry. I'll let you get to sleep. Hopefully I won't be too long."

"No problem." She took a deep breath. "No . . . problem."

"I'll see you later, sweetheart."

"OK," she said.

She rang off before he could speak again, then forced herself to stand up. She was still shivering but her head was clearer. She looked up and down the track. She could walk through Knowle to the Beckdale Road and get home that way or go back the way she had come. The last place she wanted to see right now was Stonewell Park, but there was no question that it was the quicker route by far and there was also the risk of Dad arriving home before she did or maybe passing her if she took the Beckdale Road.

She headed back toward the bridleway, her mind more lucid now. She thought again about Dad and as before decided to say nothing. It wasn't just the threat from the man with the ponytail. It was Dad himself. He simply wouldn't be able to handle this. The business with Josh had hurt him badly enough, being sacked as head chef at Oscar's hadn't helped either, but when Mum had walked out too, it had more or less finished him.

Her mind wandered to the boy again. Somehow she sensed he was the key to this, yet he was as elusive as Josh himself. The footprints disappearing in the snow were a complete mystery. As for the man with the ponytail, it was hard to know what to do apart from avoid him. He hadn't suggested he knew where she lived. It was just possible he hadn't noticed that her footprints started from Thorn Cottage and at least with the snow falling now it was likely that both sets of prints would already be covered up.

She saw the bridleway ahead and beyond it the great white expanse of Kilbury Moor sprawling away to the snowcapped fells in the distance, Raven's Fell rising high and proud among them, the lake glistening at its feet. Again she found herself struck by the strangeness of the light. Even with the snow falling it had an eerie brilliance, as though the night were somehow brighter than it should be.

Something in the air still felt wrong.

But maybe it was just herself. She knew she was in a bad way. She looked about her, searching for some sign of the boy who wanted to die. Somehow she sensed he was alive. She didn't know why she felt so certain of this and what evidence she had suggested the opposite. He had clearly swallowed a stack of pills. Yet the disappearing footprints—they had to mean something.

She thought of Silas again and once more dismissed the idea of asking him if he'd seen anything. If the old man spoke to her at all, it would be to give her an earful for disturbing him. Besides, she had to hurry home. She set off toward the gate into Stonewell Park.

She'd been right about the snow. Her earlier footprints and those of the boys had been covered by the latest fall and the snow was now so heavy it wouldn't be long before the prints she was leaving behind her were covered too. She stopped at the gate into Stonewell Park and stared through the grating. There was no sign of anyone in the park, and no footprints at all. She thought of the boy again.

"Where are you?" she murmured to him. "I know you're alive. I can feel it."

She ran her eye over the children's playground, the trees, the playing fields. All she saw was white falling on white. She climbed over the gate and walked over to the swing, silent now in the windless air. She stopped by it and pushed the seat. From the top of the swing came the familiar metallic groan, then silence as the swing stopped moving.

She wandered up to the children's playhouse and peered through the window. Nothing and nobody inside, and no sign that anyone had used it. She walked on into the trees, wary again now that there were places of concealment. She left the fountain behind her and a few minutes later came out the other side. At the top of the slope was the other gate and beyond it the lane and Thorn Cottage.

She yearned to be back now, to get warm again and clean herself up before Dad arrived, and pretend—somehow—that she had been in bed for the last two hours, and that she was all right. The best way to do that would be to feign sleep. With any luck Dad would leave her till morning and by then she'd have calmed down and be a better actress than she was now.

The snow stopped falling.

She trudged up the slope to the gate, squeezed through the gap in the fence and looked back. Below her was the silent park and beyond it the moor stretching away toward Mirkwell Lake. High above both the peak of Raven's Fell glowed as before. She stared at it and for a curious moment had the disconcerting feeling that the snow was burning, not just on the high fell but down on the moor, around the lake, and even here around her. She shook her head and the feeling left her.

Yet still the night shimmered about her.

She hurried down the lane toward Thorn Cottage. To her relief, there was no car outside. She let herself in and closed the front door behind her. All was dark. She remembered the living room light being on when she left but had no recollection of turning it off when she ran out of the house. But she must have done so and she was glad of it now. The darkness felt good.

Tears rushed through her suddenly. They took her by surprise— she'd thought she was all right now—but the feeling of being safe again was too much. She leaned against the inside of the front door and let herself cry, then, when she'd stopped, she wiped her eyes and stared through the gloom.

There on the pad was the note she'd written to Dad. She tore it up and dropped the pieces in the bin, then hung up her coat and pulled off her boots. After a moment's thought she pushed them out of sight behind Dad's old wellies, then hid her wet coat under her oilskin. She was still wet through but at least Dad wouldn't see anything here to show that she'd been out.

From down the lane came the sound of an engine.

5

SHE HURRIED toward the stairs. It was a relief to hear Dad coming back but she'd have to get into bed quickly before he rolled in. She'd have to strip off her wet things and shove them under the bed for now or he'd realize she'd been out.

She bounded up to her room and closed the door behind her. There would be no time even to towel off. He would be here too soon for that. Already she could hear the engine drawing close.

She tore off her clothes in the darkness, dropped them to the floor and kicked them under the bed. They were still wet and so was she but there was nothing she could about that now. She pulled on her nightie. It stuck to the damp parts of her body but she didn't care as long as Dad didn't see it when he put his head around the door.

Her hair was a different matter. Even in the darkness he might spot how wet and unkempt it was. She supposed she could bury herself right under the covers but that was so unlike her he'd probably come right in and ask if she was all right, and that was the last thing she needed. She wanted him to think she was asleep and leave her alone till morning.

She snatched her old pullover from the wardrobe and used it as a towel on her hair. It wasn't very effective but it took away some of the moisture. She heard the engine fall silent, then the sound of the car door. She thrust the pullover back in the wardrobe, dived into bed, and pulled the duvet up to her chin.

From downstairs came the sound of the key in the lock, then a cough, and a few minutes of stamping off snow and fumbling by the coatrack, then footsteps on the stairs. She rolled onto her side so that she was facing away from the door. It opened—and there was a long silence.

She sensed Dad peering in, trying to gauge whether or not she was asleep. She took some slow, slumberous breaths. He didn't close the door. She went on with the slow breaths, wishing she didn't have to play this game. He spoke.

"Dusty?"

His voice was soft, very soft. It was a voice that only wanted to be heard if she was already awake and didn't want to disturb her if she wasn't. She still had a choice. She could say nothing or she could answer.

Say nothing, she told herself. It's for the best. Talk in the morning. You'll be calmer in the morning. You won't give yourself away.

"Dusty?" came the voice, even softer than before.

Say nothing, say nothing, say nothing.

"Dusty?"

This time the voice was barely audible, but now she could hear the yearning in it, the need not to wake her, yet also to talk. She rolled over to face the door, keeping her eyes closed, and spoke in the sleepiest voice she could manage.

"Dad?"

She heard him close the door behind him and walk toward her, felt him sit on the bed. She prayed he wouldn't stroke her hair. He'd feel the moisture straightaway, in spite of her attempted toweling. But he didn't touch her. She sensed a movement from his body that could only mean one thing. She opened her eyes.

"Dad? Are you crying?"

He shrugged and looked down, his face too dark to read but the tears glistening in his eyes. She pushed aside her fear of him seeing her wet hair and fumbled with the bedside lamp.

"No," he said. "Leave it off. I like the darkness."

She took her hand away and lay back, looking up at him.

"I don't like you to see me crying," he said.

"Why not?"

"Just don't."

"I've seen you cry lots of times."

"Maybe that's why." He gave a long sigh. "Bit of a wimp, aren't I?"

"Crying doesn't mean you're a wimp."

"No, I guess not."

He wiped his eyes. She watched him. His face was starting to define itself as her eyes grew used to the darkness. He wasn't sobbing. These were quiet tears. It was hard to tell exactly what they meant.

"Didn't it go well tonight?" she said.

"It went fine. She was nice."

"But she wasn't Mum."

"She wasn't Mum."

Dad wiped his eyes again, then stretched.

"Sorry. I'm a bit of a disaster these days."

"No, you're not."

"Yes, I am. You don't need to be kind to me." He shook his head. "I'm not strong-minded like you. Wish I was. You're feisty, independent. Too bloody independent. You scare me to death sometimes. Josh was right. You are a tomboy. No wonder the two of you got on so well. You think you can do anything, take anyone on, and maybe you can. But me, I'm . . ."

He fell silent. Dusty said nothing. She knew from previous conversations like this that he needed to offload without prompting.

"I'm not very good on my own," he went on. "Maybe that's why your mum walked out. She couldn't take living with someone so dependent."

"We both know why Mum walked out and it wasn't that."

"Yeah, yeah."

"We all went funny after Josh disappeared."

Dad said nothing. She watched him for a moment, then said, "Dad?"

"Yeah?"

"Would you take Mum back if she walked in the door now?"

"She's hardly going to do that, is she?"

"But would you if she did?"

"I don't know what I'd do. Fall apart probably like I usually do."

He looked away. Dusty stared at him in the darkness. He'd stopped crying now and seemed a little calmer but he was clearly still distressed. She reached out and took his hand. He didn't look around but he squeezed hers and held it tight.

"Your hand's wet," he said after a while.

"It's moisture from your own hand," she said quickly. "You didn't dry yourself properly coming in."

"Oh, sorry." He let go of her hand and wiped his on his clothes. She quickly did the same with hers under the duvet, trying not to give away what she was doing. "Try this," he said, reaching out again. "Where's your hand gone?"

"Here." She took his again. "That's better," she said. "You're dry now. Has there been more snow?"

"Yeah."

"Is the car all right?"

"Yes, they fixed it."

"What about this woman you saw tonight?"

"Helen?"

"Yes. What's she like?"

"Nice. The best one the agency's found so far."

"That's not saying much."

She heard a chuckle from Dad, and felt another squeeze of the hand.

"No, she's nice," he said. "I really liked her."

"What does she do?"

"She's an osteopath."

"Nice-looking?"

"Yes."

"Not like me, then."

"You're nice-looking."

"Oh, sure."

She'd spoken lightly, meaning to make a joke of this. Her looks, or lack of looks, had never bothered her before, yet for some reason she felt a little vulnerable about it tonight. Perhaps it was that man's sneering words: *Not much of a looker, are you?*

"Not much of a looker, am I?" she heard herself say.

"You look great to me," said Dad, "and you'll look great to some hunky bloke one of these days."

"I'm not sure I want some hunky bloke. I'm not sure I want any bloke."

"Well, there's no hurry on that front. It'll happen in its own good time."

She'd never had that kind of attention from boys, not like Kamalika, who had them swarming around her. But this shouldn't matter right now. It had never mattered before. She changed the subject.

"So what does she look like?"

"Helen?"

"Yes."

"Nice. About your mum's height and build. Medium-length hair."

"Straight or curly?"

"Straight."

"What color?"

"Auburn."

"Like Mum's?"

"I suppose."

"Maybe that's why you like her. Because she looks like Mum."

"It did set me off a bit. When I first saw her, I nearly got back in the car and drove off again."

"Why didn't you?"

"Would have been a bit rude, don't you think?" Dad thought for a moment. "Maybe it was a mistake joining this agency. I was OK before I started going out on dates."

"You weren't OK. You were bloody miserable."

"I'm bloody miserable now."

"Yeah, but you were even more miserable. At least now you're meeting some new people. Even if these dates don't lead to anything."

"I did like Helen."

"That's good."

"We hit it off pretty well. We didn't . . . I mean . . . do anything. We just talked."

"Oh."

"You sound disappointed."

She said nothing. Her thoughts had slipped back to Mum and Josh, and the man and his sons, and the strange boy.

"I saw this strange boy," Dad said.

She looked sharply at him.

"What boy?"

"Least I think it was a boy," said Dad. "I'm not completely sure. It might have been anyone. Or maybe no one at all."

"What are you talking about?"

"Sorry. I'm not making much sense. Have you seen anybody tonight?"

"How could I? I've been at home."

"No, I mean . . . out of the window. You haven't seen anybody in the lane or anything?"

"No." She paused to collect herself, then said, "Why?"

"It was the weirdest thing. Almost thought I'd seen a ghost. And . . . you know . . . I don't exactly believe in spooks and all that stuff."

"What did you see?"

"I was driving to Beckdale to meet Helen. About half seven, quarter to eight. What time did I say good-bye to you?"

"Half seven."

"Well, a few minutes after that. I was still driving down the lane. I hadn't even got to the Beckdale Road. And it had just started to snow again."

She remembered the snow shower just after Dad had left, the last one of the evening before she'd run off to the park later to search for the boy; a heavy shower but it had only lasted a few minutes.

"So I'm driving down the lane, right?" said Dad. "Dark outside and snow falling but full beam on, so I'm feeling OK. And I'm about a quarter of a mile from the junction with the Beckdale Road. You know, that bit where there's a stile on the left."

"I know it."

"And I just happened to look in my mirror and there was this figure walking away down the lane."

"The way you'd just come?"

"Yes. In the direction of this house. Though that was a long way off."

"And you could see it was a boy?"

"Well, that's one of the weird things. I couldn't really see clearly. All I saw was the back of a duffel coat with the hood pulled up, so it was some kind of figure walking away. Could have been a man or a woman, or a girl or a boy. Not a kid though. Someone at least sixteen."

"But you think it was a boy?"

"Yes. Don't know why. It just kind of felt like a boy. Maybe it was something about the walk. But that's not what's really strange. What's really strange is that I didn't see him coming toward the car. I just looked in my mirror and there he was. I can't believe I didn't see him ahead or walking past me."

"Maybe he came from the field and climbed over the stile just after you drove past. And then you saw him."

Dad shook his head.

"I hadn't quite reached the stile at that point. I was approaching it and I could see it just ahead. I wasn't past it."

"Then he climbed over the wall from one of the fields after you'd driven past."

"Maybe. Still felt weird though, to see that figure in the mirror."

"You didn't stop and call out and ask if he was all right?"

"No. Do you think I should have?"

"I don't know."

"I mean, he didn't look like he was in trouble or anything. But I nearly rang you up to say keep your eyes open. I didn't like the thought of him heading toward Thorn Cottage. It's such a lonely place out here and I worry about you being on your own. Though I don't suppose it ever bothers you, Miss Bloody Fearless."

"I didn't see anyone," she said.

"OK."

They fell silent again but Dusty's mind was moving fast. A figure in a duffel coat with the hood pulled up, moving down the lane toward Thorn Cottage. It could well have been the boy. The tracks she'd seen came from the direction of Beckdale and the snowfall would have been too brief to cover them. Strange that Dad should have seen so little yet be convinced it was a boy. She remembered those opening words on the phone.

I'm dying.

Perhaps the boy was already dead. Perhaps . . .

She hesitated.

"Do you think Josh is dead?" she said.

Dad squeezed her hand again.

"What made you suddenly think of Josh?"

When am I not thinking of Josh? she asked herself. But all she said was, "I don't know. I just did. Do you think he's dead?"

"I don't know. I hope not. But we have to accept the possibility that we may never know."

"I've been accepting that possibility for the last two years."

"I know. It doesn't get any easier for me either. But Josh's life isn't something we've got any control over now. Not that we ever did."

That was true, she thought. Josh had been even more of a rebel than she was. If he was alive, she didn't suppose he'd be any different now. She thought of the boy on the phone again, and what he had said. He knew something, he knew a lot, and now he was gone. She felt she'd give anything—even risk those horrible people with the dogs again—to speak to him one more time, just to find out whatever she could.

"I'd better let you sleep," said Dad. "I shouldn't have woken you in the first place."

"I'm glad you did."

"So am I."

He leaned down and kissed her.

"Thanks for being you," he said. "Thanks for being stronger than me."

"'Night, Dad."

He stood up and headed toward the door, then stopped and looked back.

"Dusty?"

"Hmm?"

"I really did like Helen."

"Good. Did she like you?"

"I think so."

"You think?"

"No, she did. I'm pretty sure she did."

"Has she been married?"

"She's divorced. Guy walked out on her."

"Sounds familiar."

"You'd like her, I think."

"Has she got any kids?"

"Two. Daughter who's just started university and a son who's left home and works for his father in New Zealand." Dad paused. "Listen, Dusty, I might see her again. Is that OK?"

"What are you asking me for?"

"Well, I don't know . . . I just . . . "

"You don't need to ask me."

"Yes, I do. I need to know you're all right about it."

"I'm all right about it."

"You know I'd never let anybody or anything in the world come between you and me. There's just the two of us left now. I want you to know I'm here for you first, last and always."

"I know that, Dad."

"Even if I am pathetic sometimes."

"You're not pathetic. You're never pathetic." She paused, watching him watching her in the darkness. "Dad?" she said. "Can I go to sleep now?"

"Sure. Sorry. I didn't mean to . . ." She heard a long sigh in the darkness, then: "Dusty?"

"Yes?"

"I didn't imagine that figure in the lane."

6

SHE LAY THERE AFTER he'd gone and gazed up at the ceiling. It was hard to know what to make of all this. The business with Helen was no problem. It was good that Dad was dating. It had been her idea in the first place to use the agency and this Helen sounded nice enough.

The figure in the lane was another matter.

She was certain it was the boy. She lay there, her mind fixed upon him, and as she drifted toward sleep, she found herself picturing footprints in the snow, starting far down the Beckdale Road and appearing one by one behind a figure in a duffel coat with the hood up.

The figure was clear in her mind, and she was following with her eyes, just as Dad had done, only her drowsy imagination went further than Dad's and followed and followed and followed, watching the trail of prints lengthen in the snow, and the hooded form making them.

Step, step, step, and still the figure walked on up the Beckdale Road. She was heavy with sleep now but still she saw the figure walking in her mind, step, step, step, past the turning into the track that led to Knowle, and on to her lane, and then down it toward Thorn Cottage and Stonewell Park at the end.

Step, step, step, and still she was awake, still the figure walked. She saw it reach Thorn Cottage and continue toward the park gate, not even glancing at the house, and as it walked, her sleepy mind pondered what the face of this figure must be like. She wanted it to turn but it did not turn. It simply walked on, leaving the prints behind in the snow, then squeezed through the gap in the fence, and headed down the slope to the trees, and disappeared from view.

She fell asleep.

But it was a confused sleep with strange conflicting dreams. She saw dark, shapeless forms. She felt anger, hatred, pain. She saw the fangs of dogs. She saw the man and his two sons. She saw Josh's face but not as she last remembered it. He seemed different but in ways that made no sense—older, younger, she wasn't sure.

Then he vanished and there was nothing but a snowy expanse. She thought at first it was Stonewell Park, then she saw it was something else, something broader, more remote, Kilbury Moor, that was it—and then suddenly everything in the dream was gleaming white.

It was pleasant at first, but then she realized it was growing brighter and brighter and brighter, too bright now, horribly, dangerously bright, so bright she felt she was losing all form herself. She felt cut through by brightness, cut through by snow, by cold, icy whiteness. She felt her body shiver, as though it wanted to dissolve.

And then she woke.

She was sitting bolt upright in bed, the duvet thrown back. She was shivering, just as she had been in the dream. She reached out and touched the radiator. It was on. She stayed upright but pulled the duvet up around her. The sense of gleaming brightness was gone. The room was dark again. But something was wrong.

She was not alone.

Someone was here. She could see no one, yet she could sense someone's presence close by. She tried to calm herself. She knew she was still overwrought. But she also knew that this wasn't imagination. She held herself rigid, her eyes flickering from side to side as she searched the darkness.

Nothing. No figure, not even a shadow.

She moved her head now, slowly, cautiously, scanning the dusky features of the room: the bedside cabinet, the door, the bookshelf, her schoolbag on the floor, the wardrobe, the chest of drawers, the desk, the laptop, the drawn curtains.

Nothing. Nobody.

But someone was here. She listened for the sound of breathing. All she heard was the patter of snow against the window. She tried to think. There was only one person in the house apart from her and that was Dad, and he'd hardly creep into her room and conceal himself just to scare her. Yet her instinct still told her she was not alone.

"Who's there?" she said to the darkness.

The darkness did not answer. She shivered again and pulled the duvet more tightly around her. This was crazy. She couldn't possibly be right. She tried to think things through in a cold, dispassionate manner. Her eyes were good. She wasn't fanciful by nature. The simplest thing was just to check this. If she could make herself do it.

She pushed the duvet slowly back, climbed out of bed and stood there, breathing hard. She felt even more vulnerable without the duvet wrapped around her. She reached for the bedside lamp and switched it on. The light relaxed her a little. There was clearly no one in the room. She looked about her, searching again.

No sign of anyone or anything that shouldn't be here. She hesitated, then bent down and peered under the bed. Nothing but the wet clothes she had kicked under there earlier, plus her old sneakers. She straightened up again. There was only one other place a person could hide in this room.

She took a step toward the wardrobe, then another, and another. With each step, the feeling of unreality grew. She was acting like a kid seeing bogeymen that didn't—couldn't—exist. Dad wouldn't slip into her room and then hide in the wardrobe, nor would an intruder. She couldn't believe she was even bothering to check.

But she had to. She knew it. She couldn't rest until she had satisfied herself that her logical mind was right and her instinct was wrong. If she checked every possible hiding place in the room, then perhaps she would be able to persuade herself that this was imagination after all.

She was close to the wardrobe now. The big mirror on the door was shining with the light from the bedside lamp glancing over it, and as she drew closer, she saw the outline of herself spreading upon it. With her untidy hair, still partly wet, she looked like an apparition, a strange, formless thing quite unlike her normal image of herself. She stopped a couple of feet from the wardrobe, her eyes on this shadow of herself, and on the door.

It was a fraction open.

She hadn't noticed that before and she was certain she'd closed it properly when she put the pullover away after rubbing her hair with it. She was sure she remembered hearing it click shut.

She stared at it, ready to turn and run if it suddenly swung open, and in spite of the scornful inner voice that chided her for such foolishness, she heard herself say, "Come out of there. Whoever you are, come out of there."

The wardrobe door didn't move. She went on staring at it, trying to summon the courage to open it. But she was frozen.

Get Dad, said a voice inside her. Get him to check.

But she knew she couldn't. He'd think she was nuts waking him up for some nonsense like this, especially when she was supposed to be the strong one in the house. She took a deep breath and jerked back the door so forcefully that the wardrobe rocked on its base. Something dark and hairy fell out. She jumped back with a start.

But it was only her pullover tumbling down from the top shelf where she'd shoved it back. There was no one in the wardrobe, just clothes on their hangers still swinging with the motion, drawers closed, shoes jumbled in their familiar higgledy-piggledy way about the bottom.

Her normal, untidy wardrobe.

She swung the door shut and stared at her reflection in the mirror again. She could see her face more clearly now that she was closer. It seemed so solemn she wanted to laugh. But she could not. She clenched her fists. She had proved there was no one in the room, yet still her mind clung to the feeling that someone was close.

She even felt that she was being watched.

"Get a grip," she murmured. "It's just that business with those horrible people. And the boy."

It must have unhinged her, made her imagine things that weren't there, and that was serious. She'd never been this way before. She walked slowly back to the bed, climbed in again, and switched off the bedside lamp. Darkness settled once again. She lay on her back, pulled the duvet over her as far as her chin and peeped out over the top.

She was breathing fast—too fast. Something still felt wrong. She knew this was stupid. She'd checked everything and found nothing. Again she felt her eyes move about the room, searching. She even felt her hand reach out from under the duvet and stretch toward the bedside lamp.

"Don't be silly," she murmured. "You've got to get over this. It's all in your mind."

She let her eyes check things again, slowly, methodically: the bedside cabinet, the door, the bookshelf, the schoolbag, the wardrobe, the chest of drawers, the desk, the laptop, the drawn curtains.

The drawn curtains.

She stared at them and immediately rejected the idea. There was no way anybody could hide behind them. They didn't stretch all the way down to the floor. They barely extended below the top of the radiator. All they did was cover the window. If anybody was standing behind them, she'd see the person's legs and feet at the bottom.

There was nobody there.

Yet she sat up. She let the duvet fall back and climbed out of bed again. She stood there in the darkness, staring toward the window. Again she had the sense of someone watching her. Again logic screamed at her: no one could be hiding behind the curtains and no one could be outside the windowpane. She was on the first floor of the house and there was nothing to climb up unless somebody had brought a ladder—and that was too preposterous for words.

She took a step toward the window. She had to sort this out once and for all. She'd check the window and reassure herself, and then she'd go back to bed and sleep. She wouldn't even bother putting the light on again. There was nothing to be afraid of. She'd just check out the window and go to sleep.

She walked toward it. The curtains were still. No draft was pushing through. She reminded herself that the window was closed—another good reason for her to be reassured. No one could have climbed in from outside. All was well.

She drew closer to the curtains. For some reason they seemed brighter than usual. They were brown and normally dark but they seemed to be brightening the closer she came. It had to be the brightness of the snow pushing through from outside. She could think of no other cause. She stopped a few feet away and ran her eyes over them. In spite of the stream of logical thoughts running through her, she could feel that unease again. Whatever her rational mind was saying, her instinct still told her something was wrong.

She stared at the strange, almost glowing curtains. Before her eyes they were burning with a chilly fire. Even as she watched, shivering in the night, a snowy blaze was moving up them like an icy conflagration. She reached out a hand and touched them. The warmth of the velvet was still there. She relaxed and pulled back the curtains—and saw to her horror a face staring in at her.

"Ah!" she gasped.

But it was not a real face. It was a snow-face. The latest shower had ceased but flakes from it had somehow stuck to the window, covering the pane in a thick coating of white. This in itself was unsettling. She was sure snow couldn't do this. She would have expected it to slide off down the pane and collect on the sill.

But this had stayed. The flakes had built up and built up, clinging somehow against gravity and compacting themselves against the glass. But what was even more disturbing was the shape they had formed.

For this was a face, an unmistakable face. She saw the mouth, the eyes, the snowy mane of hair tumbling down over the shoulders, and then—nothing. There was no body to go with it. Just a face, suspended in glass, looking in at her with gleaming eyes.

And then suddenly, as she watched, almost as if it had waited for her to see it, the face started to disintegrate. The snow slipped down the pane to form an untidy pile on the sill. She shuddered and pulled the curtains quickly across, then after a moment's thought, pulled them back again, thrust open the window and elbowed the pile of snow over the edge into the garden. Then she closed the window, drew the curtains across again and stepped back.

She was trembling. The arm of her nightie was sodden and cold where she had used it to brush away the snow. She thought of Dad's figure—the duffel coat, the hidden face—and on an impulse walked to her desk, picked up her sketchpad and pencil and took them over to the bed. She was still trembling but she forced herself to ignore it. She sat down on the edge of the bed, switched on the bedside lamp and started to draw the snow-face.

It was easy to picture and easy to draw. She finished quickly and held it close to the lamp. The glow gave it a strange, ethereal look. She tore out the sheet from the pad and sat there, wondering what to do with it. She had no idea why she had drawn the face in the first place. It certainly didn't make her feel any less frightened. She stared at it for a moment, then placed it on top of the bedside cabinet, threw the pad and pencil into the corner of the room, and climbed into bed.

The arm of her nightie was still cold and wet and she supposed she should have changed, but she couldn't be bothered. She felt sure she'd fall asleep now. She pulled the duvet around her and rolled over so that she was facing the bedside cabinet. There on top was the drawing of the snow-face. She wasn't sure whether it comforted or scared her. She reached out and touched it, then switched off the lamp.

Darkness fell upon the room again. She lay there, breathing hard, thinking of Josh and the strange boy. There was no feeling of being watched now, not even from the drawing by the bed. She gazed at it in the darkness, aware of it even as drowsiness crept over her. It was the last thing she saw before she slipped into sleep.

7

AND THE FIRST THING she saw on waking. She stared at it, somewhat startled. She was facing the cabinet in exactly the position she last remembered being in when she fell asleep. It was as though she hadn't moved at all during the night, though she didn't suppose that was true. She frowned, then sat up in bed, reached over and picked up the paper face.

A fair likeness of the image she'd seen on the window, yet why was it only now that it reminded her of Josh too? Something in the eyes, perhaps, or maybe the mouth. Or maybe it was just foolishness. It was only a drawing after all.

She reached back to the cabinet, opened the top drawer and pulled out the photos. Josh's face stared up at her with its familiar wicked smile. She bit her lip and went through the pictures one by one, then she looked at the paper face.

Yes, there was a similarity but she was starting to mistrust herself now. A face made from snow could be made to look like anything, especially a dream. Maybe Josh was still alive. Maybe the strange boy who'd phoned last night did know something about him. Maybe the snow-face and this papery imitation meant something.

Or maybe not.

She climbed out of bed, reached for her trousers and thrust the paper face in one of the pockets, then she washed, dressed and made her way downstairs. From the kitchen came the sound of Dad preparing breakfast. She glanced at her watch.

Ten o'clock.

She'd slept several hours but didn't feel rested at all. She felt tired and tense and in no mood to put on a front with Dad and pretend all was well, though she knew she'd have to. She wondered what state she'd find him in this morning. She pushed open the kitchen door and saw him standing by the stove, cutting bread.

"Hi, Dad."

He looked around at her.

"Hi."

"You all right?"

"Fine." He turned back to the bread. "Sorry I kept you awake last night."

"It's OK."

"Want some tea?"

"Could I have some coffee?"

"You don't normally have coffee first thing. Need perking up, do you?"

She shrugged.

"Maybe."

She glanced out of the window. Beyond the back garden the snow-covered fields stretched away toward Knowle. Again she noticed the strangeness of the atmosphere. Where last night the snow and the darkness had glowed, now in daylight the air seemed somehow thinner, fainter, as though a transparent veil had been drawn across her line of vision, and for a moment she had the curious feeling that the hedges, trees and even the distant peak of Raven's Fell were hanging like clouds in weightless suspension before her. Dad's voice broke in upon her thoughts.

"Coffee it is, then."

She looked around at him.

"Thanks."

He seemed fairly calm this morning, calmer than last night anyway. He filled the kettle and switched it on.

"You sit down and get started," he said. "Scrambled or poached?"

"Scrambled, please."

"OK."

She sat down at the table and started her cereal, her eyes still drawn to the window, her mind on last night.

"There was a phone call for you this morning," said Dad.

She looked sharply up at him.

"Who?"

"Just some boy asking for you."

"What boy?"

Dad grinned.

"Only joking."

"What do you mean?"

"It was Kamalika."

"Oh."

"Sorry to disappoint you."

"I'm not disappointed." Dusty turned back to her cereal. "Didn't believe you anyway."

"Why not?"

"When's the last time I got rung by a boy?"

"Yes, well . . ." Dad started to break the eggs into the bowl. "There's plenty of time for that stuff and there'll be plenty of boys. Don't you worry."

"I'm not worried. They can take as long as they like about it. I'm not looking for a boyfriend. I'm more interested in getting you fixed up with someone."

"I noticed."

She looked up at him again.

"Is it a problem? I mean, I don't want to—"

"No, it's OK." Dad started to whisk the eggs. "You were right to encourage me to try the agency. I need to get out and meet people.

I've turned into a bloody recluse." He stop whisking and frowned. "It's just that . . ."

"What?"

"Sometimes I think about your mum, you know?"

"I bet she never thinks about you."

"I don't suppose she does."

"You haven't heard from her once since she left."

Dad said nothing.

"Have you?" she said.

"No."

"Honest?"

"No, of course not." Dad threw an angry glance at her. "Why should I lie to you? I haven't heard a word from her." He paused. "Have you?"

"No."

"Well, then."

"Easy, Dad," she said. "I'm not having a go at you."

Dad didn't answer.

"I don't want to hear from Mum anyway," said Dusty. "Or see her."

"You might feel differently one day."

"I won't ever. She dumped us both. So I've dumped her."

"She cracked up when Josh disappeared."

"So did you. So did I. But we didn't clear off. She did. And she was horrible to you. Have you forgotten that?"

"No, I . . ." Dad turned back to the stove. "I haven't forgotten that. She was horrible, no question."

"Really horrible."

"Yes, well . . ." Dad wiped his brow with the back of his hand. "She never was easy to be around. But then, I'm not either, am I?"

"You're great."

"Oh, sure. Like I believe you."

She reached out and gave him a pat on the leg.

"What time did Kamalika ring?" she said.

"About nine."

"I didn't hear it."

"You must have been out cold."

"What did she want?"

"Just to speak to you. I said you weren't up. Told her to ring back later this morning. She said she might text you instead."

Dusty pulled out her mobile and switched it on. There was no text message waiting for her. Neither spoke for a few minutes. Dad put the coffee on the table and carried on with the scrambled eggs. She finished her cereal, glad of the silence. She could sense the tension in Dad but it was hard to tell what the problem was. It could be Josh or Mum or this new woman he was seeing.

Or it could be her. She knew he worried about her being so independent and getting into scrapes like Josh did and now, with Josh gone and Mum too, he'd become almost obsessively frightened of losing her. She saw him approaching with the scrambled eggs.

"There you go." He put the plate down in front of her. "Enjoy."

"Thanks. Looks great." She smiled up at him. "As I'd expect from a head chef."

"A head chef without a job."

The phone rang.

"I'll get it," said Dusty, standing up. "It'll be Kamalika."

Dad stopped her.

"Finish your breakfast. I'll tell her you'll ring back in a quarter of an hour."

"OK. Thanks."

Dad left the kitchen and closed the door behind him. A moment later she heard the phone stop ringing and Dad's voice in the hall, then it faded and she caught the sound of the living-room door closing. She frowned. It certainly wasn't Kamalika. Dad would hardly take the phone into the living room for a secret chat with her. She thought of the boy and felt a moment's panic.

Her mobile beeped with a text message. It was from Kamalika.

Thers a weird boy on ravens fell dont go ther

She stared at the words, thoughts of last night flooding over her again, and with them more anxiety about Dad's phone call. He definitely wasn't speaking to Kamalika. It was someone else, someone he wanted to talk to in private. It could be quite harmless—maybe Helen. It was possible he'd given her his home number. Yet all she could think of was the boy. She could almost hear his voice.

No sound of Dad returning. She forced herself to finish her eggs, drink her coffee. Still the phone call went on. She walked over to the window and stared toward Raven's Fell.

A weird boy.

There could only be one. She knew it was him. She had to ring Kamalika, had to find out what her friend knew. She picked up her mobile, but before she could ring, it beeped with another text. Kamalika again.

Meet at macs 1130?

She texted straight back.

Ok

Then she heard the sound of Dad's footsteps in the hall. She turned toward the door. It opened and she saw him standing there, staring.

"Are you all right?" she said.

He didn't answer. Again she thought of the boy. Again she heard his voice in her head.

"Dad? Who was that on the phone?"

He walked slowly into the room and sat down at the table.

"A head chef without a job?" he murmured. "Maybe not."

"What do you mean?"

"I've got an interview."

"What!" She sat down next to him. "Who was it? Come on. Who was it?"

"The Pied Piper. They're looking for a head chef."

"You didn't apply to them, did you?"

"No, they've headhunted me. They've got new management. Guy said he knew I hadn't worked for a bit. But he's a mate of Gary Warrby. Remember him?"

"No."

"You were probably too young. He was my boss when I was head chef at the Sea Trout. Nice man. I only left because the job at Oscar's came up. Except they went and fired me."

"It wasn't your fault."

"I went to pieces."

"It wasn't your fault. It was the Josh and Mum thing."

"Anyway," said Dad, "it was nice of Gary to put in a word for me at the Pied Piper. I haven't had any contact with him since I left the Sea Trout. I thought he might have borne me a grudge for dumping them to go to Oscar's."

"He wouldn't do that. He knows you're a good man." She took his hands and squeezed them tight. "I'm so pleased. You deserve a break. And now there's Helen as well. Are you seeing her tonight?"

"Well, I . . ."

"You have arranged another date, haven't you?"

"Not exactly. I didn't want to presume or anything. She might want to think things over. I don't want to push it."

"But you said last night you wouldn't mind seeing her again."

"Yes."

"Did you mean that?"

"Yes."

"And would you like to have seen her again tonight?"

"Sure I would."

"And do you think she'd like to see you?"

"Don't know."

"Dad!" She looked him hard in the face. "You must have an idea."

"Well, we did exchange mobile numbers."

"There you go." She leaned forward. "That means she's happy to have further contact with you. If she didn't want that, she'd make sure everything went through the agency."

"I suppose so. But it still doesn't mean she'd want to see me tonight. And anyway, she might have another date. She might be seeing another bloke. She's probably got a list of people from the agency waiting to see her."

"Like the list you've got?"

"Very funny."

"Exactly. She might not have a list at all. And even if she has, there's no reason why you shouldn't ring her. If she can't meet up tonight, you'll still get an idea of whether she wants to meet up some other time." She felt his hands fidget in hers, saw him glance away, shift in his seat. She knew the signs and leaned back. "Sorry," she said, "I don't want to push you."

"No, you're right." He looked back at her. "I should ring. I want to ring. I mean . . . she even said . . . it would be nice to hear from me sometime."

"She said that?"

"Yes."

"When?"

"As I was leaving."

"Well, get on with it. Ring her. And then go and get that job. What time do they want to see you?"

"It's all very relaxed. The guy just said pop in around lunchtime today, see the setup and talk things over."

"And you said yes?"

"Sure."

"Good. You can give me a lift into Beckdale."

8

THE CAR BUMPED and skidded along the lane, now thick with snow. The change in Dad was dramatic. The chance of a job and the immediate acceptance by Helen of his offer to cook her a meal that evening had turned him into as happy a version of himself as Dusty had seen since the day Mum walked out.

He chattered about the job at the Pied Piper, how badly he wanted it, how ready he was to work again, how he just needed this break and they'd climb out of debt and wouldn't need to sell Thorn Cottage after all. Dusty let him talk, glad that he didn't appear to notice that her smile was a mask.

Inside she felt nothing but fear: fear of the boy, fear of never seeing Josh again, fear of those people with the dogs, fear of the ghostly light spreading all around them. Dad clearly hadn't noticed it, any more than he had noticed her unease. He talked cheerfully on as they made their way down the lane.

But progress was slow. The wheels kept spinning in the snow and the engine sounded even more labored than it usually did.

"That's another thing I'm going to sort," said Dad.

"What's that?"

"The car. Can't have it conking out all the time like it did last night. It was really embarrassing with Helen standing there. Trouble is, it's getting so old now I'm not sure how much life it's got left in it."

"It might help if you stopped trying to service it yourself and took it to a garage once in a while."

"Can't afford to," said Dad. "You know that. But things'll be different now. If I can just get this job." They drew close to the end of the lane and he nodded ahead. "That's the place where I saw the boy in my mirror."

"If it was a boy. You said the hood was up, so you couldn't tell."

"Well, that's the place anyway." Dad drove on a few yards and stopped just before the stile. "Here. This is the exact spot. I just looked in my mirror and saw him."

"Or her."

"I'm sure it was a him."

Dusty looked over her shoulder and pictured the figure with the duffel coat. She too had no doubt it was a him. She wasn't sure why she was being so stubborn with Dad and suggesting otherwise.

She glanced at him. He'd said nothing and was already driving on but his mouth was set, his face hard to read. He didn't seem angry but she'd broken his flow of talk and she was annoyed with herself for that. He was always better chatty than moody. They reached the intersection at the end of the lane and turned right onto the Beckdale Road.

She stared out of the window. The fields on either side were seas of unbroken white, but unlike the lane, the snow in the road had already been churned up by the traffic heading into town. It was clear that the bad weather wasn't going to stop this being as busy a Saturday as it usually was in Beckdale.

They passed the track to Knowle. She glanced down it and shivered at the memory of last night.

She'd been looking for the white van since the moment they set off but there was no sign of it here. She went on searching even so, as surreptitiously as she could. Again Dad didn't seem to notice her. He'd retreated into a silence as deep as her own. She glanced at him a few minutes later.

"You all right, Dad?"

He didn't answer.

"Dad?"

"What?"

"Are you all right?"

"Yes."

"Do you mean that?"

"No."

"So you're not all right?"

"I'm about as all right as you are," he said.

"What's that supposed to mean?"

"It means I'm about as all right as you are."

She looked away, unsure what to say.

"I'm nervous about the job interview," he said.

"You sounded really confident a moment ago."

"Well, I was really confident a moment ago. But now we're getting closer to it, I'm feeling a bit nervous. And I'm not being helped by seeing you nervous as well."

"I'm not nervous," she said.

"You're nervous as hell. You're fidgeting in your seat. You're looking this way and that. You're as edgy as I've ever seen you. I suppose it means you've got something going on with Kamalika or Beam or someone. And I don't imagine you're going to tell me about it. Just like Josh never did."

She looked back at him.

"There's nothing going on."

"Then what are you so edgy for?"

"I'm not edgy."

"I'm not stupid." Dad shook his head. "I know you play games with me, Dusty. You do it all the time, just like Josh did."

"Can you stop saying 'just like Josh' all the time?"

"I'll keep saying it because it's true. You're just like him. You play games with me, and I don't know if you're being devious or just trying to protect me because I'm a crap dad."

"You're not a crap dad."

"I am a crap dad. We don't have to beat about the bush. I am a crap dad. But I told you—I'm not stupid. You've been funny ever since you got up this morning. You were jumpy in the kitchen and you're jumpy now."

"I've just been sitting here doing nothing."

"You've been looking hard at every car that's gone past us. Both directions."

"So?"

"So what's going on?"

"Nothing, Dad. Honest. Nothing."

"What's this thing with Kamalika?"

"She just sent me a text."

"What about?"

Dusty took a slow breath.

"Dad, it's none of your business."

"Oh, right. It's none of my business. It's never my business, is it?" Dad scowled at her. "You're off on your own all the time, just like Josh. I'm starting to think you're worse than Josh. Off on your own, off on your own. And I'm not supposed to ask questions because it's none of my business."

"Dad, listen—"

"You disappear for hours on end. You fall out with people at school or in town. You get into scraps because you're too feisty for your own good."

"I'm only going to have a coffee at Mac's."

"Nothing else?"

"No."

"Then why all the fuss about 'Dad, it's none of your business'?"

She shrugged.

"I don't know. I just . . . don't like being interrogated."

"Christ, have I ever heard that before?" Dad glowered over the wheel. "It's like listening to Josh all over again."

They drove on in silence for a while.

"I'm only seeing Kamalika," said Dusty eventually.

Dad didn't answer.

"Dad? I'm only seeing Kamalika."

"I heard you."

"And she's not the sort of person to get into any trouble. You know that."

"Apart from fending off boys."

"Exactly. And she's pretty good at that anyway. Her father doesn't want her to have boyfriends yet. He's really strict about the people she sees."

Dad grunted.

"So nothing's bugging you?"

"No, honestly. You shouldn't be worrying about me. You should be thinking about your interview at the Pied Piper."

"And what about your sudden interest in cars?"

"I didn't know I was looking at cars."

"Well, you were."

"Nothing's wrong, Dad. OK? Nothing's wrong."

She sensed he still knew she was lying but he said nothing and they drove on again in silence. She slumped back in the seat, staring out at the snowy landscape, fields to the left and, off to the right, the sweep of Kilbury Moor toward Raven's Fell. She thought once more of Kamalika's text, and the strange, elusive boy. Then Dad spoke again.

"Wish that bloody van would make up his mind."

She looked quickly around at him.

"What van?"

"He's been stuck up my backside for the last few minutes."

She felt her muscles tighten. She forced herself to relax, to act calm, then eased herself forward so that she could see into the wing mirror. All she caught from this angle was a flash of white, but it was enough.

She sat quickly back, keeping her head below the top of the seat. It was hard to tell whether she'd been spotted. Dad glanced in the mirror.

"What's the matter with him?" he said. "Clear stretch of road and I've even slowed down for him to get past."

"Pull away from him, Dad."

"What?"

"Pull away from him. We should be a lot faster than a van."

"I didn't want to go too fast in this snow. Still, you're probably right. I'm getting a bit fed up with him."

Dad pressed the accelerator, and to Dusty's relief, they started to surge forward. Dad waited for a few moments, then checked the speedometer.

"Good girl," he said, patting the wheel. "You might be decrepit but you've still got a bit of poke." He glanced in the mirror again. "Damn!"

"What?"

"He's put on speed too."

Dusty felt a shudder run through her.

"Bloody idiot!" said Dad. "He's right on our tail again."

Dusty heard the roar of an engine directly behind them, then it moved to the outer edge of the car. She looked warily to the right and saw a white shadow ease alongside. It didn't continue past. It hovered there for a few moments, then slowly edged forward again. She clenched her fists, waiting to see those hateful faces staring at her.

But she was wrong.

It was another van altogether: a larger, smarter white van than the one she'd seen yesterday. At the wheel was a heavyset man with a thick, black beard, accompanied by two other men and a woman. Dad slowed right down and the van lurched past and continued on up the road ahead.

"Dreadful driving," he said. "I've half a mind to report him."

Dusty frowned, her eyes still on the van. After a few minutes it disappeared from view ahead. She looked at Dad but he had fallen into silence again. He didn't break it until they'd reached the outskirts of Beckdale.

"What time do you want me to pick you up from Mac's?"

"You don't need to," she said. "I'll get the bus back."

"I don't like you doing that."

"I've done it enough times."

"I still don't like you doing it."

"Why not? There's no danger. It drops me off at the end of the lane and all I've got to do is walk from there."

"What you really mean is you want to buzz off somewhere and not be tied down, right?"

Dusty shrugged.

"Maybe."

She didn't know what she wanted right now. She only knew that she felt afraid. They crossed the ring road and drove in toward the town center. She stared out of the window.

"Dad?"

"What?"

She hesitated.

"Do you think the light's a bit funny?"

"In what way?"

"I don't know. Just . . ." She looked about her. Still the strange thinness of the air, the sense of a veil hanging over her, over everything. "Just . . ."

"Looks bloody cold to me," said Dad. "That's all I know. If I can see anything in the air, it's snow coming. Which is another reason why I'd rather pick you up after my interview."

"I'll get the bus, Dad."

"Please yourself."

"Drop me here," she said. "No point going around the one-way system."

Dad pulled over to the side of the road.

"Good luck," she said. She leaned across and kissed him. "I'll be thinking of you."

"I'm getting a bit panicky again."

"You'll be fine. You're a fantastic chef. One of the best there is."

"If not the best."

"Don't get cocky."

"I was joking."

She kissed him again.

"See you later."

She climbed out of the car and closed the door. Dad gave her an awkward smile and drove off. She waited till he had disappeared around the corner of the street, then closed her eyes and felt the tension tighten within her. She had never felt so vulnerable, so unsure of who or what her enemy was.

She opened her eyes and looked about her. No sign of the people with the dogs. No sign of any danger at all. Just the light glistening all around, the light Dad couldn't see. She crossed the road, cut through to the square and headed for Mac's Coffee House.

9

KAMALIKA WAS SITTING at the corner table by the window, but she wasn't alone. Beam was with her, his huge form overflowing the seat, and there was another girl, someone Dusty didn't know.

She watched from the door, still unseen by the three of them. She'd hoped to find Kamalika by herself. She was in no mood for other company. She considered the situation. If she slipped out now, before they caught sight of her, she could ring Kamalika from down the road and say she hadn't been able to make it into town, and maybe find out at the same time about the boy. Mac's voice put paid to this idea.

"Morning, Dusty."

She saw the big man smiling at her from behind the bar.

"Hi," she said, with some reluctance. Mac nodded toward Kamalika and the others.

"Come to see that lot?"

"Yes."

"Guessed as much."

Kamalika had spotted her now and was wandering over.

"Want some coffee?" said Mac.

"Yes, please."

"Same as usual?"

"Thanks."

"I'll get someone to bring it over."

Kamalika arrived.

"Hi, Dusty."

"Hi."

"We've got some company."

"I noticed."

Mac leaned on the bar.

"Who's the girl?" he said.

"She's called Angelica," said Kamalika. "I met her in Scamps."

"You amaze me! A clothes shop!"

Kamalika gave him a withering look.

"She's just arrived in Beckdale," she said. "She'll be coming to our school when term starts again on Monday."

Mac studied the figure in the corner.

"Nice-looking kid. No wonder Beam's behaving himself." He glanced back at Dusty. "You paying for this coffee or what?"

Dusty handed him the money.

"Thanks." Mac gave her a wink. "I'll get it sent over."

"Come on, Dusty," said Kamalika, and she set off toward the corner table. Dusty caught her by the arm.

"Hold on. What's this stuff about a boy on Raven's Fell?"

"Didn't Mac tell you?"

"What's it got to do with Mac?"

"It's his story. I got it from him. I thought that's what you two were talking about just now."

Dusty shook her head.

"We didn't have time to say much."

"Well, come and sit down and I'll tell you."

"But what about Beam and that girl?"

"Angelica?"

"Yes. Do we have to talk about it in front of them?"

"It's not private. Half of Beckdale probably knows about it. Mac's been blabbing about it all over the place. Anyway, I'll tell you about it at the table. Beam and Angelica both know and you need to know too."

Dusty frowned. She still wished the others weren't here. She needed to think, not make meaningless conversation. They joined the others by the window. Beam turned and grinned up at her.

"Hi, Dustbin."

She cuffed him on the head.

"Ow!" He gave a grimace and looked at Angelica. "This is Dusty. She's a bit wild."

Angelica gave a smile.

"Hi, Dusty."

"Hello."

Dusty and Kamalika sat down.

"I was just giving these out," said Angelica.

She handed Dusty a little card.

"What's this?" said Dusty.

"Just a card with my mobile number on it. In case you want to phone or text me."

Dusty glanced at it. A small white card with nothing on it except a handwritten phone number and a smiley face drawn underneath that was clearly meant to look like Angelica.

"Have you got a mobile?" said Angelica.

"Yes," said Dusty, but offered no more. She ran her eye over the girl. She seemed pleasant enough. She was certainly pretty. Blond hair, blue eyes, slim figure, almost like a model—a strange contrast to Kamalika's duskier Bengali beauty.

She could see why Beam was interested, though she didn't suppose he'd have much luck. Angelica was almost certainly the kind of girl who was used to attention and could probably pick and choose who, if anyone, she wanted to go out with. But at least she was being friendly.

"I've been hearing a lot about you, Dusty," she said.

"If it's from Beam, it's a pack of lies."

"He said you've played for the boys' rugby team."

"Only once when Damien couldn't make it."

"Who's Damien?"

"Their normal scrum-half. He dropped out at the last minute one time so I took his place. I usually play for the girls' team."

"Wasn't it dangerous playing against boys?"

"The lot we played were too thick to be dangerous."

"Dusty did really well," put in Beam, quick to regain Angelica's attention. "She's actually better than Damien in some ways. She's not as fast but she's got a smoother pass. And she's fearless at the rucks."

Dusty gave him a wry glance.

"I can't believe I'm getting compliments from a prop forward."

A waitress put down the coffee and left. Dusty fiddled with the sugar and milk, the tension still heavy upon her. She desperately wanted to talk to Kamalika about this business of Mac's but Angelica was clearly determined to be polite.

"I think you're amazing playing for the boys' team."

"Yeah, well." Dusty took a sip of coffee. "Where do you come from anyway?"

"Birmingham originally, but that's a long time ago. I've moved around quite a lot."

"Bit of a one-horse town here. Not much going on."

"I don't care."

"What does your dad do?"

"He's dead."

"Oh, sorry,"

"It's OK." Angelica shrugged. "It happened a long time ago."

"Have you got any brothers and sisters?"

"No."

Dusty hesitated.

"Have you . . . I mean . . ."

"I've got a mum, yes."

"OK."

A faint smile passed between them. Dusty turned to the window and saw snow falling once again, just as Dad had predicted. Yet still the air shimmered and glimmered with light. She spoke again, to no one in particular.

"What's this stuff about a boy on Raven's Fell?"

Kamalika answered.

"Mac said he was walking his dog on the moor yesterday evening around dusk and he saw this figure hanging around those big rocks a little way up the slope. The dog ran up toward it, and when it got to about fifty feet from the figure, it started acting strange. The dog, I mean, not the figure."

"What do you mean—acting strange?"

"Whimpering and whining and stuff. And then it came tearing back and—"

"Ran straight past me," said Mac.

Dusty looked around with a start. She hadn't sensed Mac's approach. He gave a laugh.

"Can't have someone else telling my story, can I? No, he was out of his tiny little mind. Never seen him like it before. He's a bit of a thicko, my dog, but he's friendly. Likes company. Well, he didn't like this company."

"Who was it?" said Dusty.

"Couldn't tell," said Mac. "He was standing up there by those rocks, everything snowcapped. Couldn't see his face. He had a duffel coat on with the hood up."

Dusty bit her lip.

"How do you know it was a he?" she said. "Could have been a she."

"True." Mac pondered this for a moment. "Could have been

female. But it just didn't feel like it was a female. Something about the body shape. Maybe that was it. Struck me as male, even though I couldn't see the face. And I'm also pretty certain it wasn't a full-grown man. More like a boy about sixteen. But that's not the really freaky thing."

"What's the really freaky thing?"

"The freaky thing is I'm looking up the slope at this figure—right?—and my dog charges past me at ninety miles an hour. I turn and shout after him to come back, which he doesn't, and then I turn back to look at the figure and he's gone. Vanished."

"He walked behind the rocks."

"Nope. He wasn't close enough to do that. I looked away for a split second. No way did he have enough time to walk behind the rocks."

"It was dusk," said Beam. "The light was fading."

"I could still see clearly," said Mac. "One moment he was there, the next he wasn't. And I don't believe in ghosts. So where does that leave us?"

No one answered.

Dusty turned back to the window and stared out. So many pictures were forming in her head and all of them seemed threatening, even the pictures of Josh.

"Have you told the police?" she said.

"Yes, I thought I'd better. I mean, I know the guy wasn't actually doing anything wrong but he was weird. You know what I mean? There was something really strange about him. The way he freaked out my dog, and then just vanished, I definitely did the right thing telling the police."

"And what did they say?"

"That they'd keep an eye open for him. Not much they could say. I mean, he might not be dangerous but I still reckon he's someone to be avoided. My advice is to keep away from the moor and fell until the police find out who this guy is. That's what I've been telling people."

"What happened to your dog?" said Angelica.

"Oh, he was waiting for me back at the car. He's not right though, even now. Off his food. Not himself at all."

And Mac left them alone.

Dusty finished her coffee in silence. On the far side of the square a small knot of people had formed. She narrowed her eyes: a stocky man standing with two other figures. She stiffened for a moment, then relaxed.

It wasn't the man with the ponytail and his sons. It was some of the travellers who'd camped around the back of the school: a guy with streaky hair and two gangly-looking boys. Two more figures appeared but these weren't from the travelling community. They were from school.

She watched with distaste. Denny and Gavin were the last people she wanted to see right now. She had nothing much against Gavin but Denny was another matter. She wasn't sure what it was about him that she disliked, but it was a strong dislike, and it was mutual. If the boys came in here, there'd be trouble.

But they appeared to have no such intention. They wandered across the square as far as the monument, then stopped and began to scoop up snowballs. It was quickly apparent who their targets were. Vicky Spence and Sarah Moon were crossing the square from the other side. Seconds later the girls were ducking as the snowballs flew at them.

They responded by scooping up snowballs of their own and flinging them back. The battle raged for several minutes, with bursts of laughter on either side, the girls finally throwing snowballs at each other and the boys doing the same, then they all tired of the game, withdrew to the monument and lounged there, talking, in spite of the falling snow.

Dusty watched them, her mind distracted. Dimly she took in the fact that Beam and the others had been talking continuously while she was staring out of the window. She had no idea what they'd been saying. She felt as apart from the group in here as she did from the group out there. Her mobile rang in her pocket. She pulled it out and answered it.

"Hello?"

There was a long silence, then a voice she recognized at once.

"I feel apart too," said the boy.

10

SHE STIFFENED and glanced around at the others. They were staring at her with fixed expressions. Out in the square she saw Denny and his friends still standing by the monument. They had seen her now and were staring too. Everyone, it seemed, was staring at her. Again she heard the boy's voice in her ear. He sounded weary, even spent.

"I feel apart from everything and a part of everything. Does that make sense?"

She didn't answer. She couldn't answer.

"I wish this pain would go," he muttered. "But it's getting worse. It's . . . it's so bad now. It's like walking with a shadow you can't shake off. And now this new vision. I can't make sense of it. All I know is it's . . ." He breathed heavily out. "It's something to do with the light. Something not many people can see. But you can see it. You think your biggest mystery's Josh. But it isn't. It's this other thing."

She looked awkwardly around at the others.

"I've . . ." She stood up. "I've got to . . ."

But she could say no more. She turned from them and took the phone over to the door of the coffee bar. But there was even less privacy here with customers hanging around, waiting for the snow to stop.

She pushed through the door and stepped outside. Over by the monument Denny, Gavin and the two girls continued to watch. They were too far away to hear her but she lowered her voice even so as she spoke into the phone.

"I don't know what the hell you're talking about."

"It doesn't matter," said the boy.

"All this . . . stuff."

"It doesn't matter."

"What happened last night?"

"I don't know."

"You must know. You took an overdose. I thought you were going to die."

The boy said nothing.

"Are you there?" she said. "I thought you were going to die."

"I might already be dead," he answered. "I'm not sure."

"What's that supposed to mean?"

"I don't know what life and death are anymore."

She squeezed the phone, wishing she could squeeze this boy's neck instead and wring some sense out of him.

"How did you get my mobile number?" she said.

"I don't know."

"Don't keep saying 'I don't know'! Stop playing games with me!"

"I'm not playing games with you."

"Then how did you get my number? And don't just say you made it up like you did my landline number."

"I don't know how I got it. I just thought of you and rang it."

"Don't be so bloody—"

"Please, Dusty. Don't push me. Most of the things I do I don't understand."

She shook her head. This boy was mad.

"You're right," he said. "I am mad."

She shivered at this chill echo of her thoughts.

"What do you keep ringing me for?" she said.

"I'm frightened."

"Why phone me?"

"I like your strength. It helps me."

She didn't believe him.

"You must believe me," he said. "I'm telling the truth."

"Can you stop doing that?"

"I can't help speaking your thoughts."

"You're doing it again."

"I told you. I can't help it."

"But it's not natural. It's not . . . right."

"I don't know what's natural or right. Do you?"

She didn't answer. He gave a long sigh.

"All I know," he said, "is that sometimes . . . it's like I see and feel everything that exists. Then other times it's like nothing makes any sense at all. That's when I get frightened. Like I am now."

"What are you frightened of?"

"Being me," he said.

She stared out at the snow, her mind on Josh again.

"I don't know where he is," said the boy.

"You knew I was thinking of Josh?"

"I knew you were thinking of Josh."

"And you know who he is?"

"I'm guessing he's your brother."

"You're not guessing. You know who he is. And you know where he is."

"I don't."

"But you said you see things. Everything that exists."

"Sometimes."

"So you should be able to see Josh."

"I can't see him at the moment."

"You could look for him."

"I don't look for people," said the boy. "People look for me. There are people looking for me right this moment."

Like I am, she thought.

"Yes," said the boy. "Like you are."

She felt another shiver run through her.

"Dusty?" said the boy. "I really don't know where Josh is."

"I don't believe you."

"I don't know where he is. That's all I can say." The boy paused. "But I know where you are. You're outside. I can sense it. You're standing in the snow somewhere."

She said nothing.

"You're outside some kind of building," he said. "Standing on a porch or in a doorway or something, some kind of place where you buy stuff. Food and drink maybe. Or a bar of some kind. You're watching the snow. You're fascinated by the light, even though you're feeling angry and a bit scared again. And you've got people with you. Friends maybe. And . . ." The boy hesitated. "And some other people. People you don't like. They're nearby."

She looked uneasily about her, searching for some sign of the boy. He could only know all this if he was following her around. But all she saw was Denny and the others watching her from the monument, and people crossing the square, and cars, and snow falling as before. She spoke again into the phone.

"And you're wearing a duffel coat with the hood up."

There was another silence, a long one. She was determined not to break it first.

"You're right," he said at last. "I am wearing a duffel coat. But the hood's down, I pulled it down so I could speak on the phone more easily."

She squeezed the mobile again. So this boy was the figure Dad and Mac had seen.

"Then your phone's getting wet," she said. "From the snow, I mean."

"How do you know I'm outside?"

"I just do."

"You don't know. You're guessing."

She didn't answer.

"And you guessed wrong. I'm in a call box. Hang on. I want to put some more money in so we don't get cut off." There was a pause, then the boy's voice came again. "Listen, Dusty—"

"What's your name?" she said.

"You're going to hear rumors about me."

"What's your name?"

"You're going to hear rumors about me."

"Why won't you tell me your name? I've told you mine."

"Dusty, listen. Forget about the name thing. It's not important. Call me anything you want and I'll answer to it. But listen—you're going to hear rumors about me. Maybe you've heard them already. I can't tell you what to believe and what not to believe. I can only tell you I don't mean any harm. But I have to defend myself, OK?"

"What does that mean?"

"I've killed two dogs. Pit bulls. They were coming for me. I told you, Dusty. There are people looking for me. Some of them have got dogs."

"Some of them?" Dusty's mind was in a whirl. It was obvious which dogs these were and who they belonged to. But were there more people after this boy? "Who are all these people after you? What do they want?"

"They want to kill me."

"But . . ." She remembered the fangs, the eyes, the powerful bodies. "How did you kill the dogs?"

No answer came. She stared over the square toward the monument. Denny and Gavin were still looking at her. So too were Vicky and Sarah. She felt the eyes of Beam and Kamalika and Angelica upon her from inside the coffee bar. The boy spoke at last.

"I don't know. I just did."

Another silence: a hard, painful silence. She saw Angelica walking toward the door. Kamalika and Beam were still sitting at the table. Beam's eyes were on Angelica's back. The girl stopped on the other side of the door and looked through the glass at Dusty standing on the porch. The boy's voice sounded again inside the earpiece.

"Someone's just joined you. Or about to join you. You're not alone anymore."

Dusty said nothing.

"A girl," said the boy. "It's a girl. I can feel her. But she's not right next to you."

Angelica pushed open the door and stepped into the snow.

"She's coming closer," said the boy.

Dusty tightened her grip on the phone. Angelica had not spoken. Her footsteps made barely a sound, certainly nothing that the boy could hear.

"I've got to go," he said suddenly.

"Wait," said Dusty.

But the line went dead.

She glared at Angelica, who stopped sharply, a couple of feet away.

"Sorry, Dusty. I just came out for some air. Don't stop talking."

"I've finished," said Dusty flatly.

"Oh, I hope I didn't . . ." Angelica hesitated. "I hope I didn't spoil anything."

Dusty said nothing. She was trying to retrieve the boy's number on her mobile. She didn't suppose it would be traceable. The boy would probably have been too careful. She was right: *number withheld*. She frowned and looked up to see Angelica still watching her.

"I hope I didn't spoil anything," the girl said again.

Dusty turned and stared across the square. Over by the monument Denny was patting together another snowball.

"I was sorry to hear about Josh," said Angelica.

Dusty whirled around.

"How the hell do you know about Josh?"

"Your brother . . . I mean . . ."

"How do you know about Josh?"

Dusty glowered at her. The girl took a step back toward the door of the coffee bar. Through the glass Dusty saw Beam watching. His eyes were enough to explain Angelica's sudden need for air. But they didn't explain this business about Josh.

"How do you know about Josh?" she demanded.

"I didn't mean to cause offense."

"What have you been told about him?"

"Only that he walked out two years ago and no one knows what happened to him. And your mum . . . I mean . . . she . . ."

"She had a nervous breakdown and walked out six months later." Dusty went on glaring at her. "What else have you been told?"

"That's it."

Dusty was still bristling with anger. She scowled at Angelica, then through the glass at the others.

"Kamalika had no right to tell you about Josh," she muttered.

"It wasn't Kamalika," said Angelica. "It was Beam. He was telling me about you while you were talking to Kamalika at the bar. And he mentioned Josh. I'm sorry if I upset you. I didn't mean to."

Dusty clenched her fists. Now she understood. In Beam's desire to impress Angelica, he'd told her about a family tragedy that was none of her business. Not that the girl wouldn't have heard about it eventually. Most people in Beckdale probably knew about Josh's disappearance from all the news bulletins at the time. But that still didn't make it right. It wasn't Beam's story to tell and now, to make matters worse, here he was lumbering toward them with an irritating grin on his face.

She looked darkly at him, so worked up with anger and confusion she was ready to jump on him and lash out. But before she could move, she heard a thud nearby, then a scream. She looked around, startled.

Angelica was bent over, both hands clutching her face. The remains of a snowball lay scattered on her neck and shoulder. Dusty leaned closer.

"Are you all right?"

Angelica was sobbing.

"Caught you in the face, did it?"

Angelica said nothing and went on sobbing. Beam pushed through the door and hurried over.

"You OK?" he said.

She didn't answer.

"Dusty? What happened?"

But Dusty was staring toward the monument. Denny and Gavin had their backs toward her and were talking to the two girls. All four seemed to be making a strenuous effort not to look this way.

"It was Denny," she murmured. "He threw it."

Kamalika appeared in the doorway.

"Is Angelica all right?"

Angelica straightened up and took her hands from her face. There was a gash under her left eye.

"There's no way a snowball did that," said Dusty.

"What do you mean?" said Beam.

She didn't answer. She was already bent over the ground, searching in the snow. Then she saw it: an ugly, sharp-edged stone. She grabbed it and straightened up.

"There," She held it out in front of Angelica. "That's what was inside the snowball. That's what hit you." She turned toward the monument. "Except it was meant for me."

"Dusty," said Angelica. "It's not worth it."

"Yes, it is." She shot a glance at Beam. "Are you in?"

"Well, I . . . I don't know if it's . . . I mean . . ."

"Pathetic."

Dusty raced off across the snow toward the group by the monument. Her blood had been up since the business last night and now, after all that had happened this morning, she was more angry than she'd been for a long time. She knew she couldn't beat Denny up before Gavin and the others stepped in but she could do some damage. She headed straight for Denny.

"Clever boy," she called as she drew near. "Stone inside a snowball. Well done."

He turned and saw her.

"I don't know what you're talking about," he said.

She jumped on him. He was clearly expecting this as he was braced and ready but the impact still knocked him to the ground. He recovered quickly and tried to push her back but she was already thumping his face with her fists.

"Bastard!" she shouted. "Bastard!"

She went on thumping him. She knew she wouldn't have long before the others intervened but she was determined to draw blood.

"Get her off me!" Denny bawled to his friends.

She felt something hard smash into her face, Gavin's fist probably, and here were arms tugging at her, trying to pull her clear. She squirmed free of them and went on punching Denny. But he was fighting back now and with his greater strength he managed to roll her over in the snow.

She knew she was in trouble. If she didn't break free, he'd pound her unconscious. She saw Gavin looming over her, and Sarah and Vicky. She saw Denny's bloody face fuming above her. She saw his fist come down. She twisted to the side and it drove straight into the snowy ground.

"Crap!" shouted Denny.

A large form thundered in from the right as Beam threw himself into Denny. His body drove the boy off Dusty and the two lads rolled together in the snow, punching each other fiercely. Gavin ran forward and threw himself on top of both of them. Kamalika arrived, shouting at them to break it up, but, like Sarah and Vicky, hung back and didn't get involved. There was no sign of Angelica.

Dusty scrambled up and ran forward. Gavin and Beam were on their feet again, trading punches.

Denny was still struggling to get up. Dusty jumped on him and they went down in the snow once more.

But here were hands pulling at her again, pulling at Denny, and there were voices too, Sarah's and Vicky's and Kamalika's, all yelling at them to stop—and suddenly it was over, Denny half stumbling with the two girls across the square, Gavin a few yards behind, holding his hand to his head.

11

Beam stood motionless, watching them go, then he turned to Dusty.

"You all right?" he said hoarsely.

Dusty grunted. All right was the last thing she felt. Her head was thumping and her body seemed to ache all over. But that was nothing to what she felt inside. The rage was still there. The confusion was still there. The fear was still there.

Nothing had changed—and Josh was no nearer.

"I'm OK," she muttered.

She stared blankly around her. The snow was still falling. Strange how she'd almost stopped noticing it. Strange too how few people there were in the square. It seemed suddenly a chilly, remote place. She glanced toward Mac's Coffee House and saw faces turned inward, as though no one wanted to see them.

"Angelica's gone," said Beam.

"I don't blame her," said Kamalika. "She won't be wanting to hang around with us anymore. She'll be thinking we're nothing but trouble. Or Dusty at least."

Dusty looked at her.

"Me?"

"Yes, you." Kamalika narrowed her eyes. "And I'm starting to think the same thing myself."

"Thanks for nothing," said Dusty. "Denny chucks a snowball at me with a stone inside. I fight my corner. And you say I'm nothing but trouble."

"It hit Angelica, not you."

"But it was aimed at me. He's had a thing about me for ages."

"You've had a thing about him for ages."

"Meaning?"

"Meaning you've had a thing about him for ages."

"He's a pain."

"He's like Josh."

Dusty glared at her.

"Say that again."

"He's like Josh."

"You saying Josh was a pain?"

"I'm not saying that at all."

"What she's saying," said Beam, "is that you still haven't worked out why you hate Denny so much."

"I told you. He's a pain. Are you telling me he's not?"

"No, I agree with you. He's a jerk." Beam paused. "He also happens to look like Josh did."

Dusty glowered at him. She knew he only meant one thing by this remark and that had hit her hard enough. But the other thing—the thing he hadn't meant to say—had hit her harder still.

"You speak about Josh like he's dead," she snapped.

"I didn't mean to suggest—"

"Like Josh *did*. That's what you said. He also happens to look like Josh *did*."

"Yeah, well. It's just the words I used. You're reading too much into it."

"He's alive," she snarled. "OK? He's alive."

Beam held her eyes for a few moments, then reached up and wiped some of the snow from around his mouth. It was tainted with the blood oozing from his nose.

"I'll see you," he said quietly, and he lumbered off.

Kamalika watched him go, then turned back to Dusty.

"He's right, you know. Denny does look like Josh."

"Can't say I've ever noticed."

"I think you have."

Dusty said nothing.

"I've got to go," said Kamalika. "I promised I'd be back for lunch."

Dusty looked down. Kamalika was so bad at lying but that wasn't the hardest thing to accept. The hardest thing was to see how badly her friend didn't want to be with her right now.

"Listen," said Dusty. "I've had some weird phone calls. This boy. I don't know who he is but he got my number somehow. I think . . ." She hesitated. "I'm pretty sure he's the figure Mac saw on the fell."

"Then you need to tell your dad." Kamalika's voice matched the expression on her face: formal, detached, noncommittal. "Or the police. Or both."

"But he hasn't done anything wrong. And anyway, I don't think he's dangerous. I think he's desperate."

"What do you mean?"

"The first time he rang, he'd taken an overdose. He was trying to kill himself. I can't report someone for that. And anyway, I've got no way of proving the boy I spoke to is the same as the figure on Raven's Fell."

"Then why did you say you think they might be the same person?"

Again the formal tone. Kamalika didn't sound remotely sympathetic. There seemed little point in pursuing this. Dusty forced a smile.

"I don't know . . . I just . . . I suppose I just wanted to tell you this. It's made me a bit stressed out and that's maybe why I flew off the handle at Denny."

"Maybe."

They looked at each other in silence, then Kamalika gave a nod.

"I've got to go."

"OK. See you around."

Kamalika looked her over.

"I expect so," she said, and turned away.

Dusty watched her go. She was close to tears and she hated it. Everything was going wrong. First the boy with his strange talk, then the fight, and now she'd fallen out with her friends. She stared down at her hands. They were stinging around the knuckles where she'd punched Denny and they were growing cold. She reached into her trouser pocket and pulled out her gloves. As she did so, something fluttered to the ground.

A piece of paper.

The face she had drawn last night. It stared up at her as the snow fell upon it, just as that other face had stared in at her last night from the windowpane. She gazed down at it. The flakes were soaking the image already and in a moment it would be lost. She thrust her gloves back in her pocket, then reached down and picked up the paper. The image was still visible but it was starting to blur.

She crumpled the paper into a ball inside her fist, yet still the image remained, as clear to her mind as it had been to her eyes, perhaps more so. Once again the likeness to Josh struck her. She reached into her pocket for the thing she always carried—his last photo, the picture she had taken of him out in the garden. No smile on his face, just an uncharacteristically wistful glance past the camera as if toward a distant horizon.

And the snow fell on that too.

She pushed the photo and the crumpled picture back into her pocket. She still felt angry, confused, close to tears, and there was something else: she was certain she was being watched. She stared about her and caught a movement on the far side of the square by the entrance to Station Road.

But it was nothing. Just a figure in an anorak walking across the street, the hood up against the snow. She thought of the boy and frowned, but this wasn't him. This was just a man, and a fairly elderly man at that. She caught another movement a few doors down Station Road.

Someone in a dark blue raincoat, also with the hood up. Yet there was nothing suspicious about this person either. It definitely wasn't the boy, or the man with the ponytail or one of his sons. It was nobody dangerous-looking. She glanced back at Mac's Coffee House.

The windows were now moist from the snow but she could still see through them. The table where she and the others had sat was being cleared by the same waitress who had served them. Nobody was looking out and there was no sign of Mac.

She pulled on her gloves and squeezed her fists tight. Her hands still smarted, still felt cold. She no longer knew what to do. She supposed she should catch a bus home. There seemed no point in staying here. Dad certainly wouldn't want her turning up at the Pied Piper and cramping his style. Yet she didn't want to go home.

She wanted . . .

She wanted to see Josh standing before her. More than anything in the world she wanted that. She stared about her, searching, as she had so often done, for some trace, some explanation. But she knew it was in vain. She started to walk across the square.

She didn't know where she was going, nor did she care as long as it was away from Station Road. She didn't know why but Station Road felt wrong. At least the bus stop was in this direction. She supposed that was where she should be heading. She left the square behind her and dipped her head to shield her face from the snow.

It was growing heavier by the minute. She glanced over her shoulder toward the entrance to Station Road and saw the figure in the dark blue raincoat again, still with the hood up. She pressed her lips tightly together. She too had a hood but she had no intention of pulling it up.

Anger still bubbled inside her—anger toward the boy, toward Kamalika and Beam, toward Denny, even toward Josh—and as she walked, she could feel it transmuting into a deep, irrational defiance against the snow. She stared up at the glowing flakes. They would not defeat her. They would not stop her going wherever she wanted. They might even invigorate her, clear her thoughts.

But they only made her colder, and despite her determination not to bother Dad, she soon found herself outside the Pied Piper. She knew she shouldn't be here. She could ruin everything for him. But she was desperate to see him. She wanted to run in and hug him. She wanted him to hold her and be something he wasn't. She wanted him to be strong.

She stared through the glass. Most of the tables were taken and she could see waiters moving with unearthly serenity about the room. There was no sign of Dad. She set off down the road and finally reached the bus stop. There was no one here and the exposed bench seat—now that vandals had finally smashed away what was left of the old shelter—had a thick layer of snow across the top.

She brushed some of it aside and sat down. The surface was still wet under her trousers but she didn't care. She was wet through already. She waited, shivering, and the snow continued to fall.

Her mind had ceased to work, or so it felt. The cold and damp seemed to seep not just through her body but through her every thought. She reached inside her pocket and felt for the crumpled paper. It was still there. She pulled it out, unfolded it and forced herself to look at the blurred face again.

It seemed to glow with the same eerie light she felt all around her.

She crumpled the paper again and put it back in her pocket,

then gazed about her. Everything was dazzling white, as in the dream she'd had last night of Kilbury Moor. But as in the dream, it felt dangerous—too bright, too white. She could feel the brilliance cutting through her body, her mind, her very essence. For a queasy moment her body seemed to fade, like the boy's footsteps in the snow.

"Please," she murmured to it. "Please."

She didn't know what she was trying to say. She heard a rumbling noise at the end of the street and saw the bus heading down toward her. Something in the sight and sound of it brought her back. She clung to her body, fighting the brightness that threatened to wipe her away. The bus drew nearer, wipers swishing, engine growling. She thrust her head back, face to the sky, and the driving snow drowned her back to life.

She gulped in air and peered back over the street, her eyes still swimming with snow. The bus was alongside now. She could see people moving about inside. The door opened and she saw the driver staring out at her. She stared back, unable to move or speak, unable almost to think.

Passengers were climbing out through the other door. She glanced at them but none looked her way. They simply put up their umbrellas or hoods and hurried off toward the town center. She looked back at the driver. He was still watching her.

"You getting on?" he said.

She thought for a moment, then shook her head.

"You all right?" he said.

"Yeah."

"What you sitting out in the snow for?"

She said nothing.

"Doesn't seem like a particularly good idea," he added.

The snow went on falling, falling, falling. She closed her eyes and thought of Josh.

"You sure you're all right?" said the driver.

She opened her eyes.

"I'm waiting for my dad," she said.

"Oh." The relief in the man's voice was palpable. He gave her a quick grin. "Well, take care and keep dry."

The bus moved off and soon disappeared around the corner of the road. She stood up and stared dumbly about her. The snow was still pouring down. Everything looked white now, wherever she turned. She felt as though she were filled with snow, made of snow. But at least the brightness, the almost unbearable brilliance, had faded to a point where she could think again, and there was only one thought that rose into her mind.

"Josh," she murmured.

And she trudged off toward Raven's Fell.

12

SOMEHOW IT SEEMED the obvious place to go. Perhaps some part of her had been intending this all along. She didn't know. It was hard to understand her own motives right now. She plodded on. There was only one lead in the search for Josh and that was the boy. Not that he was much of one, given that he denied all knowledge of Josh's whereabouts.

Yet she still didn't believe him. For all his clever mind reading, he couldn't have spoken Josh's final words to her on the phone last night unless he'd learned them from her brother. They must have met somehow or spoken. He couldn't have guessed Josh's words, any more than he could have guessed her landline and mobile numbers, as he claimed to have done.

So, slender lead though it was, she had to follow it. Mac had seen the boy halfway up Raven's Fell, so Raven's Fell it had to be, however scary a prospect that was. She didn't suppose the boy would be there or that there'd be any clues, but it was somewhere to start.

At least the snow was easing a little, but she was still cold, still shivery, still broken up with anger and fear and bewilderment, and to confuse things further, she once again had the sense that she was being watched, even followed. She looked over her shoulder.

No one was visible in the street behind her, yet the feeling remained. Perhaps she was imagining it. She knew she was dangerously emotional right now. Even so, she was starting to trust her fears a bit more. She'd been right last night when she had sensed the presence of the snow-face and it was quite possible she was being watched. She was close to the school now and Denny lived near here. Not only that but he had mates here too, none of whom would be friendly toward her after today's incident.

She stopped at the perimeter fence that marked the edge of the school playing field. There were two ways she could go and neither appealed to her. The quicker route was to take the footpath and cut around the field past the old caravan site where the travellers had their encampment—but that meant skirting the estate where Denny lived—or she could go past the school and take the lane that ran straight down to the head of Mirkwell Lake. But that was risky too. With its high walls on either side, there was no escape if Denny and his mates blocked both exits.

She decided on the latter. Denny would hopefully be at home and it was unlikely anyone dangerous would be hanging about the lane in weather like this. She set off again, passed the school gate and stopped at the entrance to the lane. She hated this place but there was no avoiding it if she wanted to reach Raven's Fell by the route Mac would have taken with his dog.

"Come on," she told herself. "Walk."

She started down the lane. At least the way ahead looked clear. She could see all the way down it to the long jetty at the head of the lake. She walked on, faster, anxious to be through it and out on open ground again. The walls rose above her on either side, blocking the light, blocking even the snow. She pushed herself on, watching the end of the lane, aware as before of the feeling of being followed.

She glanced over her shoulder.

Nobody.

She glanced back ahead.

Nobody.

She hurried on, half running now. A figure appeared at the end of the lane. She stopped and stared. A figure in a long coat. A duffel coat with the hood up. She glanced over her shoulder. Another figure, the figure she'd seen earlier in the dark blue raincoat, also with the hood up. Neither showed their faces, neither moved.

She looked this way, that way.

The duffel-coated figure turned and disappeared from view behind the extremity of the wall. The figure in the dark blue raincoat started forward. Dusty turned back toward the lake and started to run. Whoever the person in the raincoat was, she had to speak to the boy.

The walls slipped past her as she drove herself on down the lane. Dimly she took in the fact that the snow had stopped falling. She didn't look back at the figure in the raincoat. The boy was the one she wanted—and yet again he'd disappeared. But he couldn't have gone far this time.

She was nearly at the end of the lane but the snowy ground was hampering her. She was skidding with almost every step. At last the wall ended and the ground opened up. Ahead of her, beyond the jetty at the end of the lane, she could see Mirkwell Lake stretching away. To the left of the great lake was the extremity of the school field and the path that twisted past Denny's estate. To the right was the car park and the path that led across Kilbury Moor around the shore of the lake and on to Raven's Fell. She could see its snowcapped peak rising in the distance.

Just a few feet away the duffel-coated figure was climbing into a car in the car park. The door slammed shut; the engine kicked into life. She ran forward and saw the car turn toward her. She stopped, her eyes on the driver. The hood was back; the face was clear. It wasn't a boy. It was a woman she knew all too well.

The Head.

The car drew up beside her and the driver's window came rolling down.

"Dusty?"

She tried to collect herself.

"Hello, Mrs. Wilkes."

"What are you doing out here?"

"Same as you probably."

Mrs. Wilkes pulled the hand brake up and turned off the engine.

"Somehow I doubt that."

Dusty said nothing. Out of the corner of her eye she could see the dark blue raincoat moving across the car park. The hood was still up and it wasn't possible to see the person's face. It didn't look like anyone dangerous, probably just a walker or someone wanting some air.

The figure stopped at the far end of the car park, leaned on the fence and gazed over it toward the bridleway that curled around the eastern edge of the moor and ran on to Stonewell Park five miles away. Mrs. Wilkes, however, had no interest either in the walker or the bridleway.

"I came to see the lake, Dusty. I wanted to see if it's frozen over."

"Oh."

"Which it hasn't. But I don't suppose that's why you're here."

"I came out for a walk."

"I don't think so but of course it's none of my business."

"No," said Dusty.

"No, it's none of my business? Or no, you didn't come out for a walk?"

Dusty shrugged.

"Both, I guess."

Mrs. Wilkes went on watching her.

"Well, you're not in school now and it's not for me to poke my nose in where I'm not invited. I'm not your head teacher when you're out of school. But as a woman in a car in a bleak spot like this, I'm worried when I see a fifteen-year-old girl out on her own."

"Like I say, I'm having a walk." Dusty glanced at the figure leaning over the fence. "Like that person over there."

"You don't look like a person having a walk. You look like a drowned rat. And you've got a black eye coming."

"I bumped into a door."

"And I bumped into Sarah Moon."

They looked at each other in silence for a moment, then Mrs. Wilkes frowned.

"Let me drive you home, Dusty."

"I'm all right."

"You're not all right."

"I am."

"Then let me ring your father. He can come and get you."

"He's out."

"So how are you getting home?"

"He's coming to collect me."

"Where are you meeting him?"

"In town."

"So what are you doing wandering around here?"

Dusty looked away. She knew Mrs. Wilkes wasn't buying a word of this. It was hard to know what to say. She looked back.

"I had this fight with Denny," she said eventually. "Sarah probably told you about it."

"She did."

"And I just came out here to cool off. Got caught in the snow. Dad's tied up in town. He's got a job interview but he should be through soon. We're meeting up in about an hour."

It was hard to tell from Mrs. Wilkes's expression whether this latest fabrication had done the trick. The Head watched her in silence for a few moments, then shrugged.

"Well, Dusty, like I say, it's none of my business. But can I say one thing? No, two things. Firstly, I think you need to understand just why you've got a problem with Denny."

"Yeah, I know. He looks like Josh."

"So you do understand that?"

"Yeah, Beam's been ramming it into me. So's Kamalika."

"That's good."

"The guy's still a prat, whoever he looks like."

Mrs. Wilkes gave a half smile.

"Well, whatever else you think of him, it's time you realized that your main problem with him is probably because of his likeness to your brother."

Dusty looked away again. The figure was still leaning on the fence, gazing over the bridleway. She turned back to Mrs. Wilkes.

"What's the second thing you wanted to say?"

"Keep away from Kilbury Moor and Raven's Fell. It's even risky coming to this end of the lake. You shouldn't be here."

"You're here."

"I came by car, and just to look at the lake, but I wouldn't have walked here on my own. There's a lot of talk in town about some weird figure wandering about. I gather the police are looking into it. Probably nothing to worry about but you need to watch out. Being a free spirit is one thing. Being foolhardy is another. I'd keep away from this place if I were you. At least until the police have sorted things out."

Dusty felt in her pocket for the crumpled paper. There it was, a little ball, oddly reassuring. She eased her hand out of its glove and closed her fingers around the paper. It felt strangely warm. She let it go and drew her hand out again, ungloved. The palm tingled for a moment in the chill air.

Mrs. Wilkes started the engine again.

"Come on, Dusty. Jump in. At least let me give you a lift back into town."

"I'm OK."

"I don't like you being out here on your own."

"I'm not on my own. There's someone over there. And it's only a woman."

"You can't tell it's a woman."

"She's got a handbag. I just noticed."

Mrs. Wilkes studied the figure in the dark blue raincoat.

"You're right," she said after a moment. "But I'd still rather you came with me into town."

Dusty said nothing and at last Mrs. Wilkes gave up.

"OK, Dusty, if you're really sure. But please remember what I said about keeping off the moor and fell."

"OK."

"And listen—at school, anytime you need to talk, you come to my office. Got that?"

"Thanks." Dusty forced a smile. "I'll try and remember."

"Take care of yourself."

"OK."

And with a somewhat anxious look, Mrs. Wilkes drove off. The moment she was gone, the figure in the raincoat turned. Dusty's mouth dropped open.

It was Mum.

13

DUSTY," she said.

But Dusty was already hurrying back toward the lane.

"Dusty, wait!"

She didn't wait. She put on speed.

"Dusty! Please wait!"

She started to run.

"Dusty!"

She carried on running, not looking back. Mum's voice rang out.

"I'll turn up at the house if you don't stop!"

Dusty stopped, breathing hard, then turned and stared back. Mum was standing on the spot where Mrs. Wilkes's car had been and there was something pathetic about her. Maybe it was just the contrast with Mrs. Wilkes. The Head seemed so confident, so in control. Mum seemed exactly what she had been the last time they met eighteen months ago—only worse.

They watched each other in silence for a few moments, then Mum started forward. Dusty waited, hating this feeling of entrapment. Life without her mother had been hard enough but life with her back was impossible to contemplate, especially now that Dad was starting to pick himself up again.

Mum was close now, just a few yards away, and her face was a battleground of emotions. What those emotions were Dusty had no idea. She had long since given up trying to read her mother's feelings from the expression on her face. Mum stopped in front of her.

"Dusty, you look terrible."

"So do you."

"You've got a black eye coming and you're soaked through."

"I'm all right."

"What's happened?"

"Nothing you need to worry about."

"But—"

"I had a fight."

Mum shook her head.

"Still getting into fights. You shouldn't be doing that."

"What do you want to talk to me about?"

"It's good to see you, Dusty."

"What do you want to talk to me about?"

"I don't know. I just . . . want to talk."

"What about?"

"Dusty, please don't make this so hard." Mum fumbled in one of her pockets and after a moment pulled out a misshapen cigarette. After more fumbling she found a box of matches. She lit the cigarette and breathed in the smoke. "Dusty, I just want to talk, OK? I haven't turned up for the express purpose of making your life difficult."

"Glad to hear it. You've done enough of that already."

Mum took a slow drag of the cigarette.

"I know," she said quietly, "and I don't feel good about it. Listen, I've parked my car just around the corner. Can I drive you back to Thorn Cottage?"

"No."

"I'm not going to come in. Not if you don't want me to. I won't even drive all the way up the lane. I'll stop halfway along, out of sight of the house, and then turn around and drive away. Your father won't even know I've been there. Unless you choose to tell him."

"Which I won't."

Mum looked hard at her.

"Is that because you're ashamed of me? Or because you're afraid he may still love me?"

"I don't want to talk about this."

"Dusty—"

"And I don't want a lift home."

But here she knew her face betrayed her. She was so cold now there was no disguising it.

"Come and sit in the car at least," said Mum. "Get warm. Then you can decide what you want."

"I already know what I want. I want you to go away and never come back."

Mum looked away toward the lake.

"I've hurt you that badly, have I? What a monster you must think me." She glanced back. "My car's around the corner. I won't force you. But if you want to come and sit with me for a bit and get warm, or have a lift home, just follow. No pressure."

And she walked off down the lane.

Dusty stared after her, fuming. No pressure, no bloody pressure, she thought. Only it's all the pressure in the world. You know I'll come, if only to make sure you don't roll up at the house and mess up Dad's life again.

And because I'm freezing cold.

She set off down the lane, glaring at her mother's back. Mum didn't look around. She simply carried on to where the lane met the road, then turned right toward the school gate. Dusty reached the road and turned the same way.

Mum's car was parked on the far side of the road. Dusty could see her already inside, lighting another cigarette from the butt of the previous one. Mum saw her and beckoned her toward the passenger door. Dusty opened it but stayed in the street.

"I'm not getting in the car with you puffing like a chimney. The smoke'll stick to my clothes and Dad'll smell it when I get home."

"He'll think it's your friends, won't he? I'm sure some of them must smoke. Come on. Get in."

Dusty looked away. She could feel herself being drawn back into that world of conspiracies that Mum seemed to need to create. Five minutes together and they were already forging lies to tell to Dad.

"OK," said Mum suddenly. "I don't want us to fall out over a cigarette." She wound down the window and threw it out. It hissed in the snow as it landed. She wound up the window again. "Come on, Dusty. Get in."

Dusty climbed reluctantly in.

"I'll sit with you for a bit," she said. "That's all. No driving anywhere."

She glanced about her. The car looked as tatty and unkempt as Mum did. Whatever Mum had been doing with her life since she walked out, moneymaking clearly hadn't been part of it. She was gaunt too. Dusty frowned.

"You look like you haven't eaten for the last eighteen months."

"Thanks a lot," said Mum.

"And you've colored your hair."

"Do you like it?"

"Not much."

"Did you like it better before?"

Dusty turned away. She could sense there was a game being played here but she wasn't sure how to play it.

"I'm not playing a game, Dusty," said Mum.

Dusty looked back at her. Something about that last remark reminded her of the boy. Then she remembered his disconcerting habit of speaking her thoughts aloud, as Mum had just done.

"I'm not playing a game, Dusty," said Mum. "I'm really not."

"Can we just drive?"

"I thought you didn't want to."

"Well, I do now. I'm freezing and I want the car heater on. So we'll have to drive."

"Where do you want me to take you?"

"You might as well take me home. Only you're not to go—"

"I know. I'm not to go more than halfway up the lane. Don't worry. Your father won't see me."

Mum turned the key and the engine spluttered into life, a very different sound from Mrs. Wilkes's suave motor. Once again Dusty found herself struck by the contrast between the two women.

"Put your seat belt on," said Mum, fastening her own.

Dusty snapped the belt on without a word and Mum pulled away from the curb.

"This snow's treacherous," she said. "You'd better hold on tight. We may skid a bit."

"Can you just put the heater on?"

Mum fiddled with the controls.

"It takes a while to get going," she said.

"Just get the thing started."

The heater grumbled into life. Dusty huddled on the seat, praying that the feeling of cold would go away soon. Mum seemed focused only on the road. It certainly was treacherous—the snow was deeper than ever and it was hard in places to see where the pavement was— yet Dusty sensed that Mum's silence stemmed from something other than the need to concentrate on the driving.

"I thought you wanted to talk," she said after a few minutes.

"I do," said Mum, "but I'm scared."

"What of?"

"I don't know. You, maybe."

More silence. At least the heater was starting to work. Dusty stared out of the window. Raven's Fell was clearly visible, rising in clean white slopes. She could even make out the rocks where

Mac had seen the figure in the duffel coat. There were no figures there now; at least, none that she could see. It looked like a bleak, snowy place: no refuge for a duffel-coated boy. Mum spoke at last.

"Dusty?"

"Yeah?"

"How are you? Really, I mean."

"I'm fine."

Mum glanced at her.

"Don't you want to know how I am?"

"You're obviously going to tell me anyway."

"But don't you want to know?"

"Not particularly."

"I miss you. I miss your dad. I—"

"He's met someone."

"Oh."

"Someone really nice."

Mum bit her lip.

"I'm glad to hear it," she said eventually. "Who is this person?"

"A woman."

"I gathered that, Dusty, but who?"

"I told you. A woman. That's all you need to know."

"You can tell me more than that, can't you?"

"Why should I? It's none of your business."

"What's she like?"

"I just told you. She's nice. He's really happy."

"He's never happy."

"He is now."

"What's her name?"

"None of your business."

"Dusty, come on! It's not going to be a problem; I mean, me

knowing who she is or whatever. What do you think I'm going to do? March over to her house and beat her up?"

"No, you wouldn't have the guts."

"Thanks a lot."

"But you might go and tell her off. Cause a scene or something. Put her off wanting to see Dad."

"You really think I'd do that?"

"You might."

"Well, I wouldn't." Mum stared at her. "Dusty, I just want to know about her."

"I'm not telling you anything."

"Is that because you're bluffing?"

"What do you mean?"

"Kidding me along. Because you don't actually know her properly yourself."

"I know her really well."

"Or maybe there isn't a woman at all. Maybe you're just making it up."

"You can believe that if it makes you feel better."

Mum shrugged.

"So how long have they been seeing each other?"

"Quite a while."

"What does that mean?"

"It means it's time you changed the subject."

Mum said nothing for several minutes, yet it was clear she was deeply unsettled. Dusty watched her out of the corner of her eye. She was gripping the steering wheel tightly, her head kept bobbing this way and that and she kept biting her lip.

"What's the problem?" said Dusty. "Is it a cigarette you want?"

"No."

"Have one if that's the problem."

"I don't want a cigarette."

"You look so nervous."

More silence. They pulled out onto the main Beckdale Road and joined the other traffic heading out of town. Dusty caught a flash of metal in her wing mirror and stiffened: a white vehicle overtaking them. Mum glanced at her.

"Now you're the one looking nervous."

Dusty said nothing, tried to look calm, but she knew it wasn't working. She gripped hold of the seat. Over to her right she sensed the vehicle moving alongside. She couldn't look at it. She heard the roar of its engine, then the sound of Mum winding down her window and yelling out.

"Don't just stay there! Go past or go back!"

Now Dusty looked and, to her relief, saw it was only an elderly couple in a station wagon crammed with garden utensils. Mum eased off the accelerator and they struggled past and away up the road.

"Bloody farmers," she muttered, winding up the window again.

"They're not farmers," said Dusty. "They've got a stall in the market. I've seen them."

"Well, they shouldn't be driving if they're not safe."

Dusty felt the tension drain from her, but Mum seemed worse than ever: not just tense but bad-tempered as well. They drove on in uneasy silence and finally reached the lane to Thorn Cottage.

"You can drop me here if you want," said Dusty.

"Is that what you want?"

"I'm just saying."

"We agreed halfway. Then I'll turn and come back."

"OK. If you want."

They drove off down the lane, neither talking. The stile appeared ahead, then slipped slowly past. Mum carried on for another few minutes.

"This'll do," said Dusty.

"Just a bit further."

"No."

"I can't turn very easily here. It's wider just up there."

Dusty looked quickly at her.

"You're not to go all the way to the house."

"I won't."

"You promised."

"I know. So you don't need to worry."

They drove on another hundred yards, then Mum pulled over to the side of the lane. Dusty looked around her. It didn't seem any easier to turn here than it had been earlier, but at least they'd stopped out of sight of Thorn Cottage. Mum turned off the engine and sat back in her seat.

"Dusty, you know why I walked out, don't you?"

"Because you're a cold, unfeeling witch."

"No, not because I . . ." Mum paused. "I had a breakdown . . . as you well know . . ."

"You're still a cold, unfeeling witch."

"Well, we . . . we don't have to argue about that now. When you have a breakdown, you're not always in your right mind." She was biting her lip again, clenching and unclenching her hands. "Dusty, listen, can I—"

"Have a bloody cigarette, for God's sake!"

"Thanks." Mum jerkily lit a cigarette, then wound down the window and blew the smoke out. "Dusty, when Josh left, we didn't know what happened to him, did we?"

"Of course not."

"And you haven't . . . in the last eighteen months . . . I mean, you haven't heard anything more?"

"How would you know? You haven't been here."

"Yes, but . . . I just assumed someone would have told me if there'd been any news."

"Why the hell should we tell you anything? You walked out."

"Dusty, I've tried to explain. This . . . breakdown, it just . . . knocked me over. I haven't been right since. I'm still not right. Look at me. Do you ever remember me smoking like this?"

Dusty said nothing. Mum took some more drags of the cigarette, then stubbed it out against the side of the car.

"But there's something I didn't tell you or your dad." Mum hesitated. "After Josh walked out and the months went by and he didn't come back, I . . . I went to see this medium. She told me Josh was dead. She said she'd spoken to him in the spirit world."

"You should have said."

"I didn't want you or your father to lose hope and I couldn't . . . I mean . . . I just couldn't face the possibility either. I was in denial. And that's what tipped me over the edge. But, Dusty, listen . . ." Mum gripped her by the arm. "I'm convinced now . . . utterly convinced . . . that he's still alive."

Dusty looked away over the snowy fields.

"How do you know?" she said.

"I met this strange boy."

She turned sharply back.

"What boy?"

"I don't know. I didn't really see him properly. It all happened so quickly."

"Was it Josh?"

"No, definitely not. And he didn't give me a chance to ask him any questions."

"What happened?"

"It was a few weeks ago. I was in the car."

"Where? Around here?"

"No, back home. You know I've been staying in different places but some of the time I've been with Mum and Dad in—"

"Yeah, yeah. What happened?"

"I was thinking of Josh. When am I not? And I was crying. I was in the car on my own and I was stuck at some traffic lights and I had the window down, and I was just bawling my head off. I couldn't stop. And this figure comes from nowhere, this . . . this boy in a duffel coat . . . and he just bends down and says, 'Don't cry, Mumsligum. It's all right.' And then he walks on and disappears around a corner before I can even think. Mumsligum! He called me Mumsligum! That's exactly what Josh used to call me!"

"I know."

"His voice even sounded like Josh's. Only it wasn't him."

"What did he look like?"

"I barely got a glimpse before he disappeared. But he was strange. Sort of snowy-white features. And then he was gone. When the lights changed, I turned right to look for him but there was no sign. Dusty, I know it's a message. I know Josh is alive."

Dusty reached into her pocket and squeezed the paper ball tight. As before, it felt strangely warm. Mum reached over her suddenly and opened the passenger door.

"Go home, Dusty. I know you've got to. But take this."

She held out a card. Dusty glanced at it.

"Mobile hairdresser? Since when have you been a mobile hairdresser?"

"Since I qualified. I'm trying, Dusty. I'm really trying. But look— will you promise me something?"

"What?"

"My mobile number's on the card. Will you promise you'll ring me if you ever want me back in your life?"

"What's it got to do with me? It's between you and Dad."

Mum shook her head.

"It's not. I know your dad too well. He might not want me as his wife anymore, especially if he's found someone else, but he'll forgive me. He'll take me back as a friend. I know he will. He's that kind of man."

"He's a good man."

"I know. But your forgiveness is something else. I won't come back without it."

Dusty put Mum's card in her pocket, next to the paper ball.

"Don't say any more," said Mum. "I know you're confused. But remember . . . just remember . . . you've got my mobile number if you ever need me."

And without another word Mum started the engine again. Dusty climbed out of the car, then, after a moment's hesitation, leaned back in and gave Mum a kiss on the cheek. Mum reached out and drew her close, then quickly kissed her back and pushed her away.

"Go," she murmured. "Please go."

Dusty closed the passenger door and straightened up. Inside the car Mum was lighting another cigarette. Their eyes met again and she saw her mother wave her away. She hurried off down the lane, not looking back. From behind came the sound of wheels spinning in the snow.

She walked on, listening still, and gradually it became clear that Mum had turned the car and was driving back to the Beckdale Road. Dusty walked on, fighting the tension inside her, and now desperate to reach Thorn Cottage. But when she arrived, her anxiety only deepened.

A police car was parked outside.

14

CHRIST, DUSTY!" Dad stood in the front doorway staring down at her. "What's happened to your eye?"

She peered past him into the hall. There was no sign of any police officers but she could hear voices in the kitchen. Dad pulled her inside and closed the door behind her.

"You've been in a fight!" he muttered. "Another bloody fight!"

"Yes." There seemed no point in denying it. She wasn't prepared to talk about the strange boy or Josh or Mum or the weird stuff, but the business with Denny had nothing to do with any of that. "I bumped into Denny in town."

"For God's sake, Dusty, how many times have I got to tell you? You can't just pick fights with all the people you don't like. And this thing with Denny's gone on long enough. Are you hurt?"

"No."

"Not that you'd tell me." He looked her over. "You're soaked through as well."

"We rolled in the snow. Don't worry about it. Did you get the job?"

"Never mind that."

"But did you?"

"Yes, yes, but listen." He lowered his voice. "The police are here."

"I saw the car. What do they want?"

"I was hoping you might tell me. They've only been here a few minutes. Said they wanted to speak to the two of us together. I told them you might not be back for ages but we agreed they'd hang about for a bit in case you turned up. I'm just making them a cup of tea. What's going on?"

"No idea."

Dad looked at her, clearly unconvinced.

"Well, whatever it is," he said, "they can wait while you have a shower and clean up your face. You look an absolute bloody mess, and you reek of cigarettes."

"Kamalika had a friend with her. She was smoking."

"I don't want to know. Go on. Upstairs. I'll tell them you'll be down in . . . what? How quick can you be?"

"Ten minutes."

"I'll make that fifteen."

"OK."

But it was a good twenty minutes before she was down again. She stood outside the kitchen door, clean and dry at last, and in warm comfortable clothes, but her heart was racing. There was enough to worry about right now without the police involved as well; and her face still looked a mess.

She listened to the voices on the other side of the door: a man's voice, deep and gravelly; a woman's, clipped and clear; Dad's, somewhat tense. Nothing much under discussion, just a time-killing conversation about the snow on the moor. She sensed the impatience of all three beneath their studied politeness.

She pushed open the door.

They were sitting at the table drinking tea. All twisted around to face her. Dad looked pale and nervous. The policeman and the policewoman were harder to read.

"This is Dusty," said Dad.

"Thank you, sir," said the policeman. "Nice to meet you, Dusty."

She nodded but said nothing and sat down at the table.

"You won't know us," he went on. "We're not from this part of the country. We've come to assist our colleagues here. They've obviously filled us in on your family background and circumstances. I'm referring of course to Josh, your . . . er . . . brother."

"I know who Josh is, thanks."

She caught a warning glance from Dad but ignored it. The policeman shrugged.

"Yes. Well, anyway, I'm DC Brett."

"And I'm DI Sharp," said the woman.

Dusty glanced at her. Sharp by nature too, she thought, and with a clear sense of her own authority, in spite of having allowed the man to open the proceedings.

"Nasty shiner you've got there, Dusty," she said.

"Yes."

"How did you get that?"

"I had a fight in town today."

"Oh, dear. I hope you're not hurt."

"I'm fine."

"Dusty's not scared of anybody," put in Dad. "She'll take on anyone, even boys."

"Really?" said DI Sharp in an unimpressed voice. "Well, we'll try not to get on the wrong side of her. Now we've just got a few routine questions we need to ask, if you can both spare us a few minutes of your time."

"Of course," said Dad. "What's this about?"

"We're looking for a boy," said DI Sharp, and her eyes fixed on Dusty.

Dusty swallowed hard. The woman's gaze was so intense it seemed to stab her. She stared back as blankly as she could and tried to give nothing away.

"What boy's that?" said Dad. "Someone from the school?"

"No," said DC Brett, "but it's someone we're very anxious to trace.

He's a rather unusual boy. Someone you'd definitely remember if you'd seen him."

"What's his name?"

The two police officers exchanged glances.

"We're not actually sure," said DI Sharp.

"You're not sure?"

"I know it sounds strange but the boy himself is a little strange. He's probably been given lots of names, or given himself lots of names. But we're not actually certain what his original name was."

"How old is he?"

"We're not sure of that either but probably about your daughter's age."

"Dusty's fifteen."

Again Dusty felt DI Sharp's eyes upon her. Again she found the scrutiny uncomfortable. She turned and stared out of the window. Nothing moved outside save the snow falling once more in the glistening air. The boy's words came back to her.

It's something to do with the light. Something not many people can see. But you can see it.

She gazed out, wondering.

"Dusty," said DI Sharp.

It wasn't a question, just a flat statement. Dusty turned back to face the officer again.

"Good name," said the policewoman. "One of my favorite singers was called Dusty."

Dusty said nothing. She didn't trust those eyes. They saw too much.

"So what about this boy?" said Dad.

"We can't say much about him," said DC Brett, "for the simple reason that we don't know much about him. But he's been involved in a few incidents in other parts of the country and we're anxious to have a word with him."

"What kind of incidents?"

"We can't go into that, I'm afraid. But we do need to speak to him urgently."

"So why should Dusty or I know anything about him?" DI Sharp answered.

"He's been spotted in this area over the last few days. A man reported seeing a boy yesterday evening who matched his description and we think the boy may have stolen this gentleman's mobile phone."

"How do you know that?" said Dad.

"We don't but it seems possible. The man said he left the mobile phone on top of the water tank outside his home."

"Water tank," said Dusty.

"Yes."

"Was his home a tumbledown kind of place? More like a hovel?"

"It might have been."

"An old man? Bad teeth and no hair?"

"It might have been."

It could only be Silas. She thought of how he hated being pestered by people. He wouldn't have enjoyed an interview with the police. He didn't much like talking to anyone, including her.

"I can't imagine Silas having a mobile," she said. "I wouldn't have thought he'd know how to use it."

"You're obviously acquainted with the gentleman," said DC Brett.

"Dusty knows everyone," said Dad. "Including one or two people I wish she didn't."

"Silas is all right," she said. "He wouldn't harm a fly."

Dad turned back to the two officers.

"And the old man's seen this boy?"

"We think so," said DI Sharp. "Not to speak to, just hanging around the moor not far from his home. And then his mobile phone went missing. The old man's pretty sure he left it on the water tank, and when he remembered what he'd done and went out to fetch it, he found it was gone. And he saw the boy running away across the moor."

"But what's this got to do with us?"

"We've been checking calls made from that mobile since the old man reported it missing. There's only been one call so far and that was at eleven forty last night. It was to your landline number."

Dusty saw Dad's eyes flicker toward her. The police officers were watching her too. She tried to master her thoughts. If the boy had done something wrong, she should tell them everything. Yet somehow all she could think of was the voice at the end of the phone: the boy wanting to die, the boy frightened of the people hunting him. Perhaps he was a criminal, yet he hadn't sounded like one. He'd sounded like a boy in despair.

She thought of the footsteps fading in the snow. Everything about this boy was a mystery, yet he seemed to know something about Josh, or at least have some connection with him. She stared back at the two officers. They had their own agenda. So too did the boy's enemies. Once he was caught by either party, he'd be lost to her and any chance she might have of finding out about Josh would be gone.

She couldn't give away what she knew just yet.

"I answered the phone," she said. "Dad was out. But there was nobody at the other end. So I put the phone down again."

DI Sharp's eyes seemed to darken but it was her colleague who spoke next.

"You heard no voice at the other end of the line?"

"No."

"Just silence?"

"Yes."

"No background noise? Breathing? Music? Traffic?"

"Nothing."

"So you put the phone down?"

"Yes."

DI Sharp spoke.

"Why didn't you put the phone down at once, Dusty?"

"What do you mean?"

"It's a simple question. Why didn't you put the phone down at once?"

Dusty tensed. She could feel herself being steered somewhere she didn't want to go. DI Sharp pulled out a notebook and glanced at it.

"According to our information, the phone call lasted fourteen minutes twenty-eight seconds. And you say it was a silent call. I'm just wondering—why didn't you put the phone down sooner than that?"

"I don't know. I just . . . hung on. I suppose I thought someone might speak."

"But no one did?"

"No."

"Wasn't that rather a strange thing to do?"

"What do you mean?"

"Well, I can understand you hanging on for a minute or two to see if the other person's going to speak. Maybe you thought it was a friend, or perhaps even an emergency at that time of night. Your father was out, you said. Perhaps you thought it was him trying to get through."

"I did. That was the reason I hung on."

"For fourteen minutes twenty-eight seconds?"

"Yes."

Dusty frowned. It was clear that neither of the police officers believed this. She tried again.

"I just . . . wasn't sure what to do. The phone rang. I thought maybe it was Dad. The snow had started again. He was later than I expected. I thought maybe he was in trouble or something. And there was this phone call. I just . . . hung on. I thought it was the right thing to do."

There was a long silence, then DI Sharp spoke again.

"You don't need to be defensive, Dusty. You're not under suspicion of anything. We're just trying to piece together what happened." She paused. "So you stayed on the line for over fourteen minutes. What happened then? Did you hang up first or did the line go dead at the other end?"

"The line went dead at the other end."

"Then what?"

"I put the phone down."

"OK. And you've no idea who might have made this call?"

"No."

The eyes watched her, heavy with accusation.

"I haven't," Dusty added.

"OK."

"But I've seen a strange boy," said Dad.

Both police officers turned to him. Dusty breathed out, grateful to be released, if only for a moment, from DI Sharp's attention.

"Tell us what you've seen, sir," said DC Brett.

Dad told them about the figure in the duffel coat.

"And you're convinced it was a boy?" said DI Sharp. "Even though the hood was up and the figure was walking in the other direction down the lane?"

"Yes. I mean, I just . . . well, I just thought it was a boy. Maybe it was the walk. Can't remember exactly. I know that sounds pretty flimsy."

"It doesn't sound flimsy and it does match other descriptions we've had from people in the area."

"What? A figure in a duffel coat?"

"Yes."

Dad looked at Dusty.

"See? I was right. It was a boy."

"It might have been," DI Sharp corrected him. "It's still only a guess. Even so, it's very helpful to have this information."

"This boy," said Dad. "You say you can't tell us what he's done or how old he is or what his name is. Can you tell us what he looks like? You said we'd remember him if we'd seen him. Have you got a photo of him?"

Dusty caught an awkward glance between the two officers and for the first time they seemed slightly less confident.

"We don't have a photo of him," said DC Brett after a moment. "It's an odd thing but . . ." He glanced at his colleague again. "Well, we just don't have one. Not one that tells us anything anyway."

"What does that mean?" said Dad.

Another awkward look between the two officers.

"As I mentioned earlier," said DI Sharp, "he's a rather strange boy. Neither of us has seen him personally. We're forced to go on descriptions that other people have given us about him. But he seems to be so distinctive that those who have seen him never forget him."

"In what way is he distinctive?"

"He's as white as snow."

Dusty stared out of the window again at the bright flakes falling.

"An albino, then?" she heard Dad say.

"It's more than that," said DC Brett. "We've seen pictures of albino types but this boy seems different from them. He's got white hair, white skin. They say his eyes are very pale. And also . . ."

His voice faded away. Dusty went on staring out of the window.

"Also what?" said Dad behind her.

"Well," said DC Brett, "it appears his face and body shape are a little out of the ordinary. A sort of—how shall I put it?—mixture of male and female."

"But he's a boy, isn't he?" said Dad. "You've been talking about him as a boy. So there must be something about him that makes you feel that."

"Oh yes, we're quite clear that he's a boy. Everyone who's ever seen him refers to him as a boy. And we do have some pretty conclusive reasons, which we can't go into here, for asserting that he's a boy. As DI Sharp just said, neither of us has personally seen him, nor have any of our colleagues at the Beckdale branch. We've been relying on reported sightings of the boy from members of the public and from what we've been told by our colleagues around the country."

"Around the country?" said Dad.

"Yes," said DI Sharp. "He's been seen in lots of places and there've been a number of incidents that make us very anxious to speak to him."

Dusty thought of the figure Mum had seen at the traffic lights. Where had this boy been? How many other places? Were there other lives apart from hers that he had thrown into confusion?

She went on staring out of the window. The sky had darkened in spite of the snow, yet the eerie radiance still hung over the garden and fields. She forced herself to speak.

"Is he dangerous?"

"We don't know for certain," said DI Sharp. "But there's one particular incident . . . one alleged incident . . . that we need to follow up as quickly as possible. He certainly shouldn't be approached."

Dusty turned back from the window to see DI Sharp's eyes upon her again.

"So if you come across him, Dusty," she said, "you're to keep well away. If you're the fiery type your father says you are, you need to take in what I'm saying. You're not to approach him. If you see anything, you report it to the police and we'll deal with it. Is that clear?"

"Yes."

"This is not someone you're to take on. It's all very well being fearless and getting into scraps with boys. This is different. Do you understand?"

"She understands," said Dad.

"I'm asking Dusty."

"I understand," Dusty said.

"Good," said DI Sharp. She glanced at her colleague, who nodded.

"We've kept you long enough," he said. "Thank you for your time."

"I don't think we've helped you very much," said Dad.

"Yes, you have. You've explained about the phone call. It doesn't tell us how he got your number or why he phoned—if it was him who phoned—but it's another lead followed up."

"So if we see this boy," said Dad, "we're to keep away from him and report him to you."

"Yes."

"Even though we don't really know what he looks like."

"Yes." DC Brett smiled. "That's correct."

The two police officers stood up. Dad did the same.

"Good luck with your search," he said.

"Thank you."

Dusty shifted in her chair.

"You still haven't explained about the photo."

Yet again she caught an awkward glance between the two officers.

"You said earlier that you don't have a photo of him," she went on. "And then you said: 'Not one that tells us anything anyway.'"

"Yes, well . . ." said DC Brett.

"What did you mean by that?"

The officer cleared his throat.

"Well, now we're getting into the realms of what might sound a bit fanciful. And that's not something I'm happy with. It might be a lot of nonsense. It probably is. And it's all hearsay anyway."

"What do you mean?" said Dad.

"It's not something we've seen ourselves, so we can't verify it." He glanced at DI Sharp but she said nothing. He cleared his throat a second time. "The . . . er . . . boy has actually been in police custody once. Not in Beckdale. In another part of the country. He's been interviewed and photographed."

"So there is a photograph of him," said Dusty.

"I'm afraid there isn't," said DI Sharp. "For some strange reason the picture came out blank."

"What?" said Dad. "Nothing on it at all?"

"No, everything's quite clear. Everything except the boy, that is."

"What's different about the boy?"

"He's just not there. It's like a photograph of everything else that was there except the boy. He's vanished from the picture altogether like he was a ghost." DI Sharp paused. "Except he's not a ghost. He ate police food and drank police tea. His body is solid. All the police who've dealt with the boy have confirmed that. He might look weird, like he's made of snow, but he's flesh and blood. Everyone's confirmed that."

Dusty remembered the sounds she'd heard on the phone the first time the boy rang: the rasping breaths, the retching. Yes, he was no ghost. He was solid. He was real.

But his realness was unlike anything she'd ever dreamed of. She tried to picture him in her mind: the snow-boy, who seemed part female as well. For all his strangeness, for all his mystery, for all his hint of danger, he sounded eerily beautiful.

"We really must go," said DI Sharp. "We've taken enough of your time. Thanks again for your help, and don't hesitate to get in touch if anything happens. Or if either of you remember anything you forgot to tell us."

Dusty caught the flicker of a glance in her direction, but nothing more.

15

DAD WAS SOON BACK after showing the officers out and she knew what was coming. "Right," he said. "What are you keeping from me?"

She looked up at him. She desperately needed to think. The last thing she wanted was Dad on the rampage as well.

"Nothing, Dad," she said.

"Sure about that?"

"Quite sure."

"Then why don't I believe you?"

"I don't know."

"Don't mess around with me, Dusty."

"I'm not messing around with you."

He glared at her.

"I don't mind you keeping stuff from me if it's personal. Those things are none of my business. But anything dangerous or illegal is my business."

"I understand."

"So there's nothing you need to tell me?"

"Everything's fine, Dad. Tell me about the job."

"Some other time."

"But I really want to know. When do you start?"

"Monday," said Dad. "Now can we drop it? I've got other things to think about."

"Like cooking for Helen tonight."

"Yes. I've just remembered she's a vegetarian."

"Do you want me out of the way?"

"No. I want you to meet her. And I want her to meet you."

"OK." She leaned forward and kissed him on the cheek. "I'll see you later."

He frowned and said nothing.

Back in her room, she lay on the bed and tried to sleep. But it was no use. Her mind was moving too fast. Downstairs she could hear Dad clattering about the kitchen. She stood up and wandered over to the window. The snow had stopped and dusk was falling but the familiar glow still hung upon the air. She stared out at it, pondering the boy's words again.

It's something to do with the light.

"But what?" she murmured. "What's something to do with the light?"

As if in response, more of the boy's words fell into her mind.

You think your biggest mystery's Josh. But it isn't. It's this other thing.

"What other thing?" she whispered.

No words came to answer this.

She stared out at the glowing dusk, then closed the curtains and walked back to the bed. She yearned for sleep now. She pulled out Josh's photo and stared at it for a few moments, then lay back and tried again to doze. The next thing she remembered was a knock at the door. She sat up, startled. How long she'd slept she didn't know. The knock came again, then Dad called out.

"Dusty? You in there?"

Before she could answer, the door opened and Dad's face appeared.

"Oh," he said. "You are here."

He looked edgy and slightly wary of her.

"Where did you think I was?" she said.

"I don't know. I just . . ." He shrugged. "I just thought you might have run off somewhere. And I don't want you doing that, OK? Not tonight."

"I was asleep."

"Oh." Dad shifted on his feet. "Well, sorry I woke you."

"It's OK. What did you want to ask me? Or did you just come up to check on me?"

"No, I wanted to ask you something as well. Can you do the usual?"

"What do you mean?"

"I've put some clothes on the bed. I just wondered if—"

"Oh, sure. Let's have a look."

She followed him through to his bedroom and saw shirts, jackets, and trousers spread over the bed. He nodded to a combination he'd put to one side.

"I thought maybe this jacket with this shirt and these trousers?"

"Don't be silly, Dad. You can't wear those things."

"Why not?"

"You'll look like a dog's dinner. Hang on."

She studied the clothes for a few moments.

"What happened to that blue shirt I got you?"

"It's in the wardrobe."

"Get it out."

"Are you sure?"

"Get it out."

He fumbled in the wardrobe and eventually pulled it out. She held up a pair of jeans.

"Put it with these."

"Isn't that a bit casual?"

"You want to be casual. You're eating here, not going out. And you don't need a jacket."

"No jacket?"

"No, honestly. You don't want to be too formal. Those trousers and that shirt. That's all you need."

"What about shoes?"

"Sneakers. Your best ones, not the other ones."

"You're joking."

"Put them on. They look good on you."

"If you say so. What are you going to wear?"

"Exactly what I'm wearing now."

"But—"

"Dad, I'm not eating with you two."

"Of course you are."

"Don't be stupid. This is you and Helen. I'm not being the third wheel."

"But I want you to meet her."

"I will meet her. I'll come down and say hello, and then I'm leaving you together."

Dad looked sharply at her.

"I don't want you going out," he said. "Not tonight. I just said."

"I'll be in my room."

"Well, come down now and have something to eat. I can't have you starving while Helen's here."

They walked downstairs and Dad made her some cauliflower cheese. She ate in silence, aware of his continuing nervousness, and aware too of a thought growing in her mind: something the police had said and which she'd forgotten but would have to follow up. It was going to take some fixing, though, especially after what Dad had said about her not going out tonight.

Her mobile beeped with a text message. She reached for the phone, hoping it would be Kamalika with some reassurance that they were still friends. But it wasn't.

Beam gav me ur tel no sory i wlkd off im scared of
fites r u ok angelica xxx

"Who's it from?" said Dad, bent over the stove.

Before she could answer, the doorbell rang. Dad whirled around in alarm.

"Christ!" he said. "Helen's early!"

"That's a good sign," said Dusty.

"Not when I'm nowhere near ready."

"Do you want me to let her in?"

"Can you?" Dad was frantically brushing himself down. He stopped suddenly and looked at her. "Or do you think it looks bad if I don't answer the door?"

"Dad, it's fine. I'll let her in. Just tidy yourself up a bit."

"What about your meal?"

"I've finished. See?"

She handed him her empty plate, walked through to the hall and opened the front door. Mum was standing on the step.

"Hello, Dusty!" she said.

Dusty stared, unable to speak, then finally managed to collect herself. This wasn't Mum after all.

"My name's Helen," said the woman.

It was someone who looked like Mum, so very like Mum it was scary. But no, the hair was slightly longer, the face fuller, the smile different: warmer, less complex.

"It's nice to meet you," said Helen.

Different voice too: deeper, calmer. Dad strode up to join them.

"Hi, Helen," he said.

"Hi." Helen kissed him on the cheek. "How are you?"

"Fine, thanks. Good to see you. Come through to the kitchen. I'm not quite ready with the meal, I'm afraid."

"Typical chef," said Dusty.

Helen laughed.

"No hurry with the meal. I'm just glad to have got here without skidding off the road and burying the car in a snowdrift."

They made their way through to the kitchen.

"Have a seat," said Dad.

"Thank you."

Helen sat down at the table.

"You won't mind if I carry on cooking?" said Dad.

"Not at all." Helen's eyes wandered around the room for a moment, then settled on Dusty. "You looked a little startled when you saw me on the doorstep," she said.

"Sorry," said Dusty. "I didn't mean to be rude."

"Oh, it's no problem at all. You were probably taken aback because I look so like your mum."

Dusty stared at her, then at Dad. He shook his head.

"I didn't tell her anything." He looked at Helen. "How did you . . ."

Helen laughed, in an oddly infectious way, then nodded toward the far corner of the room. Dusty turned and understood: the family photo on top of the fridge, the last one ever taken of all four of them. Even two years ago Mum's likeness to Helen was clear. Dad looked noticeably younger, as Dusty herself did. Josh looked ageless, just as he always did in her mind.

"Sorry, Helen," said Dad. "Perhaps I should have moved that photo."

"You shouldn't think of moving it," she said. "Your family's a part of your life. I've still got a photo of my ex-husband in the living room."

"Don't you hate him?" said Dusty. "After he walked out on you."

"Dusty," said Dad. "That's a little personal."

"No, it's fine," said Helen. "Ask anything you want, either of you."

She looked at Dusty. "No, I don't hate him but I don't love him either. I haven't loved him for a few years. That's probably why he went off with someone else. He's getting married again later this year."

"Oh."

"But I don't have much to do with him. He lives in New Zealand with my son."

"Do you get on with him? Your son, I mean."

"Yes, really well, but he's got his own life and he's probably going to settle in New Zealand. That's fair enough. And I've still got Lydia."

"Is that your daughter?"

"Yes. She's at university."

Dusty considered the woman before her. There was a refreshing directness about her. Her words didn't seem loaded with hidden motives like Mum's usually were and her eyes were steady. Dad was fidgeting and it was clear he was awkward with both her and Helen there. She held out her hand.

"It was nice meeting you."

"You too," said Helen, taking the hand in a firm grip.

"Have a good meal."

"Thank you."

"I'll say good-bye now."

"Oh," said Helen. "Won't I see you again tonight?"

"I'll probably go to bed early."

She saw Dad watching her.

"I'll be in my room, Dad," she said, and hurried out of the kitchen.

She closed the door behind her and stood there, frowning. The thought of what she planned to do next scared her, and there was the added feeling of guilt from deceiving Dad again, yet there was just a chance it might lead to a clue about the boy. It was surely worth the risk, and if she was quick and quiet, she might even get back before Dad realized she'd been out.

She tramped upstairs as noisily as she could, then opened her bedroom door and loudly closed it again—keeping herself outside on the landing. Then she crept back down to the hall. Dad and Helen's voices reached her through the closed kitchen door: a polite, harmless conversation about Lydia's university.

She took a slow breath, then slipped her coat from its peg and put it on. No change to the voices in the kitchen. She tied her scarf around her neck, then bent down and picked up her boots. Too risky to put them on here. They were a bit of a struggle to get into and she might make a noise.

She took them through to the living room and half closed the door behind her without clicking it shut. The front door was out of the question—Dad would hear it for certain, or Helen would—but the big window in the far corner of the living room was another matter.

She pulled her boots on, fastened her coat and tightened her scarf, then listened one final time for sounds of detection. Nothing, not even the voices. That made her feel slightly better. If the voices were too far away for her to hear, then the sound of the window opening shouldn't reach them either.

She fiddled with the catch. There was a light snap but the window made no further complaint and opened onto the night. Before her was the snowy lane stretching away. She climbed out of the open window, pushed it back until it was almost shut, then set off past Helen's car toward the gate into Stonewell Park.

16

THE SNOW WAS still deep, and though none was falling now, the air seemed colder than ever. She forced her mind to the task in hand. It made her shiver as much as the cold. She knew it was risky going out on her own again like this, especially now that darkness had fallen. If the boy had as many enemies as he claimed, there were all kinds of unsavory people she could run into, and he himself might be the most dangerous of them all.

The police had said to keep away from him. Yet for all that, she knew she could not. She had to find him, whatever her fears. Something told her he was the key to the mystery of Josh. As for that other, greater mystery he had spoken of, perhaps he was the key to that too, whatever it was.

She reached the park gate and squeezed through the fence. Memories of last night flooded back—the chase, the dogs, the confrontation—but she pushed them aside and hurried on toward the trees. The snow was smooth and rich and deep. There was no sign of any footprints. She reached the little wood and carried on through. Still no sign of anyone. All was quiet. She stopped at the end of the trees and glanced around her.

Silence, whiteness, static air. A chilly sculpture of night. The ground seemed to gleam against the darkness. She walked across the children's playground toward the gate that led to the bridleway.

Below her, on the glistening snow, she pictured the footprints she'd seen tapering into nothing. Here was the spot just down from the gate where they'd ended altogether. She walked on to the gate and stopped.

Again the silence of the night. She stared through the bars. The bridleway was a smooth white, undisturbed by footprints as far as she could see. Beyond the bridleway, the moor stretched away like a shroud. She climbed over the gate. It was cold against her gloves and wet with snow along the thicker bars. She slid over onto the ground on the other side and set off down the bridleway toward the track to Knowle.

The cold was now so sharp, the snow so bright, she felt disconnected from herself, as though she were in some pocket of life detached from the world of her senses. She walked on. From far away came a hum. The sound of night traffic perhaps. She didn't know. She felt like a disembodied mind passing through a place where nothing moved or breathed except her.

Yet this feeling did not last. The more she walked, the more she felt she was wandering through an illusion. For all the passivity of the night, everything about her seemed awake and watchful and conscious of her: the ink-black sky, the gleaming snow, the cold air snaking up her nostrils, even the presence of her thoughts. Again the stillness of the night pressed itself upon her.

She stopped by the track to Knowle and looked about her.

No sign of anyone in any direction. She pushed on down the bridleway, still wary of the silence and the stillness, and as she walked, she checked ahead for danger. All seemed clear, though it was impossible, even with the brightness of the snow, to see every hiding place from here. The bridleway was fairly wide but there were banks of snow-covered bushes to the side where a person could hide easily enough.

She walked on, struggling again with her fears, her eyes moving constantly. But it wasn't far now. She clenched her fists and carried on, and at last, around a twist in the bridleway, she saw the old hovel where Silas lived.

She stared at it: an ugly, single-room cottage with a patched-up roof, shabby brickwork, and windows shuttered from both inside and out. She'd never seen them open, even in summertime, but she could see a taper of light around the edges and a trickle of smoke rising from the chimney.

It was a promising start. She'd been worried the old man might be out. She wasn't expecting any kind of welcome—nobody got that from Silas—but if she handled him right, she might just glean something about the boy he'd seen. She hurried to the door and knocked.

"Silas!" she called.

There was no answer, but she caught a sound of movement inside the hovel. She tried again.

"Silas!"

"Go away!"

"Silas! It's me! Dusty!"

"I know who it is. Go away!"

"I want to ask you about the boy."

"Don't know no boy."

"The boy who took your mobile phone."

There were more sounds of movement inside but nothing that suggested the old man was coming out. She took a step back from the door. This whole thing might be a waste of time. Silas had grown increasingly difficult with people over the last few years. He'd never been good-tempered but he was now so cantankerous he'd been banned from most of the pubs in Beckdale.

She was just wondering whether to call out again when, to her surprise, the door opened a fraction and the old man's eyes peered out.

"Silas, it's me," she said quickly.

"Seen that, ain't I?" He looked her over, his bald head glinting from the flickering fire inside. "Any case, you told me. Think I'm stupid?"

"No."

"What d'you want?"

"The boy who nicked your mobile—"

"Ain't got no mobile. Ain't seen no boy."

"Silas, I know that's not true."

"Ain't seen nobody. Ain't seen nothin'. An' if them folks with the dogs comes asking, you tells 'em I ain't said nothin' neither."

She frowned. So that was it. The man and his sons had been asking questions as well. No wonder Silas was jumpy.

"Silas, listen—"

"I ain't got nothin' more to say."

"I'm not here to get you into trouble."

"I ain't got nothin' more to say."

"Silas, the dogs are dead."

The old man said nothing, but he didn't close the door. He stood there, his eyes flicking this way and that.

"The dogs are dead, Silas," she said.

His eyes went on searching the night, then suddenly fixed on her.

"You seen 'em die?"

"Well, not actually—"

"Seen 'em dead, then? Corpses, like?"

"No, but—"

"Then you don't know nothin'. You just heard a rumor."

The silence fell upon them once more. The old man's eyes started searching again. Hers too were searching now: the snow, the bridleway, the glistening moor. Again she felt the wakefulness of the night.

"Whatever happened," she said, "those people aren't here now."

"You don't know." The old man looked back at her. "They come sudden, like. One minute they ain't here, next they is. And them dogs brayin' and snarlin'."

"They're dead, Silas."

"What difference does it make even if they is? That man ain't dead. Nor them foul-face boys."

"What did they do to you?"

"Nothin'. Just asked questions. Only they wasn't polite. Least the police was polite. Man with the ponytail scared the living daylights out of me."

"You should tell the police if he threatened you."

"Oh, yeah. Like I'm going to do that." The old man started to close the door. "I'm done talking to you."

"Silas, the boy used your mobile to phone me."

The old man stopped, his hand tight around the door.

"The police came to our house," she said. "A man and a woman. DC Brett and DI Sharp. Is that the two you spoke to?"

"Might be. Might not."

"They came to Thorn Cottage. They traced a call from your mobile to our landline phone." She hesitated. "I took a call from the boy late last night. I don't know how he got our number. But he rang. I don't . . . want to tell you what he said. I haven't told anyone, not even Dad. He and the police think I got a silent call. But the boy said some things I need to ask him about."

The old man was silent but his eyes were still now and they were watching her.

"The police said you reported the mobile stolen," she said. "They told us you left it on the water tank." She glanced toward it. "And when you remembered it and went to fetch it, you found it gone, and saw the boy running away across the moor."

"I didn't see nothin'. I didn't see nobody. And I ain't got no mobile."

She gave a sigh. She knew Silas was lying but she couldn't make him open up if he really didn't want to. It was clear he was terrified of what the man with the ponytail might do to him. Perhaps he was frightened of the boy too.

"OK, Silas," she said. "I won't push you. Sorry I bothered you."

And she started to walk back along the bridleway. She hadn't gone more than a few steps when she heard him call after her.

"It was for my brother."

She stopped and turned.

"What?"

He was watching her through the gap in the doorway.

"For my brother," he muttered.

"I didn't know you had a brother."

"Nobody knows I got a brother. Been an invalid all his life. In a home for years and then in a hospice. I ain't been to see him for forty years. That's why I got the mobile. So I could ring the hospice and find out the news anytime I wanted without going out to look for a phone."

Silas scowled at her.

"Only I didn't use it. Kept putting off ringing. Don't like hospices and all that dyin'. Didn't go and see him neither, even when they told me he wasn't going to make it. Kept telling myself I would. Only I never did. And when I managed to make the call, I was too late. Bastard had died on me. Now I'm never going to get a chance to tell him what I wanted."

The old man sniffed.

"Then the mobile got nicked and today I find it back on the water tank."

She gave a start.

"What did you say?"

"It turned up again. Whoever nicked it put it back. Only something's wrong with it."

"What do you mean?"

"I switched it on and it made some funny noises. Ain't never done that before. Something's not right with it."

"Can I see it?"

He looked her over warily.

"What for?"

"Silas, I'm not going to do anything to it. I might be able to help."

He hesitated, then disappeared inside the hovel. A moment later he was back at the doorway.

"Here," he muttered, holding out the mobile.

She walked back and took it.

"Don't do nothin' to it," he warned.

"Like what?"

"I don't know. Like make it worse."

She switched on the mobile and at once noticed a possible explanation for the sounds Silas had heard.

"Do the funny noises for me, Silas."

"What d'you mean?"

"Make the sounds you heard. As best you can."

Silas made an attempt—an awkward, squeaky sound—but it was enough.

"You've had a text message," she said.

"A what?"

"A text message. That's what the beeps were telling you. And there's a symbol on the screen telling you the same thing. See?"

Silas didn't look at the phone. He was watching her face.

"What's it mean?" he said.

"It means someone's sent you a message."

"What message?"

"You can read it if you press this button."

"You read it for me."

"It's your message, not mine. I'll call it up for you and you can read it for yourself."

"You read it for me," he said again. "Read it aloud."

"Are you sure you want me to?"

"Just do it."

She heard the fear in his voice. She called up the message.

"It was sent today," she said.

"Just tell me what it says."

It was short and unsigned. She read it out into the still night.

sorry i took yr mobile give em hell kid never say die.

She heard a sniffling sound and looked at Silas. To her surprise, he was crying.

"What's wrong?" she said.

"It's what Jonah used to say."

"Jonah?"

"My brother. When we was nippers—before 'e got ill—'e used to say, 'Give 'em hell, kid. Never say die.' In the days when we used to talk, 'e always finished with that. 'Give 'em hell, kid. Never say die.' You reckon the boy sent that message?"

"Yes."

"Then how'd 'e know what my brother used to say? I ain't told nobody in the world that."

She shook her head.

"I can't explain it. He knows things about my life too. Maybe lots of other people's lives as well. But, Silas, listen . . ."

Silas pushed his face closer, his wariness suddenly gone.

"What?" he said.

"If this message is right, then your brother's telling you he's OK. He wouldn't tell you to give 'em hell and never say die if he was angry with you for not visiting him."

The old man was silent for a moment, then suddenly he disappeared again inside the hovel. But he was soon back.

"Here," he said. "I found this."

He reached out his hand. He was holding a small white object: shiny and smooth with tiny holes over the surface that pierced through into what appeared to be a hollow chamber. The edges of the chamber were intricately carved and gave the impression of a white leaf. Yet this image did not last. A stronger one soon replaced it.

"It's like a snowflake," she said.

"A what?" said the old man.

"A snowflake. Look at it. It's just like a large snowflake."

"It ain't no bloody snowflake," muttered Silas. "It's an ocarina."

She looked up at him.

"An ocarina?"

"Musical instrument. You blow in that hole there and put your fingers in the others to make the notes. I seen 'em before. Lots of different types, funny shapes and stuff." Silas thrust the ocarina at her. "Go on. Take it. I don't want the damn thing."

She took it from him. It was light and fragile. Just like a snowflake.

"Where did you find this?" she said.

The old man nodded toward the moor.

"Over there. By them snow-covered bushes."

She studied them, then looked back at him.

"Is that where you saw the boy running away?"

The old man narrowed his eyes.

"I didn't see nothin'," he said. "All right? I didn't see nothin'. Now leave me alone."

He pulled the door closed and this time she knew he wasn't coming out again.

17

BACK IN HER ROOM she examined the ocarina. Now, under the glare of her desk lamp, she could see more clearly how exquisite the carvings were, and how subtly the instrument had been constructed. She'd thought when Silas first handed it to her that it was made from bone or clay but now she saw that it was handcrafted from wood and then painted white. The holes, like the carvings, were perfectly formed and did nothing to take away the impression that had forced itself upon her out on the bridleway.

"You really are like a snowflake," she said to it. "A musical snowflake, a kind of . . ." She thought for a moment. "A kind of snow-pipe."

She liked that. A snow-pipe.

"I'll call you a snow-pipe," she said. "Other people can call you an ocarina if they want."

Not that she had any intention of showing it to other people. It came from the boy—she was certain of that; indeed it might well have been made by the boy—and it was something she shared with him alone: another connection between them, another secret. She raised the snow-pipe to her lips and made ready to blow into the mouthpiece, then, not quite knowing why, put it back on the desk.

It didn't seem right to play it.

She stared at it for a few moments, then—also not quite knowing why—reached into her pocket and pulled out the paper face. It was still scrunched together in a little ball. She unfolded it and smoothed out the creases. The face was still visible but it had faded slightly and some of the ink had run where the snow had fallen upon it earlier.

She thought of the photo the police had taken: the photo of a boy whose image had faded into nothing. Perhaps this drawing was fading into nothing too. She took her pen and reinforced the edges of the face, then rested the snow-pipe upon the paper.

An odd little combination they made but she rather liked it. They could stay there for a bit, she decided. She'd put them out of sight later when she turned in properly, though to be on the safe side it might be best to give Dad the impression she'd done so already. She switched off the desk lamp and the main light, then lay down on the bed and listened.

No sounds from Dad and Helen. As far as she could tell, they hadn't left the kitchen all evening. Creeping back into the house had been the easiest thing in the world. But then, as if to contradict that, she heard footsteps and voices downstairs, followed by the sound of the living-room door closing—and then music.

She frowned. Dad had put on one of his more obscure jazz CDs. She listened doubtfully. This was high-risk music to be playing to a woman you wanted to impress. If Helen was enduring it out of politeness, the relationship could be dead in the water by tomorrow. If she was a fan, however, that was quite another matter.

"Please be a fan, Helen," she murmured.

She was feeling drowsy now. She supposed she ought to clear the things off the desk and turn in for real, but sleep overwhelmed her first: a short, unsatisfying sleep with stabbing images of fire and flame and the fangs of dogs. When she awoke, all was silent and dark. She sat up on the bed, groggy and confused for a moment as to why she was still in her day clothes. Then recollection returned. She glanced at the clock.

Half past one in the morning. Dad clearly hadn't looked in on her.

If he had done so, he'd have woken her and told her to change into her nightclothes and get into bed. He'd also have commented on the things she'd left on her desk. She glanced toward them and gave a start.

An eerie glow was rising from the desk. She stood up. It appeared to be emanating from the paper and the snow-pipe. She walked slowly toward them. Now she could see more clearly. It wasn't the paper that was glowing; it was the drawn face. The snow-pipe too was emitting a soft yet unmistakable light. She felt a trembling in the air, a movement in the night.

She sat down at the desk.

The snow-pipe and the face continued to glow. She hesitated, then reached out and touched the top of the instrument. It was warm. So too was the paper underneath. She picked both up, one in each hand, and the warmth and the light ran up her arms. She placed the two objects back on the desk.

"This is mad," she whispered.

Or maybe she was.

She pulled out Josh's photo. At least that wasn't doing anything weird. It was cool to the touch and emitted no freakish light. She peered about her. Beyond the glow of the desk all she saw was shadows. Familiar shadows mostly: the features of a room she saw every night as she composed herself for sleep.

But she trusted nothing now.

"This is mad," she said again.

She stood up. She had to speak to Dad. This was all getting to be too much. She hurried out of the room and down to Dad's door. From inside came the familiar sound of breathing, a reassuring sound, and she was sorry she was going to interrupt it. But Dad had to be woken up. She had to share this burden with him now. She pushed open the door and froze.

Two figures were sleeping in the bed. She stood there, staring down at them, new currents of emotion washing over her. She must have been asleep when they came up. She remembered hearing the jazz playing downstairs but not hearing it stop. No wonder Dad hadn't looked in on her.

She studied Helen and once again it struck her how similar she was to Mum. With her arm over Dad's shoulder she could almost be Mum. The two slept on, oblivious of her. She slipped back to her room, closed the door behind her and let the darkness settle. It felt frightening now and so did the glow over her desk. She reached out to turn on the light, then pulled her hand back.

"No," she muttered. "Don't give in to it."

She made herself sit down at the desk again. The brightness around the two objects now shimmered and danced and even the darkness seemed tinged with luminosity.

It's something to do with the light.

She could almost hear the boy's voice speaking in her mind.

She realized with a start that she was still clutching Josh's photograph. She held it close to the snow-pipe and the paper face and the light from them trickled over the surface of her brother's face. The voice spoke in her mind again.

You think your biggest mystery's Josh. But it isn't. It's this other thing.

"This other thing," she whispered, staring at the light.

She pulled open the desk drawer, dropped the paper face and snow-pipe inside, and closed it again. The light vanished at once, leaving only the darkened outline of Josh's face staring up from the photo. The silence of the night pressed upon her again.

"Josh," she murmured.

Her mobile beeped with another text message. She switched on the desk lamp and checked the phone.

Dusty pls tel me ur ok angelica x

She frowned. She'd forgotten all about Angelica. She checked the girl's previous message.

Beam gav me ur tel no sory i wlkd off im scared of fites r u ok angelica xxx

She texted a reply.

Im ok

Almost at once an answer came back.

Wanna tlk?

She sighed. Wee hours of the morning and yes, she did want to talk, even to someone she hardly knew. She thought back to the girl she'd met at Mac's. They didn't have much in common but maybe two fifteen-year-old girls who couldn't sleep could help each other for a few minutes. She texted back an answer.

If u like

The phone rang a few seconds later.
"Hello?"
"Dusty? Is that you?"
"Yeah."
"Hi."
"Hi."
There was a silence.

"Can't you sleep?" said Dusty.

"No. Dusty, listen—are you all right?"

Dusty hesitated. There was so much she wanted to say, so much she didn't want to say.

"What do you mean?" she said eventually.

"After the fight."

"Oh, that. Yeah, I'm fine."

"You could have got badly hurt."

"No, I couldn't. Beam was always going to get involved sooner or later. And no one's going to mess with a first-team prop forward."

"But you'd have attacked without Beam being there. I know you would. I can tell. You're that sort of person."

Dusty said nothing.

"Aren't you?" prompted Angelica.

Dusty didn't answer. She was staring at the photo of Josh. His face was glistening where a tear had fallen upon it. She wiped her eyes, unaware that she'd been crying. She sensed a tension at the other end of the phone, no doubt Angelica still waiting for an answer. But the girl spoke again first.

"I know about the boy on Raven's Fell."

Dusty sat up in the chair. Josh's face still glistened in the darkness.

"The boy Mac was talking about," said Angelica. "I didn't want to say anything in front of your friends. I don't know them that well."

"You don't know me that well either."

"I feel like I do."

Dusty made no response.

"Kamalika and Beam are great," said Angelica, "but—"

"You don't have to justify yourself."

"I do to you."

"What do you mean?"

"I don't know. I just feel . . . you're not someone I'd ever want to keep something from."

"Why not?"

"I don't know," said Angelica. "Maybe I'm a bit frightened of getting on the wrong side of you."

"That's stupid."

"Maybe."

"There are loads of things I'd keep from you," said Dusty.

"Like what?"

"Like if I told you, I'd hardly be keeping them from you, would I?"

"I suppose not."

Angelica chuckled, a curiously reassuring sound in the silence of the night.

"Tell me about the boy," said Dusty.

"I saw him the day after I arrived in Beckdale. Mum and I went for a walk on Kilbury Moor. That was before the snow came and we could see our way clearly. We wanted to go around the shore of Mirkwell Lake for a bit, so we followed the path around from that long jetty, and after about a mile we came to this place where there's a broken-down cottage about a hundred yards back from the lake with a little tarn just above it and a path stretching up the side of Raven's Fell."

"I know it."

Josh's photo was dry now. She ran a finger over the surface, stroked the face.

"Dusty?" said Angelica. "Do you want to meet up tomorrow? I could show you the place where I saw him and tell you what happened. It'd be easier than to describe it over the phone."

Dusty went on stroking the face.

"Tomorrow's Monday," she murmured. "We can't meet tomorrow. We're back at school. Or meant to be."

Again the chuckle from Angelica.

"Sorry, Dusty. I forgot what time it is. I meant today. Meet me today. And I'll take you to the place where I saw him."

Dusty picked up the photo and pulled open the drawer of the desk. A glimmer of light snaked up into the air from the snow-pipe and the paper face. She dropped the photo in next to them and closed the drawer. Darkness returned, though the image of Josh's face remained in her mind.

"OK," she said.

18

MIRKWELL LAKE WAS GHOSTLY and still. No further snow had fallen in the night but a thick coat from the last heavy showers still lay upon the moor and fells. Raven's Fell, the highest and nearest of the peaks that rose from the northern shore of the lake, was a gleaming white.

Dusty walked across the car park, blowing her hands. She felt uneasy being here again. It was hard to forget Mrs. Wilkes's warning. There was no one at all to be seen on the moor or up the fell. That in itself was strange. Ramblers normally came out by the score on Sunday mornings. Clearly the rumors of a weird figure were having an effect.

But Angelica was here. She was standing at the end of the jetty, staring out over Mirkwell Lake. Dusty set off toward her. The girl didn't turn and simply went on gazing in the opposite direction. She looked strangely remote, framed against the water.

So too did the jetty. It was unusually long, practically a small pier, but had no buildings on it apart from the deserted ticket kiosk for the tourist boats in the summer. Most of the year—even in winter—there were at least half a dozen craft moored along the sides but today there were none, nor were there any people wandering over it. The jetty, like the moor and fells, was a lonely place. She and Angelica might be the first or the last two people in this snowy world.

She stepped onto the jetty and started to walk down it. Angelica turned at last and saw her. No smile appeared, no acknowledgment. The girl's face was as cold as the lake behind her. Dusty felt her lips tighten. So now we're the ice maiden, are we? she thought, and she found herself wishing it was Kamalika waiting for her here instead. Then suddenly Angelica smiled.

"Hi, Dusty!"

Her voice sounded overfriendly. Dusty walked on down the jetty, unsure what to make of this girl. Through the gaps between the snow-covered planks the water blinked up at her. She met Angelica's eyes. The girl was still smiling: a forced, uncomfortable smile. Dusty stopped at the end of the jetty.

"You poor thing," said Angelica. "That's a terrible black eye."

"Are you OK?"

Angelica raised an eyebrow.

"What do you mean?"

"You look awkward."

"Oh."

"And you sound awkward."

Angelica flushed and turned toward the lake.

"I didn't mean to be rude—"

"I didn't say you were being rude. I was just wondering if you're OK."

"Yes, I'm . . . " Angelica frowned, then shook her head. "It's no good trying to hide anything from you, is it? You obviously notice everything."

Dusty shrugged.

"It's not rocket science to see you're not right. What's up?"

"I was just a bit nervous being out here on my own. I thought there'd be lots of people around. If I'd known I'd be on my own, I'd have suggested meeting you in town and walking here."

"Well, I'm here now."

"I was a bit doubtful about that too," said Angelica.

"What do you mean?"

"I didn't think you'd come."

"Why not?"

"I don't know. I just thought . . . maybe you wouldn't want to."

"Why wouldn't I?"

"I don't know. I suppose I'm just not used to people doing what they say they will."

Angelica went on staring out over the water. Dusty turned and did the same. Neither spoke for several minutes. Below them a ripple moved from the center of the lake toward the shore. It murmured against the land, then all was silent again. The moor and fells gleamed with their white mane.

"This is one huge lake," said Angelica eventually.

"Yeah. It goes on for miles."

"Is it deep?"

"Very. Even where we're standing."

"Really?"

"Look down."

Angelica looked down.

"Can you see the bottom?" said Dusty.

"No, but it's a bit cloudy."

"Come back a bit and look between the planks."

They took a few steps back and stared through the gaps.

"See the bottom now?" said Dusty.

"Yes."

"It shelves really quickly at the end. Goes suddenly very deep. They built the jetty so that the pleasure boats can call here. They have lots of trips around the lake in the summer. It's a pain. The place is crowded with tourists. Dad hates it. He's a keen fisherman. Anyway . . . " She led Angelica back to the end of the jetty. "The bed of the lake shelves here really suddenly."

"Does it ever freeze over?"

"Sometimes. It's trying to freeze now."

They stared at it in silence for a while.

"It feels spooky out here," said Angelica.

Dusty had been feeling the same thing but all she said was, "In what way?"

"No one else around. Just the two of us here. I thought . . . I mean, like I said . . . I assumed there'd be other people about. My mum would flip out if she could see us. She thinks I've gone to Mac's Coffee House again."

"Didn't you tell her about meeting me?"

"She doesn't know anything about you. I just said I'm meeting some new friends from Beckdale High School."

"What are you so secretive for?"

"She's really clingy, my mum. Since Dad died, she's been funny about me going out. She's terrified of losing me as well."

"What happened to your dad?" Dusty hesitated. "I mean, you don't have to tell me if you don't—"

"He had a road accident," said Angelica. "Didn't see the other car in time. Bang! Just like that. One moment you've got a dad, next moment you haven't." She frowned. "Doesn't seem right, does it? A split second to lose him and a lifetime to grieve over him." She took a deep breath. "Feels like a lifetime anyway. Maybe it'll ease one of these days."

"What happened to the other driver?"

"Walked away without a scratch."

"Was it his fault?"

"Mum says so. She thinks he had time to stop."

"Did you see the accident?"

Angelica shook her head.

"I was asleep in the back of the car. All I remember is being jolted awake and hearing Mum screaming and then seeing—" She stopped suddenly, her eyes still fixed on the lake. "I don't like talking about this."

"Sorry," said Dusty. "I shouldn't have asked you."

"It's OK. I was the one to mention Dad." Angelica bit her lip. "I like talking about him sometimes but I don't like talking about . . . how he died." She thought for a moment, then said, "You'd think I'd have started to get over it by now but I haven't. It still feels like it happened yesterday."

"When did it happen?"

"Eight years ago. Anyway, never mind all that." Angelica looked around at her. "I'm really sorry I upset you at Mac's. Beam told me about Josh but I should never have mentioned it."

"Don't worry about it. Beam's always had a big mouth."

"He's quite nice but he's a bit . . . you know . . . "

"Tactless."

"Yes."

They smiled at each other for the first time.

"Dusty?"

"Yes?"

"Can I ask you something about Josh?"

"Go ahead."

"Have you heard anything from him since he walked out?"

"No."

"So he could be . . . "

Angelica looked down. Dusty watched her for a moment, then finished the sentence for her.

"He could be alive or he could be dead. We just don't know."

"Did he leave a message?"

"Not a written one. Thing is, we weren't too worried at first. Josh often took off for days at a time. He'd just disappear. No explanations, nothing. He was like that. A loner, a rebel, always getting into scrapes."

"Like you."

Dusty looked hard at her. It seemed like a strange thing for the girl to say to someone she barely knew, even if it was true.

"Yes," she went on. "Anyway, like I say, we weren't too worried because it was in his character and he always turned up again in the end. He wouldn't tell us where he'd been or who he'd been with and Mum and Dad had some terrible rows with him about it. But it made no difference. He was his own boss and that was that."

"My mum would never forgive me if I did that."

"Oh, everyone forgave Josh, even the people he got into fights with. You couldn't be angry with him for long. He was too lovable. He had people eating out of his hand. Teachers, other pupils, Mum and Dad. Specially Mum."

"And you?"

"Yeah, me too," said Dusty. "I'd have jumped off the top of Raven's Fell if he told me to. Probably still would."

"So what kind of message did he leave? You said it wasn't a written one."

"He rang a few days after he walked out. I was on my own in the house. He just said he wasn't coming back. He said everything was all right and we weren't to worry about him or try to find him. But he didn't want to see us again and he wasn't coming home."

"And that was it?"

"Yes."

Josh's last words whispered through her mind as they so often did.

I'm sorry, little Dusty. Good-bye, little Dusty.

But she wasn't going to repeat them to Angelica. She thought of the last person who had spoken them to her.

"You were going to tell me about the boy," she said.

"Yes," said Angelica. "I was."

But the girl seemed suddenly unwilling to continue.

"You said you've seen him," said Dusty.

"Yes." Angelica looked about her. "I was going to show you the place but I'm not sure I want to go there now. I feel a bit isolated out here, even with you next to me."

"We don't have to go there. I know the place anyway. You said it was by the old charcoal burner's cottage."

"That derelict place?"

"Yes. The one by the lake with a tarn above it. You mentioned it on the phone."

"Right."

"And that's where you saw the boy?"

"No, not there. We were at the top end of the tarn—my mum and me—but the boy was high up on Raven's Fell. We could see this figure standing there. He was wearing a duffel coat, and though I couldn't see him clearly, I recognized him from the other times I've seen him."

"You've seen him before?"

"Several times."

"Close up?"

"Yes."

"Where?" Dusty leaned forward. "What's he like?"

"Really strange, really disturbing. I'm scared stiff of him."

"Why?"

Angelica hesitated.

"I know this sounds crazy but I feel like he's following me around the country."

"Following you?"

Angelica nodded.

"I know you probably think I'm paranoid or making it up. But I can't seem to shake him off. He keeps turning up wherever I go."

"When's the first time you saw him?"

Angelica looked sharply away. Dusty watched her, unsure whether to wait or prompt an answer. She was growing increasingly wary of this girl. Something about her didn't feel right and this sudden silence seemed suspicious. Maybe it meant her memories of the boy were too painful to talk about. Or maybe she was simply gilding the lie. Angelica looked suddenly back at her.

"It was in Millhaven," she said. "He was slumped on a street corner, busking. He had this funny-shaped musical instrument, white and really tiny. I think someone said it's an ocarina. You blow into it and it makes this beautiful sound. He was really good at it, but he wasn't very organized. He was in the wrong place for picking up money. There were much better places for busking. And he didn't have a cap out or anything to collect the change. Anyway, that's where I first saw him."

"And what happened?"

"Nothing at first. Then he started turning up in other places. Different streets, even the road I walked down to get to school. It started to get a bit creepy. Every time I went anywhere, it seemed like I was bumping into him."

"Did he speak to you or do anything?"

"Not to begin with. It was the way he looked at you that was unsettling. And I wasn't the only one who felt that. Lots of my friends said they felt the same. And not just the girls. He made the boys feel funny too."

"How?"

"Just the way he looked at you. And then his appearance. He was like no one you've ever seen. He had this strange snowy skin. I think he tried to hide it under his duffel coat. He often put the hood up. But he couldn't disguise his eyes or his . . . his manner. I don't know what it was. And then after a while he started saying things as you went past him."

"Like what?"

"Weird stuff, creepy stuff. He'd say things like what you're thinking or what you were about to say just before you said it. Like he knew things about you that he couldn't know. It freaked me out, and my mates. Then . . ."

Angelica fell silent again. Dusty watched. The girl was breathing hard, nibbling her fingernails.

"Angelica?"

Angelica looked at her.

"What happened?" said Dusty.

"My best friend went missing." Angelica went on biting her fingernails. "And so did the boy."

A buzzard flew over the lake and wheeled away toward the southern shore. Dusty followed it with her eyes.

"Are you saying that—"

"He took her away," said Angelica. "He forced her to go with him. He kept her in a lockup on the outskirts of an industrial park. He tied her up and gagged her. Then he raped her repeatedly over a period of three days."

Dusty felt a chill run through her.

"She managed to get away in the end," said Angelica. "She was found wandering the streets, crying. There'd been a full-scale search for her."

"What about the boy?"

"He disappeared but the police caught him. He denied doing anything. As if my friend would make it up. But that's not the scary thing."

Angelica edged closer.

"The scary thing is that the boy escaped. No one knows how he got out. He was in a police cell. He was locked up. They left him alone for a bit, and when they came back later, he was gone. Door still locked. He just wasn't there. I heard it from my uncle who knows someone at the station. The boy just disappeared. And then the stories started coming in."

"What stories?"

"Other people who'd seen him and had trouble with him. Not just girls. Seems he causes problems with everyone he meets. There's loads of people out there with grievances against him. He's dangerous, Dusty. I'm telling you he's really dangerous. And now I'm scared he's looking for me."

"You can't know that for sure. It might be coincidence that he's turned up here."

"It's not just here. It's everywhere I go. Mum and I left Millhaven because we wanted to start a new life. There were too many bad associations in Millhaven, especially the business with the boy. We decided to come to this part of the country. It seemed perfect. Beautiful surroundings, lakes, fells, moors. But we didn't come straight to Beckdale. We made for Barrowmere first."

"Nice town."

"Yes, we thought. Then the stories started. Locals talking about a strange boy hanging around the outskirts of the town. Same description. There was no mistaking who it was. We told the police and they interviewed us, but since we hadn't actually seen the boy ourselves, all we could do was tell them to speak to the locals."

"What did you do then?"

"Moved on. Went south to Witherbeck. Thought the boy would never turn up there. But he did. People started talking about this weird character hanging around. We told the police again, and came on to Beckdale. And now it's happening again. There's something not human about him."

Dusty said nothing. She was trying to think, trying to make sense of what she'd just heard, trying to decide how much to believe.

"Has he got a name, this boy?" she said.

"I've never heard him give it," said Angelica. "And I don't think the police have released one. There are lots of names other people have given him."

Dusty remembered the boy's words that first time they had spoken on the phone.

I've got lots of names.

She could guess what kind they were. She thought of the sketch sitting in the drawer of her desk.

"So all we have is a face," she murmured.

She saw Angelica watching her.

"You don't believe me," said the girl. "I can see it. You don't believe a word I've said."

Dusty pulled out a pen, held out her hand.

"Draw the face," she said. "Draw the boy's face on my palm."

Angelica looked down at the proffered hand, but didn't take the pen. Instead, she turned and gazed in the direction of Raven's Fell. It gleamed in the distance as the light fell upon it.

"You don't need me to draw a picture of him," she said. She nodded toward the snowy peak. "That's what he's like. Pure white."

19

PURE WHITE.

She stared about her. Everything she saw looked pure white now: the fell, the moor, even the lake itself. She studied the surface. It seemed to shimmer as though the water had frozen and snow had settled upon it. Yet she knew this was not true: the water still moved, and no further snow had fallen.

She wondered why she was still standing here. Angelica had been gone an hour and not a soul had appeared since. She thought of the boy again.

Pure white.

Pure evil, if Angelica was to be believed, but it was hard to know what to make of the girl's story. Some things rang true: the boy who seemed to know what you were thinking—that certainly fit. But the other things—stalking, abduction, rape . . .

The lake went on shimmering below her.

She scanned the shoreline, then ran her eye over the moor and fells again. Nothing moved in that vast, white desert. She wandered back down the jetty and stopped where it met the shore. Ahead of her was the walled lane that led back past the school toward the center of town.

There were no cars in the car park just up from the jetty. To her immediate left the little path broke away and headed around the edge of the lake. She thought of the charcoal burner's cottage farther down, and the tarn, and the path up the fell where Angelica had seen the boy, or claimed to have.

She had no idea what to do next.

Her mobile rang. The sound of it made her jump, but she calmed herself, pulled out the phone and studied the screen—Dad. She'd been wondering when she'd hear from him.

"Hi, Dad."

"Where the hell are you?"

"I'm fine, thanks, and how are you?"

"Don't be rude. Where are you?"

"In Beckdale. Didn't you see my note?"

"Eventually. I woke up an hour ago but I was still tired, so I just lay there and dozed. Assumed you were doing the same. Or at least you were in the house. I had no idea you'd gone out. I only found the note when I went downstairs to make some coffee. Why didn't you wake me before you went out?"

"I thought you needed to sleep. And I didn't think it mattered."

"Well, it does matter." Dad was breathing hard. "It does bloody matter. I was about to ring you when I got a call from Beam."

"Beam?"

"Yes, Beam," he said tetchily. "He rang to say there's a lot of talk in town about a weird boy in a duffel coat hanging around the area. He's been seen around our way apparently. Must be the boy I saw on the lane. And it could well be that character the police warned us about. Beam says he's thought to be dangerous. There's even a rumor of abduction and rape. That's probably what those two police officers didn't want to tell us. But anyway, you shouldn't be wandering off on your own. Where are you at the moment?"

"I told you. In Beckdale."

"Yes, but where exactly?"

"In the square. Just outside Mac's."

"Right, I'll come in and get you."

"Dad, you don't need to. And I don't want you to. I'll get a bus when I'm ready to come back."

"You can bloody well come back now. I'll meet the bus at the bottom of the lane and drive you the last stretch."

"Dad, you're worrying too much. And anyway, I can't come back yet."

"Why not?"

"I've arranged to meet someone."

"Who?"

"A girl called Angelica."

"Who the hell's she?"

"Just a girl I met."

Dad gave a heavy sigh.

"All these things you do without telling me. All these people I've never heard of."

"It's only a girl from school."

"Well, you're to hurry back home the moment you get a chance. You understand? Do whatever you're meant to be doing with this girl—"

"Having coffee at Mac's."

"Whatever. And then get on the bloody bus. All right? And ring me on your mobile just before the bus gets to the bottom of the lane. I'll drive down and meet you."

"I can walk it, Dad. That last stretch is quite safe."

"That's exactly where I saw the boy, remember? Ring me when you get close to the lane. Promise me you'll do that."

"All right. I promise." Dusty paused. "Dad?"

"What?"

"Did it go all right last night with Helen?"

"Never mind that now," grumbled Dad. "Just come back as soon as you can. And don't go anywhere stupid. I can't afford to lose you as well as Josh."

"You won't, Dad. I promise."

Dad rang off without another word. Dusty stood there, now deeply confused about the boy. First Angelica, now Dad—and here was the phone ringing again, Kamalika this time.

"Dusty?"

"Hi, Kam. Glad you're still speaking to me."

"I'm only just speaking to you."

"What does that mean?"

"My dad doesn't want me to have anything to do with you. He thinks you're a bad influence on me."

"Thanks a lot," said Dusty.

"I can't argue about it now. I've got to be quick. He's in the next room and he might come in any moment. Listen, I'm just ringing to warn you. You know that boy you told me about after the fight with Denny? You said you'd had some weird phone calls from someone who claimed he'd taken an overdose. And you thought it might be the same boy Mac saw on the fell."

"What about him?"

"Have you told your dad and called the police like I suggested?"

Dusty hesitated.

"Well, the police have been around," she said slowly.

"And you've told them all about him?"

"I've answered their questions."

"But have you told them everything you know?"

She said nothing.

"You haven't, have you?" said Kamalika. "I just know it. You're doing what you always do—keeping stuff back. That's why people don't trust you, Dusty. Well, you're getting into deep water. You've got to tell the police everything."

"Kam, this isn't your business."

"It's everybody's business. Listen—this boy's dangerous. Lots of people have seen him now. Beam's been on the phone, telling me the things he's heard. I've had texts and e-mails from all over the place. Everybody on our street's talking about it. There's even stuff on the Net. The boy's been turning up all over the region but especially on the moor and fells and around the lake. He seems to like lonely spots and Beam says someone reported seeing him around your way. You've got to tell the police what you know."

Again Dusty said nothing.

"Dusty? Are you listening to this?"

"Yes."

"He's really dangerous. There are stories coming in from all over the place—Barrowmere, Witherbeck, Millhaven, God knows where. They're saying he abducted a young girl and raped her on and off for three days before she got away. And that's not all. He's . . . "

Kamalika's voice trailed away.

"He's what?" said Dusty.

"He's not like other people. It seems he can . . . do things. Things normal people can't do."

"Like what?"

"Like read people's minds and . . . and disappear. They're saying he was in a jail cell and he just vanished. No one knows how he got out but the door was still locked and he was just gone. And there are other stories . . . scary stories . . . "

"What kind of stories?"

"People approaching him and then suddenly blacking out . . . like he's knocked them over before they even get near him."

Dusty saw the buzzard circling again, a strangely welcome companion in this white, companionless place.

"That's not possible," she said. "Nobody can do that."

"Then listen to this," said Kamalika. "One of the farmhands down at Bidwell saw this duffel-coated figure drinking from the outside tap. Thought the guy looked suspicious, so he went to challenge him. The figure turned around, and before they were anywhere near each other, the farmhand lost consciousness. He's been in the hospital ever since."

"What, in some kind of a coma?"

"He's out of it now. The police won't say anything but he's just told his story to the local radio. All he remembers is seeing the figure and then this kind of black force hit him. And that was it. His wife found him lying on the ground and thought at first he was dead. But the paramedics got him to a hospital and he came around a few days later. He's only just been able to talk about it. But he's still got no feeling all down his body."

Dusty thought of the pit bulls lying dead.

"So tell the police everything you know," said Kamalika. "And be careful. Where are you at the moment? At home?"

"Yeah. Listen, Kam, I've got to go."

"So have I," said Kamalika. "I'll see you at school tomorrow. But, Dusty?"

"Yeah?"

"Tell the police. And keep away from the lake. And the moor and fells."

Dusty stared out at them.

"OK," she murmured, and rang off.

But it was no longer possible to keep away. The mysteries that weighed upon her were too great now. The mystery of Josh, the mystery of those other, greater questions that the boy had hinted at—they were all she could see now, together with the mystery of the boy himself, and that was the one she knew she had to solve first. That surely was the key to the other two.

But this new element of violence and rape filled her with terror. There had been danger enough before from the boy's pursuers but now it seemed that the boy might be more dangerous still. He had not sounded dangerous. He had only ever sounded weird, and desperate. But a voice at the end of a phone line could be made to sound like anything. She had deceived enough people herself to know that.

She wasn't ready to tell the police. Not yet. There was too much she had to find out for herself first. She stared at the lake again, and then over the moor to Raven's Fell. Perhaps there would be a clue there. Perhaps the boy himself might be there. It was hard to justify taking such a risk. She thought of Josh and wondered what he would do.

"He'd go," she said aloud. "He wouldn't hesitate. He'd go, no matter how scared he was."

And she set off at once.

She knew it was the right decision, even though she was still scared. Doing nothing would achieve nothing. She hated deceiving Dad and going against his wishes but playing it safe would lead nowhere. She had to take risks if she was to find Josh and to find Josh she had to find the boy. It kept coming back to the same thing.

Not that she saw much likelihood of finding anything. The boy could be hiding in a thousand places. The fact that others had seen him was no guarantee that she would see him too. She walked on even so, plodding down the snowy path that fringed the lake. It was still clear to see, with the embankment to the right of her and the lake close by to her left.

The water still gleamed with that unnatural whiteness. She stared at it as she walked. It was trying to freeze, and seemed close to doing so, though a fragile sun was now starting to break through. She walked on, following the track that Angelica had taken with her mother.

The old charcoal burner's cottage was the obvious place to check first. It was hardly somewhere the boy would want to sleep—no roof, no door, no windows—but Angelica had at least seen the boy near the cottage, or so she claimed. Dusty walked on, the chill air harsh inside her nostrils. Her feet and hands were cold too, in spite of her thick socks and gloves, but she pushed herself on, her eyes questing. No sign of movement anywhere. Even the buzzard was gone.

She reached the old cottage and wandered around it, searching the shadows. It was as barren and unyielding as she'd expected it to be. No clues here. She stepped outside and made her way up to the little tarn. Here too the water was a curious white, matching the ghostly chill of the lake. She stared up the slopes of Raven's Fell, just as Angelica and her mother had done, and saw a dark form above her.

She stiffened. It was a human form, black against the snow on the ridge just below the summit, and it was male. She stared up, aware that she was just as visible to this person as he was to her. Her mobile rang in her pocket. She pulled it quickly out.

"Hello?"

"Run back into town," said a voice.

She tensed. It was the boy.

"Run back into town," he said. He was speaking urgently, breathlessly. "Do it now."

"But—"

"It's not me on the fell."

A gunshot broke the silence. It came from up on the ridge.

"Run!" said the boy.

She turned and raced back down the path toward the town. As she did so, she saw the figure on the fell set off in the same direction. She could see who it was now: the man with the ponytail. She could make out his stocky frame and the outline of the rifle swinging in his hand.

She put on speed, keeping the phone as close to her ear as she could. There was no question of the man catching her, nor did it seem likely that he could hit her with a bullet from there, if that was his intention, but his sons were bound to be somewhere near and the gunshot might have been a signal to them.

"It was a signal!" shouted the boy, answering her thought in his usual manner. "They're over to the left but they won't catch you if you're quick!"

She stared over the embankment and saw the man's sons tearing across the moor to cut her off. To her relief, neither had guns and they were still some distance away. The boy was right. They'd never catch her as long as she kept running. She drove herself on down the path, gabbling into the phone as she did so.

"Where are you?"

"Never mind."

"I must see you."

"No, you mustn't. You mustn't ever see me."

"Why not?"

"Because I'm dangerous. I don't mean to be but I am. I'm dangerous to be around, dangerous to everybody. I cause harm. I might even harm you. And I couldn't bear that."

Another gunshot rang out.

"He's not shooting at you," said the boy. "He's calling his boys back."

She glanced over at her pursuers. The man on the fell had stopped and was beckoning to his sons. They stopped too, but all three figures continued to watch her. She slowed down to a walk but kept moving, kept speaking into the phone.

"How do you know what they're doing? Can you see them from where you are?"

"I see too much. More than I can bear."

She walked on, still watched by the three figures.

"I want to find Josh," she said. "I want that so much. I want to know if he's alive or dead."

"I no longer know if I'm alive or dead," said the boy.

"I don't understand." She shook her head. "I don't understand the stories I'm hearing about you. I don't understand about Josh. I don't understand about this . . . " She gazed into the gleaming air. "This other stuff. I don't understand about anything."

"Then stay away, Dusty. Go home and live with your mysteries."

"I can't live with them. They're driving me mad. And I can't stay away."

"You must."

"But why?"

"Because things are about to get much worse."

"What do you mean?"

Before he could answer, another gunshot rang out. She whirled around in panic. It hadn't come from the fell. It had come from Beckdale. She screamed into the phone.

"Are you still there?"

But the line was dead.

●

20

MORE GUNFIRE BROKE OUT: two thunderous reports, close together, followed by a third. She thrust the mobile into her pocket and raced down the path toward the town. Something was terribly wrong and she knew it involved the boy. But who was doing the shooting? The man with the ponytail was far away from the disturbance.

All was quiet again over Beckdale but a restless air hung about the town. She reached the jetty at the head of the lake. No one here and no further sounds of shooting, but still the uneasy atmosphere. She hurried down the lane past the school and turned toward the center of town.

An eerie tension filled the streets. No one was out but she saw faces at the windows as she passed. Some of the people gestured to her to go back. She ignored them and carried on. She had to find out what had happened to the boy, no matter how scared she was.

She passed the Pied Piper. More faces at the windows, more gestures to her to keep away. Again she ignored them. She could hear voices now coming from the square: men's voices, angry, aggressive. She steeled herself and ran on. The voices grew louder, more dangerous.

She stopped outside the post office and peered around the corner of the building into the square.

The windows of the shops and Mac's Coffee House were lined with faces staring out at a crowd of men gathered outside Mrs. Binchey's sweetshop. Several were carrying shotguns. Dusty did a quick count.

Eleven hard-bitten men. She was sure they weren't from Beck-dale. Three policemen were there too, trying without much success to calm them, but as she watched, two police vans screeched into the square and more officers poured out, including DC Brett and DI Sharp.

The new arrivals only roused the men to further fury.

"We're wasting time!" shouted one, a heavy, bearded man with a double-barreled shotgun.

Dusty stared at him. The man looked familiar, though she didn't know him. Then suddenly she remembered. He'd overtaken her and Dad yesterday in the big white van she'd mistaken for the one belonging to the man with the ponytail. He'd had two men and a woman with him. She searched the crowd again and quickly spotted the two men.

"He'll get away!" shouted the bearded man.

He was answered by an animal bellow from the mob.

DI Sharp stepped forward. Dusty watched tensely. There was no doubt about it: the woman had nerve. She'd clearly worked out—as Dusty had—that the bearded man was the ringleader and was now standing right in front of him, subtly isolating him from the main body of the group and forcing him to look at her, and now she was speaking to him in a soft, calm voice. Dusty strained to hear but all she caught was the man's furious response.

"I told you! He was in the bloody sweetshop using the phone!"

More soft words from DI Sharp; another furious response.

"He's a pervert! A bloody pervert!"

Again the quiet tone from DI Sharp. She seemed completely un-fazed by the man's anger and was talking to him almost conversa-tionally, her eyes never leaving his and forcing him—clearly against his will—to look only at her.

Dusty edged closer, desperate to hear what was being said. As she did so, she saw Mac gesturing to her through the window of the coffee shop.

"Get away!" he mouthed.

She took no notice and moved on. DI Sharp was still speaking to the man. Something about her poise seemed to have frozen the group, at least for the moment, yet the specter of violence still clung to them like a frost.

Snow started to fall.

Dusty stopped a few feet back from the fringes of the crowd. None of the men or police officers seemed to have noticed her. The police were watching the men, who in turn were watching DI Sharp as she went on speaking in that soft, mesmeric voice. But now Dusty saw someone else.

Mrs. Binchey.

The old woman was staring out from behind the closed door of her sweetshop, clearly in a state of shock. She was being comforted by Mrs. Black from the greengrocer's next door.

The snow grew heavier, colder.

Dusty inched closer, more desperate than ever to hear what DI Sharp was saying. The nearest man was now in touching distance but still no one appeared to have noticed her. She could feel the anger more palpably here—a deep, implacable rage that rippled through the group.

She knew she should get away. Mac was right. It wasn't safe here, even with the police around. Yet she could not move. She sensed that the boy was near. She leaned close to the man in front of her, so close that her cheek touched the fabric of his jacket, and now at last she caught what DI Sharp was saying to the bearded man.

"So, Mr. Hicks, let's go through this again. The boy was in the sweetshop. Is that correct?"

"I just told you," came the answer.

"And he was using the phone?"

"We've been through this, for Christ's sake! Ask the old biddy in the shop. She'll confirm it."

"My colleague has already spoken to her. Mrs. Binchey says she was in the back of the shop fetching something and didn't see the boy in question. She heard the shots in the square, but when she came hurrying back to the front of the shop, all she saw was you and your friends outside. No boy in a duffel coat anywhere."

"Well, we saw him!" The man gestured to the other men. "Didn't we?"

There was a roar of agreement, but DI Sharp simply went on in the same quiet voice.

"And then what happened?"

"I keep bloody telling you! We saw him inside the sweetshop, using the old woman's phone. He looked out, saw us coming for him and bolted out the shop."

"And you shot at him?"

The man shrugged.

"We might have fired a warning shot or two."

"And which way did the boy run?"

The man pointed down Station Road.

"That way. And we're wasting time. He'll get clean away. If you lot hadn't turned up and stopped us, we'd have had him by now."

DC Brett stepped forward.

"What I don't understand is why he would have wanted to use Mrs. Binchey's phone."

The man looked at him with contempt.

"Obvious. Bastard needed to make an urgent call. Pay phone in the square's bust. No mobile on him. Sees no one in the sweetshop so he chances his luck. Nips in and uses Mrs. Binty's."

"Binchey's."

"Whatever."

Dusty stared down Station Road. Nothing much down there save a few shops, houses, and the little railway station at the end. Yet there were several alleyways off the road where the boy might have cut through to other parts of the town.

Again she sensed the closeness of the boy.

She looked about her. No sign of a duffel-coated figure, only the white square and faces still at the windows all around, and snow falling more heavily than ever. Once again the disconcerting feeling of brightness, of gleaming brilliance cutting into her, through her, through everything. She clenched her fists and looked back at the men.

They showed no signs of dispersing. If anything, they seemed angrier than ever and it was clear that the danger was not past. She shouldn't hang around here any longer, and besides, she now had a clue to follow. She started to slip away in the direction of Station Road. DI Sharp saw her for the first time.

"Dusty!" she called. "What on earth are you doing here?"

Dusty stopped.

"I—"

"You shouldn't be hanging around here! Get yourself home at once!"

Dusty saw the men in the group and the other police officers turn to look at her. She shifted on her feet, uneasy at their scrutiny, but tried not to show it. The eyes watched her for a moment, then turned away again. Dusty looked back at DI Sharp.

But DI Sharp was no longer there. She was inside the sweetshop, talking to Mrs. Binchey. The men and officers moved closer to the open doorway of the shop, blocking Dusty's view of what was going on inside. A moment later her mobile rang in her pocket. She pulled it quickly out.

"Hello?" she said.

There was no answer.

"Who's there?" she said.

"It's me, Dusty," came a voice.

She shivered and looked up, and there through a gap in the crowd she saw DI Sharp staring out at her from inside the shop. She was holding Mrs. Binchey's phone to her ear. They watched each other in silence for a moment, then DI Sharp spoke again.

"I just pressed redial to find out the number last called from this phone." A pause. "It appears to be yours."

Dusty saw the faces of the crowd turn back toward her.

Snow settled upon her eyes. It was like liquid glass. Through the blur she saw DI Sharp stride out of the shop.

"Dusty!" she called.

But Dusty was running. She didn't look back and she knew which way to go. She could see the footsteps in the snow stretching from the sweetshop across the square. They might not be the boy's but she was sure they were. There were no other prints to follow anyway.

She raced across the square toward Station Road. Her mind was a mess now. Part of it berated her for leading the others to the boy but most of it didn't care. She had to find the boy herself, had to bring this thing to a head. If she could throw off the others, so much the better. If not, too bad. They'd all find the boy together.

At least the police should stop him being killed.

"Dusty!"

That was DC Brett's voice behind her. She took no notice and ran on, still following what she took to be the boy's steps in the snow. On they went, across the square and away down Station Road. She ran with them, as fast as she could, and only as she entered Station Road did she look back.

They were all after her—men and police—and they were close. She had taken them by surprise with her sudden flight, but even with her head start, she knew she wouldn't outrun the fastest of them. She plunged on down Station Road, her eyes still fixed on the prints in the snow. Then, to her horror, they vanished, just as they'd done in Stonewell Park.

She blundered on even so, aware of her pursuers, and now running on fresh snow. Suddenly she saw the prints again thirty yards on, still leading toward the station. She felt a mixture of relief and horror. She was sure the prints belonged to the same person, yet this was an impossibility. They had tapered into nothing and now thirty yards ahead they'd emerged from nothing, as though the boy had somehow made an inhuman leap across the snow. But there was no time to ponder this. She had to run. She had to find the boy.

"Dusty!"

It was DC Brett again. His voice sounded closer, yet not as close as she'd have expected. Indeed, she was surprised no one had caught up to her yet. She glanced over her shoulder again and saw that the fastest runners were still a good twenty yards behind. They included three of the police officers and four of the men, and now it was clear why the chasers were not moving faster.

They were hampering one another. The police were trying—even as they ran—to keep the men out of this, to get them to leave off the chase and stay out of the matter, while the men were arguing back, yet running on even so.

She put on speed, determined to use this to her advantage. But here, to her frustration, were the prints petering out again. She ran beyond them across a new patch of undisturbed snow, searching as she did so for further tracks beyond. Nothing, nothing, and then—

forty yards or more down the road—there they were again, reemerging from nothingness like the steps of a ghost.

"What the hell are you?" she muttered to the boy.

She ran on, following the new tracks. They led toward the station at the end of the road. She could see it through the driving snow, the shabby little ticket office and waiting room, the two tiny platforms, the bridge. A passenger train was pulling in. She checked the footsteps in the snow. They were heading for the bridge but now—yet again—she could see them tapering away.

She looked quickly around her. All she saw was blinding snow and behind her, the closest of her pursuers: a young, fresh-faced police officer. He'd lost his hat in the chase but was steadily gaining, and now even calling out to her as he ran.

"Dusty, stop! We just need to talk to you. We won't let anybody hurt you."

She felt a sudden yearning to stop.

Then she saw the footsteps again. Yet it didn't seem possible they could belong to the boy. They were nowhere near the bridge. They were far off to the left heading into the disused engine shed. She ran on, not toward the engine shed but toward the bridge.

"Dusty!" called the policeman.

She didn't answer and put on speed. She was starting to see a way of finding the boy and shaking off her pursuers at the same time. But she would have to be quick. She heard a grunt behind her, then a curse, and saw that the policeman had slipped in the snow.

He picked himself up and continued the chase, joined by two of his colleagues who had caught up to him. The men with the guns had stopped altogether and were gathered in an angry knot about fifty yards back, watched by some of the other police officers.

Dusty reached the bridge and started to climb. The steps were slippery but she made it to the top safely and hurried across to the other side. Below her the Barrowmere train was waiting to pull out. Beyond the station the moor stretched away, snowy and clear, toward the lower end of Mirkwell Lake and the southern fells.

"Dusty!" called the policeman. "Don't get on the train!"

She had no intention of doing so but was glad he thought she might.

"We've got your father on the phone!" he called. "Come back and talk!"

She glanced at him and for a moment doubted herself. She knew she'd have to face the music sometime. Yet now might be the only chance she had to follow those prints.

She chose her moment, then ran down to the platform just as the stationmaster was about to set the train on its way. The whistle sounded and the engine began to move. She ran along the platform, snow still blinding her face and—she hoped—the stationmaster's.

Then, as he stood there watching the carriages, she climbed the low fence, the moving train concealing her from the police, and dropped down the other side of the platform to the snowy verge beyond the station. She didn't know whether she'd been seen but there was no time to lose. The police would be here soon to question the stationmaster and resume the search.

She scrambled around the back of the platform to the far end and peered around it to the figures on the other side. To her relief they had all congregated by the bridge. DI Sharp and DC Brett were there, with three other officers. There was no sign of the thuggish men.

She glanced toward the engine shed. It had to be now. She had to chance it. Keeping herself low, she set off across the railway lines back to the other side. No shout came, either from the stationmaster or the police. She crept on, slowly, slowly, then more quickly as she drew closer to the points section where one track split off and headed into the engine shed.

The footsteps were no longer visible. The snow had already covered them. Perhaps the boy had gone—if it was the boy. Yet she could feel the proof inside her. Her instinct was the proof and it was strong. She could feel that presence again, just as she'd done before seeing the snow-face, and here it was more powerful, more frightening than ever. The boy was here—she knew it—and she was about to see him.

Her mobile rang again. She switched it off. It would be Dad or the police or Kamalika or someone else. She didn't care who. It wouldn't be the boy, that much she knew, and the boy was all she wanted: the boy who could tell her about Josh.

The engine shed opened before her: a dark, derelict place, boarded up at the far end and awaiting demolition. No locomotive inside, just a track leading into the gloom as far as the buffer at the end.

Halfway along, a figure in a duffel coat sitting on the ground, slumped against the wall, head down, face hidden by the hood: a figure seemingly unaware of her. She tiptoed forward and stopped about thirty feet away. It was the boy. She could not see him clearly but she knew it was the boy.

He did not move. He seemed locked in stillness. She watched him for several seconds and the conviction grew in her that he was asleep or in an advanced state of exhaustion, or dead. She hesitated, then took another step forward. As she did so, her foot kicked a tin can and sent it rattling into the darkness.

With terrifying speed the figure leaped up. She heard a scream, caught a flash of burning white, saw an arm whip forward as though to hurl something at her. No knife flew through the air, no bottle, no stone, nothing she could see. Yet the blast of that unseen thing lifted her off her feet and flung her through the air.

She fell heavily to the ground, waves of darkness flooding over her. She tried to scramble back up but it was no good. She could not move. She tried again. No part of her would respond. She lay on her back, panic spreading through her, and saw blackness fill her eyes.

The last thing she remembered was Josh.

21

BUT HE WAS NOT her first thought on coming to. Her first thought was of someone else, someone invisible in the black fog that filled her sight. It filled her mind too, this deep, unappeasable darkness, and every tissue of her body, or so it seemed. She tried to move, tried to think. She could do neither. Yet the sense of someone remained: someone close, someone dangerous.

The boy—at last a thought with some definition. It had to be the boy. She remembered him now and with the thought came the picture: the duffel coat, the flash of white, the glimpse of a being as bright as snow. She heard a voice.

"Dusty," it said.

She tried to answer; what to say she did not know. But she tried to answer.

Nothing came, not even a croak.

"Don't try to speak," said the voice. "You won't be able to."

A long, dark silence.

But now the gloom was clearing before her eyes. Through it she could make out a body: tall, hooded. Too much darkness to make out the features, just the form of the boy, the body and head. He was looming over her as she lay there on her back.

Again she struggled to move; again she failed. The body and head leaned closer. Still she could not see the face, just the eyes buried in the darkness.

They gleamed like glass, just as the snow had gleamed as it had fallen.

Memories were flooding now: the chase, the police, the men, the guns, the little station. She peered into the murk but saw nothing of her surroundings. She supposed she must still be in the engine shed, but that was of no importance. She was terrified of the figure inching toward her.

He could do anything he wanted to her.

She tried again to speak, to snarl at him to keep back, to leave her alone, but still no sound came. She could not even whimper. She felt heat now. It was issuing from the boy's body: a powerful, heady current.

She saw a hand reach out. It too was hot. It passed over the top of her face. The lower cuff of his coat sleeve brushed against her. She shuddered at the touch. The hand passed on and then back, the hot swirling current wrapping around her. The darkness deepened once more and she lost consciousness again.

She awoke to the sound of a new voice.

"Dusty." It was soft and familiar. "Dusty."

It was Dad.

She opened her eyes. To her surprise the darkness was gone and all was brightness. For a moment she thought she was on the moor or up on the fell. Nothing was in focus. All was brilliant white.

"Dusty," said Dad.

He was close. She could hear that from the voice. Yet she couldn't see him. She blinked and looked again into this surreal brilliance. Everything burned with a dazzling effulgence. Then, as she watched, the images started to delineate themselves one from another. She could see shapes now around her, the forms of people. She counted them sleepily.

Two, three, four, five . . .

A memory flitted into her mind, a memory from somewhere in the recent past: a memory of counting. She remembered it now. She had counted the men in the square. She shuddered and looked back at the white figures.

Five of them. No more that she could see, and whoever they were, Dad was among them. So she had at least one friend there. Another voice spoke.

"Take your time, Dusty."

She didn't know this voice at all: a woman's voice, low and calm.

The faces were taking shape now, but still they were odd. The brightness was distorting them. She remembered the snow-face on the windowpane and felt another shudder pass through her. These were like snow-faces too: cold, spectral things, all staring down at her; and then the picture cleared.

She was in a hospital bed and there was Dad, and next to him DI Sharp, and three nurses. It appeared to be a private ward. She looked from face to face and saw a smile of relief from Dad as he realized she'd recognized him.

"Dusty," he murmured. "What have you been up to?"

She said nothing. She was breathing hard, still taking in her surroundings, and trying also to move. Her body ached all over and she had never felt so tired but her limbs answered her bidding.

"Dad," she said. Her voice sounded strange. It seemed to come from far away, not from herself at all. But at least she could speak again. "Dad, how did I get here?"

"You'll have to ask DI Sharp," he said. "She knows more than I do. I've only been here a short while."

She looked at DI Sharp. The woman's eyes had that familiar steel but they softened a little now.

"There's a lot to talk about, Dusty," she said. "But maybe right now you'd just like to be with your father. You and I can talk later."

"No." Dusty reached out and—to her own surprise—caught hold of DI Sharp's wrist. "I need to know what happened. I need you to tell me."

DI Sharp glanced down at Dusty's hand clasped around her wrist.

"Sorry," said Dusty, letting go.

"It's all right." DI Sharp gave a half smile. "I can understand you're in a bit of a state. That's why I thought you'd like to spend some time just with your father."

"No, I . . . I want to know."

"All right." DI Sharp glanced around at the nurses. "Is it OK for Dusty to talk so soon? I mean, will it tire her out too much?"

"I'm fine," said Dusty quickly. "I'm not tired at all."

Her body was aching now as she felt her true level of exhaustion, but she did her best to conceal it. The nurses looked at one another, then one leaned forward.

"You can talk for a bit, Dusty," she said, "but the moment you feel tired, you stop."

"I'm not tired. I'm fine."

"You are tired. And you're not fine." The nurse smiled. "But you're stubborn too, and that's probably a good thing right now." She turned to Dad. "Talk with her for a while but don't overdo it. Twenty minutes at the most and then she's to sleep and you can go home for a few hours. In the evening we'll discuss with you whether Dr. Sturton thinks she can go home today or needs to stay overnight."

"I won't need to stay overnight," said Dusty.

"We'll see," said the nurse.

"Thanks for your help," said Dad.

And the three nurses left the ward.

"What happened?" said Dusty.

Dad and DI Sharp exchanged glances.

"I'll tell you, Dusty," said DI Sharp, "but it's got to be a deal. You've got to tell me a few things too, OK?"

"Like what?"

"Like whatever I might need to know."

The bedside manner was gone and the steel was back in the eyes. Dusty looked away. This woman was chilling when she wanted to be. No wonder the bearded man in the square hadn't stepped out of line.

"You've got nothing to fear, Dusty," said Dad. "Just tell the truth. There's nothing to hide. This lady isn't out to get you."

"Very true," said DI Sharp. "You don't need to be wary of me unless you've done something wrong. And even if you have, you're best coming clean. Now then, first question. Why did you run away from the square?"

"I thought I was in trouble."

"Didn't it occur to you that running away might put you in even more trouble?"

"I was scared of those men. I panicked."

"You don't strike me as the sort of person who panics easily. And there were police officers around. You were hardly unprotected."

Dusty said nothing.

"So you ran away," DI Sharp went on. "What made you head for the station?"

"Don't know. Just ran. Didn't really think about where I was going."

"Were you following anyone?"

"No."

"Or trying to lead us away from anyone?"

"No."

"So you ran to the station and we lost you on the other side of the bridge." DI Sharp frowned. "I thought at first you might have got on the train but the stationmaster was unable to confirm that, so we carried on with the search, though with the snow falling it was hard to see any footprints."

"So how did you find Dusty?" said Dad.

"DC Brett spotted the boy in the duffel coat standing in the entrance to the engine shed."

Dusty gave a start.

"Just standing there?" she said.

"Yes." DI Sharp looked hard at her. "I saw him myself. I had the impression he was deliberately standing there in order to be seen."

"What makes you say that?" said Dad.

"Just a gut feeling. He didn't look like someone who'd just come out at the very moment DC Brett looked that way. I felt quite sure . . . and I still feel quite sure . . . that he wanted us to see him."

"What happened next?" said Dad.

"He ran back into the engine shed."

Dusty drew a breath. With the shed blocked at the far end, the way in was also the only way out. It was hard to believe the boy would trap himself deliberately when he was already standing by the exit and could so easily have run away. The moor was close by and there were several other places he could have escaped to.

"What happened?" she asked.

"We followed him into the engine shed," said DI Sharp, "and found you."

"What about the boy?"

"Gone."

"Where? How?"

"We don't know. We're clear he didn't creep out the way he went in. But however he managed it, he escaped." She stroked her chin. "It's not the first time he's done something like this."

Dusty thought back to the story Angelica had told her about the boy's alleged disappearance from a jail cell. She hadn't believed the girl at the time. She wasn't sure what to believe now.

"As for you," DI Sharp went on, "it's hard to know what to say."

An awkward silence fell. Dusty had the feeling that neither Dad nor DI Sharp wanted to break it, that they wanted her to speak, to explain something they had clearly discussed in private between themselves. But she had no idea what that something was.

"I don't know what you're talking about," she said.

"Why did you run into the engine shed?" said DI Sharp.

"I don't know. I just . . . thought I might be able to hide in there."

"And what happened when you entered?"

"I felt this . . . kind of . . . force hit me. I don't know where it came from. The next thing I remember was waking up in this bed."

"You didn't see anybody in the engine shed?"

"No."

DI Sharp watched her for a long, considering moment.

"When we found you, Dusty," she said, "you were lying on your back in the engine shed with your arms folded across your chest. There were no signs of any . . . er . . . unpleasant interference. But your eyes were closed and what was most worrying was that you didn't seem to be breathing. My first impression was that you were dead."

Dusty remembered the blast, the flight, the fall, the black mist.

The terror.

"What happened then?" she made herself say.

"I instructed one of my officers to check your pulse. The moment he touched your wrist, you coughed and started breathing again. But you remained unconscious and none of us could bring you around. We got the medics out there but they couldn't revive you either. So we brought you here to the hospital and rang your father to tell him to come over."

DI Sharp shook her head.

"I'm more relieved than I can say that you're conscious again, Dusty. I don't know what's happened to you or where you've been, but I'm glad to see you back. And your father's been worried sick."

"I'm sorry," said Dusty, looking at him.

Dad frowned.

"I don't know whether to be angry or relieved," he said. "Maybe I'm both. But I think it's time you did some talking."

She was ready to talk now, but not to tell them everything. There was so much that was still too personal and strange, so much that she knew she had to sort out for herself. Moreover, the man with the ponytail's threat of violence if she mentioned him and his sons to the police was still there and the thought of what he might do to Dad was too awful to contemplate.

Yet the police were involved now — the boy himself had seen to that—and there was much she could tell, perhaps even enough to keep DI Sharp off her back, though this might be wishful thinking. The woman was too clever to be easily deceived.

"Dusty?" prompted Dad.

"The boy phoned me," she began. "He phoned me late in the evening on New Year's Day." She looked at DI Sharp. "I lied to you when I said it was a silent call. We did speak, but it really freaked me out. First, I didn't know the boy and I had no idea how he got my telephone number. He said he just made up a number and rang it. I didn't believe that. And then he started saying things about Josh."

"Josh!" Dad looked quickly at DI Sharp but she said nothing. He turned back to Dusty. "What did he say about Josh?"

"Not much. He suggested first of all that I call him Josh, just to give him a name. And then he used a couple of expressions Josh only ever used with me. And he seemed . . ." She hesitated. "He seemed to know things. Things he couldn't possibly know."

"But why did he phone?" said Dad.

"He said he'd taken an overdose and wanted to talk to someone as he died."

"He obviously didn't take enough," muttered Dad, "since he keeps turning up. But he was probably lying about the overdose."

"It certainly sounds very dubious," said DI Sharp. The bright eyes had narrowed again and Dusty found herself wondering whether the woman's doubts related to the boy or to her. Perhaps both.

"What happened then, Dusty?" said Dad.

"He got a bit slurred. He'd obviously been drinking. And then he rang off."

"And that was that?" said DI Sharp.

"Yes."

"Did you trust him?"

"No."

"You must have trusted him a bit."

"What do you mean?"

"You gave him your mobile number. He rang it from the sweetshop."

"I don't know how he got that number."

DI Sharp studied her in silence. Again Dusty felt the thrust of those eyes. The woman spoke again.

"So if you didn't give him your mobile number, who did?"

"I don't know."

"And what did you talk about when he rang you from the sweetshop?"

"Nothing much. More of the same. Stuff about Josh."

"Like what?"

"Just . . . stuff."

"Do I look stupid, Dusty?"

"No."

"Then why did he ring you? Why did he take the risk of going into town and using Mrs. Binchey's phone? It must have been an urgent call for him to do that. So why did he ring you?"

"We didn't talk much. There wasn't time. I heard a shot and he rang off."

"But you did talk?"

"Yes."

"About what?"

"I told you. Stuff about Josh. I don't think he really had time to say whatever it was he wanted to say because the men with the guns turned up."

A long, tense silence. One of the nurses looked in, caught DI Sharp's eye and disappeared again. The silence continued, then DI Sharp frowned.

"The only reason I don't disbelieve absolutely everything you're telling me, Dusty, is because of the boy himself. What little we know of him is not dissimilar to what you're saying, though you're clearly lying in several places and covering up in others. Yet the picture is consistent with reports we have of him elsewhere."

"Doing what?" said Dad.

"Lots of things. For example, revealing knowledge of people he couldn't credibly have. Either he's an extraordinary con man with inside information of the people he deals with or he's someone blessed—or cursed—with a superhuman gift."

"We've also heard what you and your colleague wouldn't tell us," said Dad. "That he's alleged to have raped a young girl."

"Alleged," said DI Sharp, with heavy emphasis. "Not proved."

"Sounds pretty damning to me," said Dad. "And even if he's not guilty, he's clearly dangerous to be around. I had the local radio on when you rang me and they're talking about nothing else but this boy. And who are these men with guns? Vigilantes?"

"We're looking into that. But it seems pretty true to the usual pattern."

"What does that mean?"

"Let's just say the boy seems to have acquired a spectacular number of enemies." DI Sharp paused.

"The alleged rape is undoubtedly at the heart of it. And the fact that the boy is somewhat peculiar and the police still haven't been able to apprehend him—or at least keep hold of him—well, there's no doubt that's added fuel to the fire of those who like to take the law into their own hands."

She looked Dusty over again.

"What worries me about you, Dusty, is that you're in danger of doing that very thing yourself."

"Doing what?" said Dusty.

"Taking the law into your own hands. I'm not going to be hard on you here because you've just been through a horrible experience, but I'll say this: being a rebel is one thing—I was a rebel myself when I was your age—but being reckless is another. I'm aware that you like to go your own way, and I'm also aware that you're telling me only what you want me to know and keeping back the rest. But be careful, Dusty. This time you haven't been badly hurt. You may not be so lucky if you get into trouble again."

"Dusty?" said Dad. "What is it you're not telling us about this boy?"

"Nothing."

"Are you harboring him in some way?"

"No."

"Do you know where he is?"

"No."

"Because people are going to be thinking that. They're maybe already thinking that. The business in the square will have got around and your name will be on everyone's lips. People are already talking about the boy and making assumptions. Now they'll connect him with you. And the more you clam up about what's going on, the more suspicious you're going to look."

Dusty bit her lip.

"I'm telling the truth, Dad. I don't know where he is."

He went on watching her for a moment, then leaned down and kissed her on the brow.

"Well, if DI Sharp has no more questions, I think you should get some rest."

He glanced up at the policewoman. She shrugged.

"I've got lots more questions but I'm sure you're right. Dusty and I can talk again another time. She should rest now."

"But I want to go home," said Dusty.

"You're not going home yet," said Dad. "The nurse said you're to rest."

"But I've got school tomorrow."

"We'll see how you are before deciding on that."

Dusty stared up at them both. She still felt exhausted but she was desperate to get home. She hated being in the hospital and she knew she wasn't injured in any way.

"I just need sleep, Dad," she said. "And I can do that at home."

Dad kissed her again.

"The nurse said you're to sleep here for a while first. I'll come back in a few hours and see how you're feeling once you've rested a bit. If the doctor says it's all right, we'll think about getting you home then."

Dusty forced a smile.

"OK," she said.

Dad smiled back.

"See you later."

Dusty glanced at DI Sharp.

"I'll see you later, Dusty," she said.

And they left her alone.

Dusty lay back and felt the tiredness master her again. Yet sleep would not come. Her thoughts were moving too fast. She didn't care. She was just glad to rest. The doctor looked briefly in, then one of the nurses, then they too left her alone. It felt good. Alone was good. Alone was safe. Alone was what she wanted. It was only much later, as she finally started to drop off, that she realized she was not alone at all.

Someone was standing at the head of the bed.

22

SHE DIDN'T SEE HIM but she felt him, and broke with a panic back into wakefulness. She started to look around, but before she could do so, something closed over her eyes: a hand, palm over her right eye, fingers over her left; a soft, snow-colored hand. Yet from it came a living fire.

"Aah!" she said.

"Best you don't see me," said a voice.

His voice, as she'd known it would be.

"Take your hand away," she begged.

"No."

"But it burns."

The hand didn't move. She lay there, breathing hard, blackness upon her eyes. Then slowly it began to clear. Still she sensed the presence of the hand, yet she saw nothing of it now. Instead, she felt some part of her move, some inner part that seemed to slip out of her body and into a new, less tangible place.

There were no features to it save a queasy brightness. But she knew this realm well enough. She had felt this transparency before with its terrifying sense of erasure. Yet for all that, she felt the boy too. He was still there, still close.

"What are you?" she whispered.

"I don't know."

"Some kind of angel? Some kind of demon?"

"I don't know."

"How did you get into the hospital without someone noticing you?"

"I don't know."

"You must know."

"I don't know anything." The boy's voice felt like breath upon a window. "Who I am or what I am. I don't know if I'm alive or dead. I only know that I am."

"And what do you want?"

"To cease."

"Cease what?"

"Cease to be."

Dusty already felt she had ceased to be. Yet some scrap of herself remained and she clung to it, focused on it, tried to believe in it. It was hard. All she saw was whiteness. All she felt was fire. Self was just a thought. A dream undreamed.

"Let me go," she murmured.

She wasn't sure who she was speaking to, yet in that moment everything changed. Whatever had been holding her tore itself away. She sensed it was the boy removing his hand from her face. The brilliance vanished and in its place she saw the pallid ceiling of the hospital ward. The fire flickered a moment longer, then it too faded, leaving only sweat upon her cheeks. She was still breathing hard, but at least she could feel her body again.

"Let me see you," she said. "I must."

She twisted around and this time the boy did not stop her. The sight of him made her gasp. She stared at him for a moment, then jumped out of the bed and stood there, facing him. She'd been prepared for strangeness, but not this . . . this . . .

She didn't know what to call it.

Beauty, she supposed, yet of a disconcerting kind.

He stood a few feet from her, just out of touching distance, and he was looking at her through pale eyes: a kind of limpid gray tinged with white. He was wearing a duffel coat, unbuttoned and with the hood back. Underneath she saw a pale shirt hanging over pale trousers and some old scruffy boots. No pullover, no scarf, no gloves.

How old he was she couldn't begin to guess. Part of him seemed about sixteen. Another part seemed ageless. It didn't seem to matter. He was unlike anyone she had ever seen. His skin was white. His hair was white. So dominant were these two features that everything else about him seemed white too.

He glowed with an eerie luminosity, and in spite of his snowy appearance, he radiated heat. She could feel the current of it even from here: a subtle, animal force that both roused and repelled her. She tried to ignore it, tried to remain calm, tried to study him in a cool, detached way.

The beauty came from something other than himself. It wasn't the raw, primal energy that he exuded. That was too disturbing to feel in any way beautiful. It was something else, some ambiguity she could not define.

Then she saw it: the strangely feminine quality of the cheekbones and eyes, and the hands—delicate hands with long fingers. Yet this was a boy, and within those frozen eyes she sensed passion and danger. He had beauty and otherworldliness. He had hot, primitive power. He was lethal.

"Don't be frightened of me, Dusty."

"I'm not frightened of you."

"Yes, you are."

She knew he was right, but she said nothing. He spoke again.

"And don't . . ."

"Don't what?"

"Don't become obsessed with me."

She stared at him. It seemed a ridiculous thing for him to say.

"Don't flatter yourself," she said.

He shook his head.

"It's no good, Dusty. There's no point acting tough with me. I see too much. Don't let me see you lying to me as well."

"Did you rape that girl?" she said bluntly.

"I don't know."

"What do you mean you don't know? Of course you know. Did you or didn't you?"

"What do you think?"

"Don't dodge the issue. It doesn't matter what I think. Did you or didn't you?"

"I don't know what I've done. I have no memory of things."

"Then how do you remember my name? My phone number? How to wash and eat and drink? How to walk and talk and think. Eh? How do you remember those things if you've got no memory?"

"I don't know. I just do what seems right. I just . . . act. Something shows me what I need to know. Some . . . instinct. But it's not memory. I can't keep things in my mind. Maybe for a bit. Then they slip away."

"Tell me what you did yesterday."

"I don't know about yesterday."

"Tell me what you did an hour ago."

"I don't know what an hour feels like."

"What the hell are you talking about?"

"I don't know about time. I don't know what it is. I only know people say it exists."

"That's stupid."

"Days, weeks, months, years," said the boy. "Minutes and hours and seconds. I don't know about any of those things."

"That's totally, totally stupid."

"I only know about now. And now hurts."

"You still haven't told me how you remember my name and phone number."

"The important things seem to keep coming back to me. Your

name, your phone number, people I've seen, things like that. It's like ... something keeps giving them to me. But they don't come from memory. They're like ... gifts of the present."

"You're lying. Nobody can live like that."

The boy said nothing.

"Nobody can," she said. "You're just making this up to duck out of admitting things you've done."

Still the boy said nothing.

"You know much more than you're saying," she said. "Don't you?"

He looked at her through his pale eyes.

"All I know is that I seem to have made lots of enemies and people want me dead."

"What kind of an answer's that?"

"It's the only answer I can give you. I don't know how I do the things I do or see the things I see. I only know I cause pain."

"So you could have raped that girl, only you don't remember. Is that what you're saying?"

The boy looked down.

"Do you think I'm capable of rape?"

"How do I know? You're capable of knocking me over and sticking me in this hospital with a wave of your arm."

"I didn't mean to hurt you." The boy was still looking down. "But you startled me. I thought you were one of those men coming to get me."

"You remember that, then! You've got a memory of that!"

"I've got a picture of that. So I suppose it must be something I've done."

"And you've done it before. There's stories of you knocking over other people the same way, and hurting them really badly, much worse than me. And you killed those pit bulls. The same way, I suppose?"

"I think so. I'm not really sure."

"How do you do that? With just a wave of your arm."

"I don't know."

"You can't keep saying you don't know! You've got to know!"

The boy shook his head again.

"I don't understand these things either. That's why I'm going mad."

"What about all the other stuff?"

"What other stuff?"

"The other stuff you do. The way you escaped from the jail cell. And the engine shed. The way you've just turned up here. The way your footprints disappear into nothing, like you're making great leaps across the snow. And then they appear again. And the way you read people's thoughts. Are you going to tell me you don't understand those things either?"

"Yes."

"Yes what?"

"I don't understand those things either."

She glared at him.

"If you're capable of doing those things, then you're capable of raping a young girl."

"If you think so, Dusty."

He looked at her again through his snowy eyes and for a moment Dusty saw what seemed an impenetrable sadness in them. She frowned, unsure what to feel.

"You think I'm being evasive," he said. "I'm not. I promise you. I'm in as much confusion as you are. I don't know what I am. I don't know where I've come from. I don't know how I do the things I do. I see pictures of people and places and objects in my mind and before my eyes but they're all jumbled up. I act by instinct alone. I know no other way. I think what comes into my mind and speak what comes into my mouth. And all I do is cause pain." He tightened his fingers into smooth, white fists. "I'm in torment. Can't you see that?"

"You need help."

"No one can help me. Because no one can understand me."

She didn't know what to believe anymore. His words were too weird to accept. She supposed he was telling her all this for sympathy. Yet she felt none. Whatever torment he claimed to feel, one thing he had said was definitely true: he caused pain wherever he went. Her presence in this hospital was proof enough. For all this boy's unearthly power, she felt nothing but anger toward him. To her surprise, he suddenly laughed.

"What's so funny?" she muttered.

"You're so different from other people."

"What's that supposed to mean?"

"You're not afraid of me at all really. You were when you first saw me but you quickly got over that and now you're just angry with me. I'm more frightened of you than you are of me."

"Then why did you phone me from the sweetshop? Or can't you remember?"

"I can't remember but I know why."

"How can you know why if you can't remember?"

"I just told you, I—"

"Yeah, yeah. You get a picture in your head and—hey presto!—it's the right answer. Never mind. Just tell me why you phoned me."

"I didn't want to go into town. But I could feel you were in danger from those people on the fell and I had to find a phone quickly and ring you."

"Even though you claim you made up my number."

"I did the first time. I just seemed to . . . get it right. I don't know how. And then it sort of came back to me the next time."

"Yeah, it's called remembering. Most people can do it—except those who deliberately want to forget something they've done or pretend it didn't happen. You can't remember if you raped that girl but amazingly you can remember my mobile number."

"I suppose it must seem strange to you."

"Could you see me walking by the lake, then? Before you phoned me."

"In my mind. And the others up on the fell."

"Who are they?"

"I don't remember."

"How convenient."

"You're angry with me again."

"I've never stopped being angry with you." Dusty glowered at him. "You're telling me only what you want me to know and keeping back the rest." She stopped abruptly. The words had sounded familiar as she spoke them but it was only now that she realized she'd borrowed them. They were the very same words DI Sharp had used earlier about her. But she felt no shame over this, only renewed rage toward the boy. "So what have you turned up in the hospital for? And don't say you don't know or can't remember."

"I came to apologize to you."

"What for?"

"For hurting you."

"Is that it?"

"Yes."

"OK. You've apologized. Anything else?"

"One other thing."

"What's that?"

"I can feel Josh."

All her anger vanished at the mention of her brother's name. She took a step toward the boy, then checked herself as the hot current enveloped her. The boy moved back a little as though anxious to maintain the distance between them. She hesitated.

"Tell me what you mean."

"I can feel him. I felt him the first time we spoke on the phone."

"You remember that, then?"

"No, but I—"

"Yeah, OK. Never mind. Where did you feel him?"

"In your voice. I didn't know who it was. I just felt the name first. That's why I used it. Then when you reacted the way you did, I started to feel more things."

"You were just guessing. You didn't hear them in my voice. You just guessed. You could tell the name was important to me, so you guessed a bit more and got lucky."

The boy watched her in silence for a while. She shifted on her feet. It didn't seem possible he could stare for so long without blinking. But that was not the only disturbing thing. His pale eyes were changing. They were turning red.

"You're venting your anger for no reason," he said eventually.

"I've got good reason."

"Not against me. And if you keep venting it, it's going to hurt you. Because deep down you believe me. In your heart I know you believe me. But if you keep pretending you don't, there's no point in my going on."

Another silence.

"Go on," she muttered.

He didn't answer.

"Go on," she said. "I want you to."

"Don't argue, then," he said. "Just listen."

She said nothing.

"I feel things from people," he said. "Even if I don't see them, I feel things. When I hear people's voices, I feel something of their lives, especially the things or people most important to them. Sometimes I can feel a person's whole life. With you I heard Josh in your voice. Everything you said, everything you say, speaks of Josh. Whether you're talking about him directly or talking about something else, it makes no difference. He ripples through your every word. I couldn't see the whole picture that first time. But I felt him a little bit. If I hadn't been drunk, I'd have felt more."

He fell silent and she sensed he was waiting to see if she would interrupt him again. She said nothing and went on watching his face. Once again his eyes didn't blink.

"You're starting to admit to yourself that you believe me," he said. "If only a little."

"Just get on with it."

He fell silent again and she cursed herself. If she wasn't careful, he'd say no more. She mustn't make him angry. She mustn't be impatient and rude.

"You're not making me angry," he said. "But you are being impatient and rude."

She bit her lip and looked down. He went on.

"When I woke up and found the pills hadn't killed me, I felt Josh's name at the front of my mind, and a sense of him. I didn't know—I still don't know—if he's alive or dead. But some part of him is very close. I knew that even then. I know it for certain now. And I can see his face at last."

Dusty looked quickly up.

"Where is it?"

"In yours."

"In my what?"

"Your face."

"My face?"

"Yes. He's in every word you speak. Every thought you think.

And he's in your face. He's . . ." The boy paused again, watching her closely. "You've stopped believing me again. I can see it."

"It's just that . . . I mean . . . it's so hard to—"

"He's got blond hair. Not white like mine, but blond. Scandinavian blond. Quite long, untidy at the top, straight and loose at the sides, bit unkempt. He doesn't seem to bother combing it much. But it doesn't matter. Everybody likes him that way. Blue eyes, really wicked eyes. Girls adore him. Adults, old people, everybody loves him. He's used to doing what he likes. He knows he'll always be forgiven. He knows he'll always be welcomed back. But envied too, envied by lots of people. He makes enemies as easily as he makes friends. A rebel like you. Worse than you. Not as honorable as you. But he's fond of you. Likes your pluckiness. Likes you getting into scrapes with him. And the way you fight your corner. No wonder he calls you Tomboy. His little Dusty. He actually envies you a bit. He's never told you that. But he envies you. He knows deep down he's not quite stable. He likes your strength, just as I do. Your courage. He likes your honesty. He hasn't got so much honesty himself. Small cut under the right ear and a long scar on his left palm. Must be where the knife cut him in that fight in the playground. But he's been in much darker places than that."

Dusty burst into tears. The boy waited for her to finish crying, then spoke again in a low voice.

"I must go now. And you must prepare yourself."

She wiped her eyes, still desperately unsure what to feel.

"Prepare myself for what?"

"For what happens to those who make friends with me."

They stared at each other for a few moments.

"Your father will be here any moment to collect you," said the boy.

"No, he won't. He's left me here to rest. He won't be back for hours."

"He'll be here any moment. Everything's changed. I can feel him in the hospital car park. He's just bought a ticket from the machine and put it inside the car. Now he's running to the entrance of the hospital. He'll be here within a minute or two. Dusty, listen." The boy looked earnestly at her. "You must be brave now, and careful, really careful. And you must look out for your dad too. Don't hesitate to disown me. Blacken my name as much as you want if it keeps people off your back."

"But—"

"I've got to go."

"Are you leaving the area?"

"No, not this time."

"What do you mean?"

The boy seemed to stiffen, to stand taller.

"This time I'm not letting myself be driven out. I've had enough of being on the run." He threw a glance toward the door. "Look after your father, Dusty. And look after yourself."

"But what about my brother?"

"If I can help you find Josh, I will."

"And if not?"

"Then you must live with it as best you can. As for the big mystery . . ."

"The big mystery?" she said.

But she knew what he meant. He watched her through eyes that seemed now to glow like fire.

"The big mystery we must all solve alone," he said.

She heard voices in the corridor: one of the nurses, protesting, and then Dad's, louder than usual, far louder. He wasn't angry. He was scared.

"I must see her! I must see her!"

Dusty called out.

"I'm here, Dad!"

She ran to the door of the ward and looked down the corridor. Dad was only a few yards away, the nurse just behind him struggling to keep up. He saw Dusty, rushed forward and grabbed her in his arms.

"Are you all right?" he said. "Tell me you're all right!"

"I'm fine, Dad. What's happened?"

"The house has been broken into. Things smashed up. Total mess. And a warning spray-painted on the wall."

"Saying what?"

"Give him up! That's what it says! Give him up!" Dad stared at her, his eyes wide with fear. "And I think it's time you did!"

Dusty stared back at him, then turned and looked into the ward.

The boy was gone.

23

She turned quickly back to Dad.

"Have you called the police?"

"No, I came straight here to check that you were all right."

"OK. We'll go home and call them on the way."

"But you're meant to be resting here."

"I'm checking out. I'm fine."

The nurse pushed forward.

"Dusty," she said. "Listen—"

"I'm checking out." Dusty glowered at her for a moment, then forced herself to smile. "I'm really grateful to you for looking after me. But I feel fine and I want to go home."

"I'm going to speak to Dr. Sturton."

"It won't make any difference. I'm still going home."

But Dr. Sturton was already hurrying along the corridor toward them.

"What's going on?" he snapped. "Dusty, why are you out of bed?"

"I'm going home. I feel fine."

The doctor joined them, sweat visible on his brow.

"Nurse?" he said. "What's happened?"

Dad answered.

"There's been a problem at home. Some people have broken in and trashed the house. I came back to check that Dusty's all right."

"And I am," said Dusty, "so I want to go home."

The doctor ran his eye over her, then turned to Dad again.

"Have you called the police?"

"No, I . . . I mean . . . I'm going to do that, of course. But my first concern was Dusty."

Dusty tugged at his arm.

"Dad, come on. We're going."

"Dusty, wait," said the doctor.

Dusty stopped, her hand still on Dad's arm.

"I can't make you stay," said the doctor. "I've no power to restrain you if you choose to discharge yourself. But you must understand that it's my professional duty to ensure that patients in my care leave this hospital in as good a state as possible. I can understand you wanting to go and there's clearly a dreadful situation at home. But dashing out of hospital in this hotheaded way may not be the best way to sort it."

He paused.

"It's true that you don't appear to be injured but you're still tired and I'd be much happier to see you resting here while your father and I ring the police and let them deal with things in the proper manner."

"That makes sense, Dusty," said Dad. "I didn't mean for you to come rushing away with me when I turned up. I just wanted to make sure you're all right."

Dusty shook her head.

"Thanks, but I want to go home."

Ten minutes later she and Dad were in the car. The snow had stopped and twilight was falling, though the hospital buildings were still bright with the wintry coat that lay upon them. Dad turned the key in the ignition and the engine spluttered into life.

"What about the police?" said Dusty. "We'll have to phone them."

"We'll do it at home. You and I need to talk first."

He released the hand brake and fumbled with the gear lever.

"Bloody thing. Get into gear."

The car juddered but eventually pulled away.

"Time you got us a decent set of wheels," said Dusty.

Dad didn't answer. She glanced at him. She knew he was scared, just as she was, and it didn't take psychic ability to see she was in the doghouse again.

"Don't you agree?" she said.

"About what?"

"About the car. You can't pick Helen up in this thing."

"I won't be picking Helen up in anything. That's all finished."

She stared at him.

"The thing with Helen?"

"Yes."

"Is it because of me?"

"What the hell's it got to do with you?"

"Being such a pain," she said. "Getting into trouble around town. The business with those men. And that boy. She must have heard if everyone in Beckdale's been talking about it. Is that the reason? She doesn't want anything to do with you because of me?"

"It's got nothing to do with you." Dad glanced at her. "It's nobody's fault. It's just not meant to be."

She thought of the two figures she'd seen sleeping together.

"But . . ." She hesitated. "I know it's not my business but she . . . sort of . . . stayed quite a long time when she came over. I only know because I heard her drive off in the early hours of the morning, so I . . . I kind of assumed—"

"We went to bed together." Dad glanced at her again. "OK? We went to bed together. Neither of us expected it or planned it. We'd only intended to have dinner and talk. But we ended up playing some of my old jazz stuff."

"I know. I heard. I thought it was a bit of a risky idea."

"Not with Helen. She's nuts on jazz. Knows far more about it than I do. I didn't realize that till we got talking. Anyway, we sort of hit it off better than either of us expected and ended up in bed."

"So what's the problem?"

Dad took a slow breath.

"She wasn't your mum."

His eyes remained fixed on the road.

"She's a lovely woman, Helen," he said. "And she was really understanding. Couldn't have been more understanding. But when the time came, I found I just didn't want to make love."

"So what happened?"

"We just held each other and talked."

"Wasn't she cut up?"

"Yes, she was. She really liked me. But she was great about it."

"What did you talk about?"

"Mum mostly."

"Bit tactless, wasn't it?"

"She wanted to. She particularly asked."

They drove in silence for a while, then Dusty reached out and touched him on the arm.

"It'll be all right, Dad."

He shook his head.

"No, it won't. Not till you tell me what's going on. Till you trust me. I know I haven't been much of a father. I've been weak. I am weak."

"You're not."

"I am. I get flustered. I go to pieces."

"Dad—"

"Hear me out, Dusty." He squeezed the steering wheel tight. "I know you keep things from me and that's fine. I've told you this before. Everyone's got secrets. But if you're keeping important stuff from me and the only reason is because you don't think I can handle it, then that's my fault, not yours. I've got to toughen up." He looked at her again. "And I will."

They drove on into the twilight. Beckdale seemed eerily quiet. Dusty stared out of the window. Normally at this time she would have expected to see people hurrying about, catching the shops before they closed or heading for the bus stops or the station. But most of the people on the streets were police officers.

Some were carrying guns.

Snow started to fall again. Dad switched on the wipers and leaned forward, his face close to the windscreen.

"It's about Josh, isn't it?" he said. He didn't wait for an answer. "It's always been about Josh. You've been obsessed with him all your life. You've idealized him. That's the worst thing. You've put him on a pedestal."

"I haven't."

"You have. You seem to forget he was . . ."

Dad scowled and fell silent.

"He was what?" said Dusty.

"Well, hardly a saint."

"He never did anything really bad."

"How do you know?"

"I just do. I mean, I know he got into scrapes all the time but he never did anything serious."

"You don't know that."

"Are you saying he did?"

"I'm not saying anything of the kind." Dad shrugged. "I'm just saying we don't know. He kept so much from us, remember. I think you're foolish to build him up the way you do."

She thought of the boy. Some words were whispering through her mind, something he'd said about Josh. Something about dark places.

Dad shook his head.

"Don't get me wrong. I don't blame you for being in a state over Josh. I can understand that. It's not knowing what happened to him that's the worst."

Dusty stared out of the window toward Kilbury Moor. It was like a soft, snowy blanket stretching up toward the high peak of Raven's Fell. Far down, at the base, she caught the northern rim of Mirkwell Lake and the shimmer of water.

"But the other thing you seem to forget," said Dad, "is that I feel the loss of Josh too. And so did your mum. That's why she walked out. It flipped her over. It wasn't weakness of character. She got ill. Are you listening to me?"

"Yes."

"Then can you stop staring out of the window and make it look like you're listening?"

She turned and saw his eyes upon her. He looked so tired and ravaged. She wished she could make him happy. He must have been happy once.

"You're meant to be watching the road," she said quietly.

He turned and looked ahead again.

"I heard what you said, Dad."

He didn't answer.

"Dad? I heard what you said. About Josh. And I know you're right. We've all been hurt by it."

"Tell me what I need to know, Dusty."

"What?"

"Talk to me. Tell me what I need to know."

She frowned. She was so full of doubts now after what the boy had told her in the hospital. It seemed everybody in the world hated him, everybody believed him guilty of violence and rape. Yet though he had hurt her in the engine shed, though he still filled her with anger and confusion, she could not condemn him—not while there was a chance he might be innocent. She'd never forgive herself if she became the instrument that led to his capture by the police, or worse still, the mob; and there was another thing.

If I can help you find Josh, I will.

He had given that promise. Maybe he wouldn't fulfill it, but she couldn't give him away while there was a chance of finding Josh. But there was one thing she should tell Dad about now, especially after what had happened at Thorn Cottage.

"There's this guy with a ponytail," she began.

It was a harder story to tell than she'd thought it would be. The memory of it brought back the fear but somehow she managed it. She told Dad about the man, the boys, the dogs, the chase, the confrontation on the track to Knowle—and the man's threat if she didn't keep quiet.

"You should have told me about this," said Dad. "And you should have told the police." He threw an angry glance at her. "What the hell were you thinking of going out to look for this boy? And then getting caught by those people?"

She looked away. She'd known Dad would react this way and it was better to let him say his piece.

"You were brave, Dusty, but you were stupid too."

"I know."

"Incredibly stupid. And then you never said anything."

"The man threatened me. Said he'd—"

"Hurt me if you involved the police. I know. You just said. But you still should have told me. We could have discussed it and decided together on what was best. Well, we know what's best now." He frowned. "When the police come out, you can tell them what you told me. It should be fairly easy to trace that van. In fact, I wouldn't be surprised if the police already know who those people are. I've got a pretty good idea myself."

"Who?"

"Relatives of that girl who got raped up at Millhaven or wherever it was. Father and brothers, probably. They've decided to take the law into their own hands. They've heard the boy has turned up here and they're hunting him down—hence the dogs."

"What about those men with the guns I saw in the square?"

"Friends of Ponytail Man. It's never difficult to round up a lynch mob. They're clearly not locals. They've probably come down from Millhaven as well. No wonder you're in trouble, Dusty. First they see your tracks running alongside the boy's. That gets you fixed in their minds as a friend of his. Then they find out he's rung your mobile from Mrs. Binchey's shop. How he got your number no one knows and you don't seem to want to tell us. But it's hardly surprising people think you're sheltering the boy or know where he is."

Dusty looked over at him again.

"I'm not sheltering him. And I don't know where he is."

They didn't speak again until they reached Thorn Cottage. The snow had stopped and darkness was heavy around them. Dusty climbed warily out of the car. The thought of others breaking into the house made her check around her. She noticed Dad was doing the same. But there were no figures to be seen. Dad turned to her suddenly.

"Listen, Dusty, I've told you off for keeping stuff from me. But now I've got to admit there's something I've been keeping from you."

"What?"

"I said the house had been broken into and things smashed."

"Yes. And a warning spray-painted on the wall."

"Right, well . . . " Dad paused. "It's not the house that's been trashed. It's just your room."

She felt a chill pass through her. He rested a hand on her shoulder.

"You'd better prepare yourself for a shock."

They walked up to the front door. Dad put his key in the lock, turned and pushed. The door swung open. All was dark inside. They stepped in and Dad switched on the hall light.

"They got in through the back door," he said. "Smashed through the glass panel and reached in."

Dusty said nothing. All she could think of was her room. They made their way slowly up the stairs, switching on lights as they went.

"I'll go first," said Dad.

"No." Dusty stopped him. "I will."

She entered her room and switched on the light.

"Oh, my God!" she said.

It was worse than she'd expected. All was devastation. That, clearly, had been the sole purpose of the visit. Her new laptop had not been taken. It had simply been battered to pieces. Everything that could be smashed had been smashed: the window, the lamps, bottles, vases, ornaments. Shards of glass lay everywhere. The easy chair was slashed, the pillows and sheets and duvet ripped up, the pictures and posters splattered with excrement.

The words GIVE HIM UP glowed in red on the wall above her bed.

"I'm sorry, Dusty," said Dad behind her.

She was holding back the tears, just. She was determined not to cry, determined not to let the people who did this have the satisfaction of breaking her as well. She picked up the desk chair from where it had been flung against the wall and sat down on it. To her surprise they hadn't turned over the desk. They'd covered the top surface with knife marks but had otherwise contented themselves with pulling out the drawers and dumping the contents on the floor.

She stared at the mess, her mind for some reason on Josh and the strange boy, and on something she needed to look for. She wasn't sure why she had to look now. But she bent down and started rummaging on the floor through the former contents of the desk drawers.

"Don't do that," said Dad. "You'll get your fingerprints over everything and the police will need to see things exactly as we found them."

"My fingerprints are over everything anyway."

"Dusty—"

"I'm just checking the stuff from the desk drawers. That's all I'm doing. I won't touch anything else. You go and call the police."

"But—"

"Please, Dad. Go and call them. I won't be a minute."

Dad hesitated, then disappeared. A moment later she heard his voice on the phone in his study. She went on rummaging through the things from the drawers, then, in spite of her promise to Dad, wandered about the room, searching, while he went downstairs to make some tea. By the time the police arrived, she had found Josh's photo and the paper face, undamaged.

But the snow-pipe was gone.

24

WELL, DUSTY," said DC Brett, "we seem destined to keep meeting." Dusty stared across the kitchen table. DC Brett, DI Sharp, and Dad watched her in silence. From upstairs came the sound of the other police officers carrying out their examination of her bedroom.

She glanced at DI Sharp. She'd been expecting the woman to start the questioning but perhaps this was some tactic. If it was, there was no clue to be found in the self-possessed face that looked back at her. DC Brett spoke again.

"Your father tells us you've had a nasty encounter with some people with a van."

She repeated everything she'd told Dad. They heard her through without interruption.

"So who are they?" she said.

"I don't know," said DC Brett.

Dusty glanced at DI Sharp. The officer shook her head.

"I don't know either, Dusty."

"Now you're the ones withholding information."

DI Sharp smiled.

"Sometimes we do, Dusty, just like you. But in this instance you're wrong. Neither of us knows who this man with the ponytail is. But I'm sure we can find out. You didn't get the registration number of the van, you said?"

"No, I'm sorry."

"No need to apologize. You had enough to think about at the time. You were extremely brave, Dusty, taking on those people."

"Are you making fun of me?"

"No."

"But you don't really believe me, do you? I can see it in your face. You think I'm making up the story."

"Why wouldn't I believe you?"

"Because you haven't believed anything I've said right from the start."

"Well, you've been keeping things from us right from the start, so it's hardly surprising." DI Sharp's eyes narrowed for a moment. "But I do believe you about the van and we'll certainly look into that."

"It's obvious to me who the guy is," said Dad.

"And who's that, sir?" said DC Brett.

"He's the father of that girl who got raped up at Millhaven. And the boys are her elder brothers. They've decided to take the law into their own hands and carry out some rough justice. They've heard that the police had the boy in their possession and he got away, so they think it's up to them to sort the matter out."

DC Brett glanced at his colleague, then back at Dad.

"The father of the girl you're referring to," he said, "is bald. And he's been in a wheelchair for the last eight years."

There was an uncomfortable silence. Dad shrugged.

"Then it's someone connected with the family. An uncle or something. Or a hired thug and his two boys."

"It's possible," said DC Brett. "We'll obviously check that out."

"What about those other men? The men with guns Dusty saw in the square. You must know something about them. You were there yourselves. You must have questioned them. Or some of them."

Again DC Brett glanced at his colleague. Dusty saw her give a brief nod.

"We've spoken to some of the people," he said, "but by no means all. A number ran away in the confusion and more strangers have appeared in Beckdale since then. But the ones we spoke to are from around Millhaven and Barrowmere and the outlying villages. They're not staying in the town. They're driving here from wherever they live and then driving back the same evening."

"Vigilantes?" said Dad.

"Well, if you like. People who feel particularly hostile to the young man in question and who want to . . . er . . . sort matters out in their own way. We're trying to find out if someone's organizing them."

"Someone must be."

"It doesn't always follow. You sometimes get small, unconnected groups or even individuals acting alone who then form into a body. Particularly when there's a lot of strong feeling."

"As is the case here."

"Exactly. Whether they're organized or not, they're clearly bonding with the common purpose of catching this boy. I'd keep clear of them if I were you and let the police handle things."

"Do you think they're responsible for trashing Dusty's room?"

"It's possible. But we don't have any proof yet."

"It could be the man with the ponytail," said Dusty. "Or his sons."

"That's possible too," said DC Brett. "But we need to wait till the guys upstairs have finished their examination before we start making assumptions. After all, there are other people you need to be wary of as well."

"Like who?" said Dusty.

"Like local people who are frightened of the rumors of this boy and of these strangers turning up with guns, and who see you as the cause of the trouble, as someone harboring the boy."

"But I'm not harboring him. I've no idea where he is."

"Why should they believe that?" said DC Brett. "Why should anyone believe that when there are strong indications that you're in touch with him?"

Dusty felt the boy's words slip into her mind.

Do you think I'm capable of rape?

She looked down, frowning.

"What happened to that girl in Millhaven?" she said.

No one answered.

"Eh?" she said. "What happened?"

"Nothing's been proven, Dusty," said DI Sharp.

"Then what's supposed to have happened?" Dusty looked angrily up at her. "I know you're not meant to tell me stuff but just . . . tell me what you can."

DI Sharp watched her in silence for a moment.

"All we have to go on," she said eventually, "is what the girl herself claims. If what she claims is true, then we're looking for a very dangerous boy. And a very devious one."

"Meaning?"

"That he's clever."

"Allegedly."

"Very good, Dusty. Allegedly. But for argument's sake, let's pretend the girl's story is true. And the story goes like this: she first saw the boy on a street corner. He was playing a little white ocarina. Busking, she presumed, though a number of witnesses have said he had no cap to collect money and didn't seem to be begging. Anyway, the girl and her friends often saw him on street corners, playing this musical instrument."

Dusty thought back to her conversation by the lake. Angelica had claimed to be one of this girl's friends. Perhaps the police had interviewed her as well. Perhaps the girl's story was true. Yet it didn't seem possible. Surely the boy she'd seen standing before her couldn't have done something like this?

"And bit by bit," said DI Sharp, "the boy managed to gain the confidence of this girl. That's—allegedly—the way it seems to work. He makes contact through some startling insight he has with regard to the person concerned. He'll say something that reveals extraordinary knowledge of that person's life. It's not just this particular girl. There are stories from all around the region and further afield. All say the same thing. The trouble starts with the boy making contact in this eerie way. Like he did with you, Dusty, that time he first rang you."

Dusty said nothing.

"In this girl's case," said DI Sharp, "it doesn't appear to have been through a phone call as it was with you. He just started speaking to her as she walked to school. So she says. And many of her friends have testified to seeing him talking to her. He talked to them too. They were uneasy in his company. He'd say things that unsettled them too, things that revealed an unaccountably intimate knowledge of their lives. And then, of course, there's the extraordinary appearance of the boy. It does seem that while some aspects of his nature frighten and repel people, other aspects are powerfully attractive both to females and males. This boy is dangerous to be around. And he clearly has the ability to gain a powerful psychological hold over others." The policewoman paused. "Including you, Dusty."

"You haven't told me what happened to the girl."

"You're not listening to what I'm saying, Dusty. He has a powerful psychological hold over you."

"You still haven't told me what happened to the girl."

"And I won't tell you until you hear what I'm saying."

"I hear you."

"Until you really hear me, not just with your ears but with your brain." DI Sharp looked piercingly at her. "Because I'm not sure that's working right now, Dusty. Your blood's up. You're acting on instinct. But your brain's gone to sleep. If it was working properly, you'd realize that this boy has a powerful psychological and emotional hold over you."

"Allegedly," muttered Dusty.

"No, not allegedly. We're talking fact now. None of this necessarily makes the boy guilty of anything. But whether he's committed a crime or not, it's clear that he has a hold over you. We can deduce that from your own words. And it appears—if others are to be believed—that what's happening to you is true to a pattern that has happened before. And in one instance, it may well have led to a serious criminal act."

"Are you going to tell me what that is now?"

DI Sharp's eyes had turned to flint. But her voice was as calm as it always was.

"According to the girl's story," she went on, "she found herself gradually entangled in the boy's spell. Captivated by him, she said. He seemed to have a way of touching her most intimate thoughts and especially her deepest insecurities. She found herself trusting him enough to go for a long walk with him. All she remembers is something hot overwhelming her, losing consciousness, then finding herself tied up and gagged in some kind of dark place. It later turned out to be a disused lockup on the outskirts of Millhaven. She says the boy kept her imprisoned there for three days, tied and gagged at all times, coming and going and raping her repeatedly during this time. During one of his absences she managed to untie herself and escape. She was found by a farmer on a country lane, crying and in obvious distress."

Dusty looked away. Angelica's version of the story had been pretty much the same. It was hard to know what to think. Dad spoke at last, his voice cracking with emotion.

"You're to see no more of this boy, Dusty. You understand? You don't seek him out, and if he makes contact, you put the phone down or call the police or walk away or whatever. You don't have anything to do with him. And if you know where he is—"

"I don't. I keep telling you."

"If you know where he is," said Dad, "you tell us now."

Dusty saw all eyes watching her again. She glowered back at them.

"I don't know where he is," she said firmly.

Dad thumped his fists on the table.

"You've heard what DI Sharp said. You've got to take this seriously. There's a pattern to it. He wheedles his way into people's lives. He's got these . . . these strange gifts . . . whatever they are. He's weird but he's also . . . kind of . . . intriguing to people. Attractive if you like. And he gets a hold over people. He finds out their most vulnerable spots and works on that. In your case it's Josh. Josh is your most vulnerable spot and the boy's tuned straight into that, just as he did with that girl from Millhaven."

"Allegedly."

"No!" Dad bellowed back at her. "Not allegedly! Stop playing games!"

"I'm not."

"You are! You're playing games because you don't want to face this. The boy did the same thing with that girl from Millhaven. And even if it's not technically proven that he carried out this . . . this . . . dreadful rape, you have to accept the possibility that it might be true. And if it is true, then you yourself are in similar danger."

Dad breathed out with a shudder, then glanced at the police officers.

"I'm sorry," he said. "I'm a bit overwrought."

"We quite understand, sir," said DI Sharp. "I think we've probably talked this through enough for the moment. DC Brett and I'll leave you together for a bit and see how our colleagues are getting on upstairs."

The two police officers left the room. Dusty looked at Dad. He had a worn, almost resigned expression on his face. He stared back at her through bloodshot eyes.

"You look like a cornered animal," he growled.

"Bit of a weird thing to say."

"It's what you look like." His voice was bitter now. "You're turning into Josh. Did you know that? He used to look the same way sometimes. When he'd turn up at home again after disappearing for days on end without a word of explanation. And we'd just know he'd been in trouble and we'd ask him about it. And he'd make up some story. He'd never tell us the truth. He'd just make something up. We knew he was lying. He had so many secrets. Maybe he shared some of them with you. He never shared any with us. And if we pushed him to tell us, he'd look just like you do now. A cornered animal."

"Cornered animals are dangerous."

"Exactly."

They went on staring at each other in silence. Upstairs Dusty caught the sound of footsteps and low voices. It sounded as though the police officers were on the landing rather than in her room and had finished their examination. Dad clearly thought the same.

"Dusty," he said, leaning forward. "Before they come down—is there anything you need to tell me?"

She thought hard. It was so difficult to know what to say and what not to say. But perhaps . . .

"There is one thing the boy told me," she said.

"What?" he said quickly.

She thought back to what the boy had told her in the hospital.

"He said he can feel Josh's presence. Somewhere really close."

"When did he tell you this?"

"In the—" She stopped herself. "On the phone."

"You said 'in the.' What did you mean: 'in the'?"

"I meant 'on the.' On the phone."

"You sure?"

"Yes." She glared at him. "For God's sake, you're reading too much into it. He told me on the phone, OK? The last time he rang me. He said he could feel Josh's presence."

"And I suppose you fell for that. I suppose you just lapped that up."

She didn't answer. There seemed little point. Dad shook his head.

"You're right on the edge, Dusty. I'm worried sick about you. And God knows what you're bringing on us both."

"I won't bring trouble on you," she said. "OK? I'll keep you out of it."

"No, you won't." To her surprise, he suddenly took her hands. "And listen, Dusty—whatever you're not telling me, if there's trouble, we fight it together. Do you hear me? Your problems are my problems."

"And yours are mine," she said.

She felt his hands grip hers hard. She squeezed his back and caught the briefest of smiles in his haunted face. The door opened and DC Brett and DI Sharp reentered the room. Dad looked up at them, still holding Dusty's hands.

"Have they found anything up there?"

"Nothing much to go on," said DC Brett. "We've taken a few samples of things that may yield a clue but I have to tell you there's precious little to help us."

DI Sharp sat down at the table.

"I think the important thing now is to decide how we're going to proceed from here. Or rather, how the two of you are going to proceed. Do you intend to stay in this house?"

"Of course," said Dad. "What did you think we were going to do?"

"I only ask because it occurred to me you must feel pretty vulnerable here, especially as Dusty's name is on so many people's lips around Beckdale. There are clearly people around who have a grudge against her. It struck me that if you had relatives or friends in some other part of the country, you might have wished to—"

"No!" said Dad. "We're not going to be pushed out of our own house by a bunch of thugs!"

Dusty looked at him with astonishment, and an unexpected glow of pride.

"We're staying put," he said. "This is our house. We haven't done anything wrong."

"I'm not saying you have," said DI Sharp, "but for your own safety's sake, it might have been advisable—if only temporarily—to make yourselves scarce. You never know, this might blow over soon. The boy might leave the area and—"

"He won't," said Dusty.

All eyes turned to her. She swallowed hard, aware that she'd blurted out too much. The boy's words echoed in her mind.

This time I'm not letting myself be driven out.

"It's just a hunch," she added quickly.

DI Sharp's eyes narrowed again.

"A hunch spoken with great conviction, Dusty."

"Maybe."

"Any particular reason for the hunch?"

"Hunches don't have a reason. That's why they're hunches."

The eyes narrowed further, but then suddenly DI Sharp stood up.

"We'll keep as close an eye on you both as we can. But I must warn you, we can't give you twenty-four-hour protection. We're stretched as it is with all these hotheaded strangers in the area, and, of course, our main focus is on finding the boy himself."

"We don't expect protection," said Dad.

"Even so," said DI Sharp, "it goes without saying that you both need to be vigilant. And you must ring the police if anything happens. I'm especially thinking of you, Dusty."

Dusty said nothing. She just wanted the police to go now. She wanted to clear up her room. She wanted to think. She wanted to cry. There were sounds of movement from the officers out in the hall. Someone had opened the front door. But DI Sharp and DC Brett still lingered in the kitchen.

"We'll be fine," said Dad. "We'll phone if there's any further trouble."

"May I ask what you're both doing tomorrow?" said DI Sharp.

"I'm meant to be starting a new job," said Dad. "I've just taken over as head chef at the Pied Piper. Dusty's meant to be back at school, though I'm wondering if she ought—"

"And that's what we're doing," said Dusty. "Dad'll be at the Pied Piper and I'll be at school."

"I see." DI Sharp looked from one to the other. "So, business as usual."

"Yes," said Dusty. "Business as usual."

The policewoman gave a curt smile.

"Then we'll say good-bye for the moment."

And the two officers left the room. Dad saw them out, then returned to the kitchen. Dusty stood up and looked at him, then, without a word, they reached out and held each other.

"You all right?" said Dad.

"Yeah. You?"

"I'm OK."

He pulled her closer.

"Where are you going to sleep tonight?"

"In my room."

"You can't," he said. "It's a mess. Put up the camp bed in my room. Or you can have my bed and I'll sleep on the camp bed."

"No, I want to clean up the worst."

"It'll take ages. Leave it till morning."

"I've got school in the morning. And you've got the Pied Piper."

"I'm not going to work and you're not going to school. That was just for the police."

She looked up into his face.

"Dad, listen—you're going to work and I'm going to school."

He gave a sigh.

"Well, maybe. But we'll both clean up your room. And we'll get some food inside us first."

"Baked beans on toast. Something quick."

"OK."

They ate their baked beans on toast in silence, then set to in her room. She'd wanted to tidy up on her own, to think and cry alone, but her tears wouldn't come with Dad there. Yet, for all that, and for all the tension between them, she was happy he was there. When tears finally came, they were his, not hers.

They hugged and worked on, clearing away the glass and splinters and excrement, picking up and straightening and making good what they could. By the end of the evening the window was roughly boarded, the floor clear, the carpet vacuumed, the walls cleaned, the rubbish removed, the bed remade.

"Sure you want to sleep in this room?" said Dad. "It'll be cold till we fix that window."

"I want to."

"If you get cold, come and wake me and we'll set up the camp bed in my room."

"OK."

"Promise me you will."

"I promise," she said.

"We'll decide tomorrow what we're going to do."

"We've already decided. You're going to your new job and I'm going to school."

She leaned forward and kissed him.

"I'm sorry I'm difficult," she said.

"You are difficult. Like Josh. But at least you're still here."

He kissed her back.

"'Night, Dusty." And he left her to herself.

She sat down at the desk, stared at the defaced surface for a while, then pulled out the paper face and Josh's photo. She gazed at them for some minutes: two faces strangely alike, but whereas the photo was cool, the paper face was warm as before, and a glow was starting to appear around the edges of the drawing. She leaned closer, trying to understand.

The big mystery we must all solve alone.

"Why alone?" she murmured. "Why must it be alone?"

Her own tears started at last. She didn't try to hold them back. She just cried. When she'd finished, she wiped her eyes, pulled out her mobile phone and listened. No sound from Dad's room. No sound from anywhere at all. The night was still.

"All right," she said. "I'll make it hard for you. Really hard. Then we'll see what you're made of."

She started to write a text.

We r in big trubl th hse hs bn trashed & its goin 2 get realy bad ther may b violence

She wiped her eyes again, then reached into her pocket and pulled out the card she'd never stopped carrying. She stared down at it, repeating the words she'd spoken when she first received it.

"Mobile hairdresser? Since when have you been a mobile hair-dresser?"

The telephone number on the card seemed to stare back up at her.

She listened again for sounds in the night. Still the desolate silence. She punched in the final words of the text.

com back ifu wnt

And sent it.

25

THE COMMENTS DIDN'T start on the school bus. What was eerie about the journey to Beckdale was the absence of comments. Usually the bus was a noisy place with Dusty at the center of it. But this morning was different. The pupils hung back, silent even among themselves and clearly wary of her.

Everything changed once she entered the school gates.

"How's your boyfriend, Dustbucket?"

She glanced to the right and saw Adam Brice and three of his mates lounging by the fence. Big lads, all of them, and two years older than her. She couldn't take them on. But she managed a scowl.

She walked on, aware of eyes watching from all sides. The voices were hushed, almost silent. This was horrible. She'd expected embarrassment, frostiness, the odd insult, but she felt like an outcast. She made herself walk toward the main building. Now she started to hear what they were saying.

"That's her."

"Over there."

"Keep away from her."

But these were from the younger kids who didn't know her. The older ones were bolder.

"Hey, Dusty! Seen that boy lately?"

She glanced to the side, searching for the speaker, but it was hard to tell who it was. There were so many groups clustered about the playground.

"Hey, Dusty!" Another voice, somewhere behind her. "Did you know he was a pervert when you started seeing him?"

She whirled around. Again no clue as to the speaker except that it was one of the older kids, someone she didn't know. She searched the faces from her own year. No eyes met hers. She stared around at them, then caught a movement by the school gate.

Two men were peering through from the street. She recognized one: the heavy, bearded man DI Sharp had spoken to in the square. He had no gun now, nor did his companion, but there was no mistaking their unhealthy interest in her. She turned back to the main building and saw Beam standing in the entrance.

"Go on," she murmured, watching him. "Let's see you blank me out too."

As if he'd heard her, he gave an awkward shrug and disappeared inside.

"Bastard," she muttered.

"Dusty," said a voice.

"Yeah?" She whirled around again, ready for a fight, but all she saw was Angelica standing there.

"It's me," said the girl.

Dusty stared. She hadn't recognized the voice. She'd been so ready for another taunt she'd barely been listening.

"It's me, Dusty."

"I can see that."

The two girls looked at each other, and as they did so, Dusty felt the atmosphere in the playground intensify. The animosity was still there but now it had an extra charge. She stared about her, then turned back to Angelica.

"What's going on?"

"You're not the only one who's unpopular," said Angelica.

"Don't they like you?"

"Not much."

"But they don't even know you. It's your first day here."

"They know me. Least, they think they do."

"What's that supposed to mean?"

"Doesn't matter." Angelica leaned closer. "Let's go inside. I can't stand all this staring."

"Sure. But not before we've given them something back."

"Like what?"

"Like this."

And Dusty turned slowly around.

"Go on!" she shouted at the faces. "Have a good look!"

A buzz of anger ran around the playground.

"Don't like that, do you?" she yelled. "Me not being scared! Anybody want to take me on?"

Another resentful buzz but no one stepped forward.

"Nobody?" shouted Dusty. "Nobody at all?"

Angelica tugged at her arm.

"Dusty," she whispered, "you're making things worse."

"What about you lot?" Dusty gestured toward Adam Brice and his friends. "You're all big boys. Not scared of little me, are you?"

"Dusty," Angelica urged her. "Let's go inside."

Dusty felt the girl tug at her arm again.

"All right, I'm coming," she muttered. "Let go of my arm."

Angelica let go, and Dusty followed her toward the main building.

"You're trash, Dusty!" someone called.

"Shut your mouth!" she yelled back.

"The boy's a rapist!"

"How do you know?"

"Dusty," murmured Angelica. "Please."

Dusty ignored her and turned back to the playground.

"How do you know?" she shouted, to no one in particular. "Eh? How do you know?"

"Dusty," came a voice behind her.

She looked around and saw Mrs. Wilkes standing there. The Head watched her for a few moments, then nodded toward the main building.

"Come to my office," she said quietly.

Dusty threw a last glower around the playground.

"Dusty," said Mrs. Wilkes. "We need to talk."

Dusty followed her into the school. She felt a strange guilt at leaving Angelica behind in the playground. Why the girl was so unpopular it was hard to tell, but there was no time to think of that now. She had problems enough of her own.

The corridors were as packed as the playground with people hanging about, chatting before the bell. All lowered their voices as she approached. She glared at them, determined not to flinch. Beam was standing outside the drama hall with two of his mates from the rugby team.

"Going to run off again, Beam?" she called.

Beam shifted on his feet.

"It's not right," he mumbled.

"What's not right?"

"Dusty," said Mrs. Wilkes. "Not now."

But Beam spoke again.

"Not right what you're doing."

"And what am I doing?" said Dusty. "Eh?"

"Mixing with that boy. Everybody knows you're protecting him."

"Everybody knows nothing!"

"Dusty!" Mrs. Wilkes stopped suddenly. "That's enough! You too, Beam. Get off to your classroom. The bell's about to go."

Beam lumbered off with his friends.

"Keep your mouth shut, Dusty," said Mrs. Wilkes.

But it was hard. There were stares on all sides, and muttered comments, many from people in her own year, and here was Kamalika avoiding her eyes too.

"Hi, Kam!" she said quickly. "You blanking me out like Beam?"

"It's wrong, Dusty," said Kamalika. "You know it is."

"What's wrong?"

But Kamalika merely shook her head and walked away. Dusty felt a tap on the shoulder.

"Dusty," said the Head. "I'm getting a little tired of this."

"Sorry," said Dusty. "I'll keep quiet now."

They reached the Head's office just as the bell sounded for morning registration. Mrs. Wilkes waved her to the chair in front of the desk and took her own behind it. Dusty glanced around the room: a familiar place she'd been in many times before, usually for fighting. There was a long, uncomfortable silence, which Mrs. Wilkes seemed in no hurry to break. She merely sat there, studying Dusty through narrowed eyes.

"What happened to your cactus?" said Dusty eventually.

"It died," said Mrs. Wilkes.

"I thought they never did."

"Even cactuses die, Dusty."

"Yours looked like it would go on forever."

"I thought the same. But die it did, I'm afraid."

Dusty stared at the space where the cactus had been. All that stood there now was a large new shredder.

"Funny you should mention the cactus," said Mrs. Wilkes.

"Why?"

"Because Josh used to make comments about it—well, jokes really."

"Did he?"

"Yes, all the time."

"All the time?"

240

"Well, he was in this office quite a bit. Even more than you."

Dusty frowned. It was hard to know whether this was a reprimand or the prelude to one. But the Head's tone seemed quite friendly, as it usually was. She'd always got on well with Mrs. Wilkes, in spite of being so often in trouble. The reference to Josh, however, was disconcerting. She hesitated.

"How often was he in here?"

"I don't know, Dusty. I didn't count the occasions. But lots of times."

"More than anybody else?"

"Anybody else in the school? You mean any other pupil?"

"Yes."

"Probably." Mrs. Wilkes paused. "Yes, probably more than anybody else. He was always up to something."

They looked at each other.

"What's on your mind, Dusty?"

Dusty thought back to the things Dad had said to her in the car, and the boy's words in the hospital.

"Was he ever . . . I mean . . . did he ever do anything criminal?"

"I don't know," said Mrs. Wilkes. "My confrontations with your brother were over school matters. I've no idea if he ever broke the law. But if you're asking me do I think he was capable of it, I suppose I'd have to say yes."

Dusty frowned again. She didn't know why she was pursuing this and she was sure Mrs. Wilkes hadn't pulled her in here to talk about Josh. Yet for some reason this seemed important. She took a slow breath.

"Mrs. Wilkes?"

"Yes, Dusty?"

A pause. From outside came the patter of fresh snow against the window.

"Did you . . . did you like Josh?"

She looked hard into Mrs. Wilkes's eyes, and for a moment it struck her that they were not dissimilar to DI Sharp's eyes.

"Yes, Dusty. I liked him very much."

Dusty shifted in her chair, aware of something hidden behind the Head's words, something unsaid. She looked into the woman's eyes again.

"Did you trust him?"

Mrs. Wilkes shook her head.

"No, Dusty. I'm afraid I didn't."

Dusty looked down at the floor.

"OK."

They sat in silence for a while.

"I don't trust that boy either," said Mrs. Wilkes.

Dusty looked quickly up at her.

"Is that why you brought me here? To interrogate me about the boy?"

"Dusty—"

"Because I've had enough of that already from the police."

"Don't get angry with me, Dusty. You asked me an honest question about Josh and I gave you an honest answer."

"My anger's got nothing to do with Josh."

But she knew she was lying.

"I brought you here," said Mrs. Wilkes, "to save you from beating up half the school. Or getting beaten up yourself. Or both. I didn't think you'd come to school at all today but I've been watching out for you ever since the first bus arrived in case you did." Mrs. Wilkes leaned back in the chair. "I've heard all the stories."

"Who hasn't?"

"Indeed. Who hasn't? It seems everyone in Beckdale is talking about you and this boy."

"It's not a problem. I'm dealing with it."

"Yes, I'm sure you are." Mrs. Wilkes studied her. "But what worries me, Dusty, is how much is being said and how quickly the stuff's getting around. You're aware, I presume, of how much is being written about you on the Internet?"

"My computer got trashed yesterday, so I wouldn't know."

Mrs. Wilkes let the silence stretch for several seconds.

"You don't need to fight me too, Dusty. I want to help."

"I'm sorry. It's just that everybody I meet seems to want to interrogate me. And all I want is . . ."

Mrs. Wilkes smiled.

"All you want is to find out what happened to Josh."

"Is that such a bad thing?"

"No, quite the opposite. But, Dusty, this boy doesn't seem to me to be the kind of person who'll help you achieve that."

The Head frowned.

"If there's lots of stuff about you on the Internet, you wouldn't believe how much there is about the boy. No photos, interestingly, but lots of drawings and stacks of comment. I didn't know any of it existed until my kids started showing me things they've found on message boards and in chat rooms. And this morning I've had pupils coming up to me with printouts of things they've found on the Net. Seems everyone's talking about this business. They even know about your house being broken into and the boy's ocarina being found in your room."

"What!" said Dusty. "How the hell did—"

"I don't know." Mrs. Wilkes shrugged. "I've no idea who posts this information but clearly one of the people who broke into your house has put the news on the Net or got someone else to. That's why I'm worried about you, Dusty. There's a lot of bad feeling in Beckdale and you've got yourself stuck right in the middle of it."

"What are they saying about the boy on the Net?"

"All kinds of things."

"Like what?"

"He's a fallen angel, a monster the color of snow, a demon with a beautiful face who abducted a fifteen-year-old girl called Loretta Maguire and raped her. They're saying he can read thoughts, control minds, disappear, fly, throw energy at people and knock them senseless, materialize and dematerialize things."

"What does that mean?"

"Make things appear or disappear or change their constituent parts. Water into wine and all that stuff. I have to say I don't buy into any of it."

"You don't think he can do those things?"

"I don't think anyone can do those things."

"So how does the boy seem to do them?"

"I think he's a con artist. A trickster. I mean, I know one reads about people who are supposed to have these powers but—"

"Where?" Dusty leaned forward. "Where do you read those things? I've never heard of anyone doing stuff like this."

"Oh, there are stories. Most religious traditions have accounts of miracle workers doing amazing things. Saints who levitate, appear in two places at once, vanish into thin air, read minds, heal the sick and so on. But you've only got to watch a good mind magician or illusionist or hypnotist working an audience to see that what they're doing is based on a series of tricks. Brilliant, clever, convincing tricks and all dressed up to make it look like they're psychic or mystical, but tricks nonetheless." Mrs. Wilkes stopped suddenly. "Now, that's a weird thing."

"What?"

The Head didn't answer. She was staring past Dusty's shoulder toward the window. Dusty turned but all she saw was snow dissolving on the pane. She looked back at the Head.

The snow was sticking to the windowpane," said Mrs. Wilkes. "It seemed to be forming a shape. But it's gone now. Slipped down the glass."

Dusty stood up and walked over to the window. For some reason she could feel heat moving around her. It reminded her of the boy's presence that time in the hospital. She stared through the glass. Outside on the sill lay a small pile of snow. It shimmered like the embers of a fire. She looked toward the gate and saw the two men standing there as before, now sheltering under an umbrella. From behind her came Mrs. Wilkes's voice.

"Dusty, the chairman of governors rang me at home this morning to say he thinks you shouldn't be at school while this business is going on. He fears it could have a negative effect on the pupils and on you. And I have to say, after witnessing your arrival at school this morning, I'm inclined to agree with him." A pause. "Dusty, are you going to turn around and face me or must I go on talking to your back?"

Dusty turned around.

"Thank you," said Mrs. Wilkes. "Now, I'm not forcing you out of school. As far as I'm concerned, you have a right to be here, and if you want to stay, you can. But if you want to go home and be with your father—"

"He's at work. He's got a new job."

"Oh. Well, good. But it doesn't change what I'm saying. If you want to go home, or if you'd like to go and be with your father at work, or if you've got some friends or relatives nearby and you'd feel safer or happier with them right now, then I'll be happy to drive you there myself."

Dusty stared out again at the shimmering snow.

The big mystery we must all solve alone.

"Alone," she murmured. "Alone."

"What did you say, Dusty? I didn't catch that."

"I said . . ." Dusty gave a sigh. "I'd like to stay at school."

"OK," said Mrs. Wilkes. "But, Dusty, it's on the understanding that you don't get into any fights. If someone provokes you, you're to bite your lip and not get involved. If necessary, find a teacher or come and see me."

Dusty went on staring out of the window. The men were still there. The snow was still there. The mystery was still there. She leaned close to the pane.

"Josh," she whispered, and watched her breath mist the glass.

She turned back to Mrs. Wilkes.

"I'd better go," she said.

26

BUT WHERE, she did not know.

There was no place she could think of where the pain would not follow. Something else was following too: something hot, something bright, something all-enveloping. The mystery yawned, breathed its white breath.

She stood in the corridor and looked about her. She had to go somewhere. She couldn't stay here all day.

Go to English, she told herself.

She set off down the corridor, heat now swirling about her. Again it reminded her of the boy. She thought of him. A magician, a con artist, a trickster—maybe Mrs. Wilkes was right. It was hard to know what to think. She stopped outside Room 12.

From inside the classroom came the sound of Mr. Finch's voice: a light tenor, quite pleasing. She'd never really noticed it before. She braced herself and opened the door. Mr. Finch turned toward her.

"Dusty," he said. "I wasn't expecting to see you today."

She walked in.

"I had to see Mrs. Wilkes."

"OK. Sit down."

She took her place next to Kamalika, who gave her an awkward glance but said nothing. Mr. Finch turned back to the class.

"Now, we were talking about Shakespeare's extraordinary final play—*The Tempest.*"

The lesson continued but Dusty barely took in what Mr. Finch was saying. She felt utter desolation. She knew her classmates were afraid of her. The hidden glances, the averted eyes, the outright stares—all said the same thing. Only Angelica, sitting alone at the front of the class, gave her an open smile.

Mr. Finch went on talking about *The Tempest*. Dimly she picked up bits of what he was saying. Something about a shipwreck. Something about treachery and enslavement and reconciliation. A beautiful girl who falls in love. A hideous monster. An airy spirit. A character with magical powers.

"Which he renounces at the end," Mr. Finch said.

Angelica put her hand up. Mr. Finch looked at her.

"Yes, er . . ."

"Angelica."

"Yes, Angelica?"

"I don't know what *renounces* means."

"Gives up. He lets go of his powers at the end of the play. He says, 'This rough magic I here abjure.' He doesn't need it anymore. He has been omnipotent but he ends the play as a mortal man, subject to the human frailties we are all prey to."

Mr. Finch smiled at her.

"I'm glad you asked me about the word. You mustn't let things go by that you don't understand. Some of the others here probably didn't understand it either but they have a tendency to let me ramble on unchecked, though Dusty's not usually shy in calling me to account."

He glanced at Dusty but she hardly saw him. All she saw was snow forming on the window behind him: a face appearing before her, before everyone.

She thought of the boy again, murmured more of his words.

"Apart from everything and a part of everything."

She still didn't understand them.

"Dusty?" said Mr. Finch.

"Yes?"

"You murmured something."

The snow-face continued to form. It seemed only a matter of time before someone mentioned it. She felt the heat around her grow. Kamalika shifted in her seat.

"Dusty?" said Mr. Finch. "Are you all right?"

Her body was lightening. She clutched the edge of the desk. It moved with a scrape against the floor. She held on and somehow rooted herself to the spot. Nothing moved, yet she could feel a subtle upward pressure pushing through her body. She clutched the desk more tightly. It scraped against the floor again but somehow remained on the ground. The heat now raged over her skin. She felt all eyes upon her, fixed, questioning.

Her mobile beeped in her pocket. A text message. There was a murmur around the room as though the mundaneness of the sound had released some of the tension. The snow on the window dissolved and slid down, dragging the face with it. She felt her body weight return but the heat was worse than ever. She could take no more of this. She stood up and started to walk toward the door.

"Dusty?" said Mr. Finch.

She didn't answer. She opened the door, stepped into the corridor and walked down it until she was out of sight of classroom eyes. Then she waited for Mr. Finch. He appeared a moment later. From behind him came a buzz of conversation. He closed the door and walked down to her.

"What's going on, Dusty?"

"I need the bathroom."

"No, you don't. It's something else."

"I need the bathroom. It's girls' stuff."

"Don't play that game with me. What's up?"

"Mrs. Wilkes said I could go if I want to. And I want to."

"If that's what she said, then of course it's all right. But you must tell her first what you're doing so she knows. And where you're going, obviously. I'll come with you."

"No, I'm . . ." Dusty looked away, unsure what to say or do. Mr. Finch was being decent and kind and she didn't want to snap at him or do something rash. But she had to get out of here, had to go now, this moment. She didn't know where. Just somewhere, anywhere. Another second here and she'd go mad. She'd made a big mistake coming to school.

"Dusty, listen—"

"No, I . . ." Dusty looked down at her feet. She could hardly speak now. Nothing felt safe; nothing felt right. She could feel the heat growing, the lightness returning. She could feel that unearthly brilliance again. It was closing upon her, cutting through walls, cutting through the floor and ceiling, cutting through Mr. Finch, cutting through her. She saw him now as she saw herself: eyes without a face, eyes without a form.

Eyes without eyes.

"Dusty . . ."

"Go away," she murmured.

She felt herself drift away. Something seized her arm. She sensed it was Mr. Finch's hand. She tugged herself clear and drifted on. The hand caught her a second time. She tugged herself free again, and then she was moving, racing, flying, it seemed, through light. She saw nothing at all now save light, and she was spinning faster than thought, the hot, slippery air churning about her.

Something struck her and she fell back. She was still spinning with light but shadows were closing around her too, mingling with the gleaming fire, and somehow the jostling colors eased into something resembling the door to the playing field. She was lying on her back and her head was pounding. She'd clearly run into the door. From somewhere behind her came the sound of shouts.

"Dusty!"

It was Mr. Finch.

"Dusty!"

"Dusty!"

More voices: Mrs. Wilkes and someone else. It was hard to tell who but she had no intention of waiting to find out. This door would do and by going out the side entrance she could squeeze through the fence and avoid the men at the main gate.

She struggled to her feet and staggered out of the door. The cold hit her at once and for a moment she reeled, but she kept her balance and ran across the snowy field toward the fence. It seemed to loom toward her faster than it should. She watched it roaring closer, then suddenly she was past it and out in the street. She had no recollection of squeezing through the fence.

But she was moving again, as if without will. The street was deserted, though she could still hear voices calling her name. They sounded far behind her, so distant they seemed to come from a world of whispers. She let her feet take her where they wanted.

They took her well away from the main gate. Some part of her brain was clearly working, yet her mind was cloudy now and her eyes were deceiving her. Nothing was as it should be: the street, the school fence, the playing field, the parked cars—all seemed familiar and unfamiliar. As for the snow . . .

The snow scared her. She didn't know why. Perhaps because it reminded her of that gleaming face, perhaps because it hissed with every footstep. She sensed the strange, hot presence moving around her again.

"Josh," she murmured.

She clenched her fists. What the hell was she doing muttering Josh's name? He wasn't here. He was gone. He wasn't coming back. She saw a man approaching, his collar high. She stared at him. No one she knew, just a man in an overcoat. He glanced toward her as they passed.

"He's gone!" he snapped, and walked on.

She stopped and turned. The man was striding away, not looking back.

"What?" she called out.

The man walked on without a word.

"What did you say?" she yelled.

Again no answer. The man disappeared around the corner. She stumbled down the street, her mind in a daze. From somewhere behind her came more shouts. She ignored them, forced herself on down the street.

"Go," she muttered. "Go somewhere."

The somewhere was a doorway farther down the road. She had no recollection of arriving there but she recognized the place. It was the porch outside the Quaker Meetinghouse and she was slumped against the door. A woman in a tracksuit jogged past.

"He's gone!" she shouted to Dusty. "He's gone!"

Dusty sat up in alarm but the runner had already disappeared down the street. She slumped back against the door. Everything was falling apart, and now these strange messages from people she didn't even know. She thrust her hands into her pockets and one of them touched her mobile. She remembered the text she hadn't checked. It was from Dad.

R u ok?

She so wanted to see him, hold him, kiss him. But the last thing he needed on his first day at work was a lame duck. She texted back.

Fine u ok?

He answered at once.

Goin rly wel rng or txt me if probs luv u

"I love you too," she said. "I bloody love you too."

And she burst into tears.

A second woman appeared in the street outside. A woman about Mum's age but with long, untidy hair falling over a faded overcoat. She stopped in front of the porch and gazed in at Dusty.

"Who the hell are you?" Dusty snarled.

The woman walked slowly forward and bent down.

"Come and have some soup," she said.

Dusty wiped her face with her sleeve. She had no intention of going anywhere with this stranger. But the woman simply said, "Follow me," and set off down the street. Dusty stepped out of the doorway and stared after her. The woman was heading toward the bottom end of the school grounds where the street narrowed to a lane and stretched on around the extremity of the playing field.

She started to follow, slowly, as confused about her own actions as she was about the motives of this woman, and as she walked, the name went on falling from her lips.

"Josh, Josh."

"He's gone," she answered herself. "He's gone."

The woman stopped and turned. Dusty stopped too, checking around her. But there was no one else on the street. She walked forward and stopped beside the stranger.

"My name's Bernadette," said the woman. "What's yours?"

"Doesn't matter."

The woman shrugged.

"You're in school uniform, so I presume that means you're playing hooky?"

"I've got permission to leave."

"So you can slump in a doorway?"

Dusty turned to walk away but the woman caught her by the arm.

"Wait." The woman smiled. "I don't need to know anything about you. Let me just give you some soup. That's all I want to do."

"What for?"

"Do I need a reason?"

"But you don't even know me."

"Come and have some soup."

And the woman set off again. Dusty hesitated, still wary of this woman, then slowly followed. They didn't walk far, just around the perimeter wall at the base of the school grounds, then off down the lane. A twist to the right, then back to the left, and suddenly they were in front of the old caravan site.

A scruffy piece of ground, even when beautified by snow. None of the original caravans were there now, save one uninhabitable relic turned on its side down at the bottom, but the place was far from empty. There were several recently arrived caravans to be seen— tired, battered-looking things—and the rest of the space was taken up by a ragtag assortment of vans, campers, and old buses. Now she understood.

This woman was one of the travellers.

27

THERE WAS NO SIGN of the white van, the first thing Dusty checked for among the vehicles, nor of the man with the ponytail and his sons or any of the thugs she'd seen in the square. Indeed, there appeared to be nobody about at all.

Perhaps they were all inside. She didn't come this way very often and had no idea how many people lived on this site or even how long this particular group had been here. She knew that travellers often turned up in Beckdale but local feeling toward them was so hostile they didn't normally stay long. This group, however, had clearly dug in for the winter.

"Where is everyone?" she said.

"Some have gone into town. Some are keeping warm inside."

The woman walked over to the nearest—and by far the shabbiest— of the caravans and opened the door.

"Come in," she said.

Dusty climbed in after her. It was tidier than she'd expected, and warmer too. There was no one else inside but a fire was burning in a little stove in the corner. The woman called Bernadette glanced around at her.

"Close the door and make yourself comfortable. Tomato soup OK?"

"Yes, I suppose. I mean . . ."

It was hard to know what to say. The woman was being kind but Dusty still felt wary of her. She watched as Bernadette poured the contents of a soup can into a saucepan.

"Still don't want to give me your name?" said the woman.

"No."

"OK."

Neither spoke for a few minutes, and as Bernadette warmed the soup, Dusty leaned back in the squashy little chair she'd been offered. Yet she couldn't relax. Danger felt close, in spite of this woman's friendliness. Her instinct was right. Even before the soup was ready, she heard men's voices outside.

"Check the place out. Don't take any crap from anyone."

"She won't be here, will she?"

"You never know. She might have taken refuge with these good people."

"OK."

"You two take the buses and the vans. You three do the caravans over there, I'll check this one."

The curtains of the caravan were drawn across but Dusty knew at once who the voices belonged to. It was hard to know how Bernadette would react. The man had spoken the words *these good people* with unconcealed contempt.

She threw a glance at Bernadette but the woman merely said, "Stay out of sight," and went on stirring the soup. Dusty looked quickly around her.

"Go in the bathroom and close the door behind you," said Bernadette. "But do it quietly."

Dusty had barely closed the door before she heard a thump on the side of the caravan. Bernadette waited for a second thump before opening the door.

"What do you want?" she said quietly.

"Seen a girl?"

The tone of the voice—the abruptness, the arrogance—told Dusty all she needed to know about this man. She knew who it was. It was the bearded lout she'd seen at the gate, the ringleader.

"I've seen lots of girls," said Bernadette. "I'm sure you have too."

"Don't get funny with me. You seen a girl or not?"

"I don't know what you're talking about."

"A girl, for Christ's sake! You people thick or something?"

Bernadette said nothing. From inside the cubicle Dusty heard the man stamping about in the snow. From across the campsite came shouts from the other men to say they'd found nothing. She also heard a woman—presumably one of the other travellers—swearing at the men.

"Piss off!"

And there was some grumbled backchat, which she didn't catch.

The bearded man was still stamping around in the snow outside. He clearly hated having to be polite to people he saw as scum and was struggling to decide what to do. Eventually, in a more ingratiating voice, he tried again.

"Listen, there's a girl—right?—and she's wearing a school uniform. Ugly little cow. You can't miss her. Fifteen years old. Supposed to be in school but she's broken out and she might have come this way, OK? Now, we've been sent to find her because we're all worried in case she gets into any trouble. Thing is, there's this dangerous boy on the loose. You must have heard about him. And we want to make sure she doesn't get mixed up with him. So have you seen her or not?"

There was a long silence. Dusty held her breath. Then Bernadette answered.

"No."

Another silence, longer than before. Dusty heard the tramping of more feet toward the caravan. As the silence lengthened, she pictured the other men standing there, looking up, and Bernadette looking back. There was nothing the woman could do to stop them if they chose to force their way in and there was nothing she herself could do to escape from this cubicle. Bernadette spoke again.

"I said no."

Again the tense silence, but at last the stamping of feet again, and gradually the men moved off. From different parts of the campsite came the sound of catcalls from the other travellers.

"Piss off!"

"Thugs!"

"Get out of it!"

Then Bernadette's voice, calling to her companions.

"That's enough! Let it go!"

And silence fell once again. Bernadette closed the door and called softly to Dusty.

"You can come out now."

Dusty stepped out and peeped around one of the little curtains. There was no sign of the men.

"They've gone," said Bernadette. "But we'd better keep our eyes open. I wouldn't put it past them to rush back suddenly and try to catch us out. Get ready to jump back inside the loo if I give the word. Anyway, soup."

She bent over the saucepan once more.

"Thanks," said Dusty, sitting down again.

"Don't worry about it. We're used to dealing with pond scum here." Bernadette stirred the soup. "I presume you're the person they're looking for?"

"Yeah. The ugly little cow."

Bernadette poured the soup into a mug and handed it to her.

"And is that what you think you are? An ugly little cow?"

Dusty shrugged.

"I don't much care what I am." She sipped at the soup but it was too hot. She stared over the rim of the mug at Bernadette. The woman seemed remarkably self-possessed. It must have been difficult to hold in her anger or her fear with men like that. She blew on the soup and tried another sip. "What are you doing this for?" she said.

"Doing what?"

"Helping me."

"Like I said earlier—do I need a reason?" Bernadette poured herself some soup. "I don't need a reason to help someone. Though in your case, I do have one."

Dusty looked up at her.

"Oh?"

"There's one thing that thick, hairy pillock of a man said that was true."

"What's that?"

"There is a dangerous boy around these parts."

Dusty said nothing.

"And I've heard the rumors," said Bernadette, "about a local girl who's got mixed up with him and is said to be protecting him. I don't know if that girl's you—"

"It's not."

"But if it is, I'd warn you to keep well clear of him. He's not someone to get close to."

"It's not me."

"That's all right, then."

They sipped their soup in silence, Bernadette peering every so often around the side of the curtains. Dusty finished her soup and put down the mug. Bernadette did the same. They looked at each other for a few moments, neither speaking. Then Bernadette smiled.

"Take care, Dusty," she said.

"I didn't say my name was Dusty."

"No, you didn't. But take care anyway."

"And you."

Dusty stood up, opened the caravan door and stepped out onto the snow. It hissed again under her feet. The brightness glared at her and she felt that savage brilliance fill her again, and the lightness in her body return. She swayed on her feet for a few seconds, then heard the sound of Bernadette's boots in the snow.

A hand took her arm, steadied her. She gazed into the light. It was deepening, widening. It seemed to cut right through her. She could feel that terrifying sense of erasure again. Over to the south she could make out the peak of Raven's Fell. It too was white. It too was fading into brilliance.

"What's happening?" she murmured.

Bernadette didn't answer, but her hand tightened around Dusty's arm.

"It's like . . ." Dusty tried to think but her mind was so cut through now by brightness there was no space left for the shadows of thought. Then she saw one. She reached out and clasped it. "It's like . . . nothing's real anymore, everything's connected, everything's . . . part of everything else . . . and it's not meant to be."

"Maybe it is."

Neither spoke for a few minutes. Dusty went on staring into the brightness, searching for shapes.

"Have you ever . . ." she began. She was breathing hard, lost and disoriented in the strangeness of what she was becoming, and of speaking like this to someone she didn't know, but lucidity was returning and the words were falling out of her. "Have you ever . . . lost someone you really loved?"

She couldn't believe she was asking this of a stranger. The woman didn't answer, but she took Dusty's hand in hers. Dusty squeezed it, held it tight for a moment, then let go and stepped forward. The brightness did not ease but somehow, through the glare, she saw the way ahead.

She set off toward the lane out of the caravan park, then stopped by the gate and turned back. Bernadette was standing by the doorway to her caravan. Farther around the site were other faces, some inside their homes, some outside, neither friendly nor unfriendly, just watching with weird, transparent eyes. She looked back at Bernadette. The woman was swirling with spectral light.

"Thank you," said Dusty.

And Bernadette disappeared inside her caravan.

She turned back to the lane and forced herself to walk. From what, toward what, she didn't know. Perhaps there were no destinations anymore. All was just light: deep, suffocating light. Heat too. It slithered over her as before, prickling her skin, circling her spine, hissing in the snow as her feet touched the ground: a fizzing fury of burning light, scalding her very thoughts. More light, more heat, bursting about her in blinding clouds, yet still she walked, whispering her brother's name, still—somehow—she saw the lane ahead.

"Go home," she murmured.

There seemed little point in doing anything else, though no doubt people would be waiting for her at Thorn Cottage: the police, the men, Mrs. Wilkes, maybe Dad, maybe all of them. No doubt everybody was looking for her again, just as they'd once looked for Josh. But she wasn't ready to be found yet.

Take the path around the school grounds, she told herself.

It made sense. The lane still had the occasional car or tractor using it. Indeed, those men might still be hanging about. But the path, though closer to the school, was well concealed and usually deserted at this time of day. Whatever "this time of day" now meant, for even time had lost its meaning. She didn't know how or why. All she knew was that no matter how many steps she took, she had the unshakable feeling that she was walking through a single moment, a moment crystallized in blinding stillness.

Hiss, went the feet, *hiss, hiss, hiss*, and even as they hissed, she felt herself sink more deeply into the effervescence of the present. What was this place and where had she gone? Somehow her feet found the way to the perimeter wall. Beyond it she heard the shouts of pupils running about the football field. She stepped closer to the wall to hide herself more easily, then set off around it, skirting the eastern side of the school.

Snow was falling again, yet still she felt hot. Even the snowflakes felt hot. She kept on walking, the brightness pressing itself upon her and further distorted by the falling snow. Her body felt uncomfortably light now, yet still her feet touched the snow. The path around the school was a long and winding one, studded by bushes much used for concealment by the older pupils. There was no one here now, at least no one she could see in this white, timeless place.

She walked on. She felt so alone now. She supposed she should be glad of that. She knew the aloneness would not last. The path would end in about ten minutes and she would have to negotiate the town. That wouldn't normally be difficult. There were plenty of quiet lanes she could choose that would take her around the outskirts to the main road out of Beckdale, where she could catch a bus home. But today was different.

Today people would be looking for her everywhere. She should savor this aloneness while it lasted. Yet she could not. It hurt too much, and as the brightness deepened, it hurt even more. Her mobile rang—a harsh, unpleasant sound that seemed louder than normal. She pulled the phone out of her pocket and stared at the screen. It was brilliant white, quite unreadable. She felt for the button and pressed it, but before she could speak, she heard the boy's voice in the earpiece.

"You're feeling alone," he said.

"I knew it would be you."

She walked on, listening to the hiss of her feet.

"It comes from the light," said the boy.

"What does?"

"Everything. Including the fire."

"Whose fire is it?"

"Nobody's. It just is."

The hot snow continued to fall.

"You're seeing and feeling what I see and feel," he said. "Some of it anyway. Maybe by the end you'll see and feel all of it."

"I don't want to."

"I don't want you to either. But you might not be able to stop it. There's no separation now, Dusty. Not for you."

She walked on, following the path through the blinding landscape of her mind, and what little of the outside world she could see. The school grounds were still to her left, and the fields were opening up to her right, silent and still and growing more deeply shrouded with the white veil of snow.

"You're crazy," she murmured. "You know that, don't you?"

He didn't answer.

She reached the extremity of the school grounds and stopped at the fork in the path. Still no sign of anyone. It was tempting to take the left fork and cut straight down through the industrial park to the main road. It was just possible she might get there without being spotted by someone. But it was too much of a risk. The other way was longer but far more secluded. She took the right fork and set off down it.

"You've taken the wrong path," said the boy.

"How do you know?"

"I don't. It's just a feeling. Go back and take the other fork."

"Sod off."

She hated this path but she hated the boy more. All he seemed to want to do was confuse her. She walked on, squinting into the light to see where she was going. She could just make out the path. It was narrow and windy and deserted. The houses on her left, with their long, denuded gardens, were ghostly white. The fields to her right, though bright and crisp with snow, seemed chill and hard and hostile.

"I can't help you, Dusty. Not if you don't listen."

"I am listening."

"Then go back and take the other fork."

"What did you ring me for?"

"To tell you to be strong."

She stopped, clutching the phone. The snow had ceased falling. The heat still trickled over her but it was easing. So too was the light. She could see farther ahead now, and more clearly. But the pain was deeper than ever.

"It's lonely being everywhere, isn't it?" said the boy.

"What the hell are you talking about?"

"Doesn't matter."

"And what did you ring me for?" She squeezed the phone tight. "Not just to tell me to be strong and to burble on about . . . being everywhere."

"You're right. I didn't."

"Then what did you ring me for?"

"I wanted to tell you about Josh. I'm starting to get a picture of what happened to him. I'm starting to see—" The boy stopped talking suddenly.

"What?" she said.

He didn't answer for a moment, then suddenly he shouted down the phone.

"Dusty, run!"

"But—"

"Do it now!"

"But what about Josh?"

"Just run! Please, Dusty. I can hear—"

But Dusty could hear it too now: the sound of feet plunging in the snow, and sharp breaths. She'd heard those breaths before and she knew whose they were. She looked quickly behind her: no sign of the man with the ponytail but there were his sons racing down the path, just as they'd chased her from the park gate down the track to Knowle.

"Run!" shouted the boy into the phone.

She was already running. This time she was determined not to get caught. She had a lead of at least fifty yards and with any luck she'd get to the end of the path well before them and be able to disappear down one of the streets that headed in toward the center of town. She plunged on, still clutching the mobile. As she ran, she heard the boy's voice screaming inside the earpiece.

"Run! Run! Run!"

She looked over her shoulder. The gap had lessened but she'd expected that and was still confident she'd reach safety. She stumbled on, skidding and sliding over the slippery ground. Ahead of her was the stile at the end of the path, and the lane beyond. She'd climb over, turn left down the lane, and within a hundred yards she'd have a choice of streets in which to lose herself.

She glanced over her shoulder again. The gap had lessened further but she should still be all right. She heard the boy scream something through the mobile. It was hard to catch the words and she knew it would slow her down to put the phone to her ear. She ran on to the stile and started to climb over. The voice screamed again inside the phone and this time she caught the message.

"Turn right after the stile!"

She jumped to the ground on the other side of the fence.

"Turn right!" screamed the boy.

She turned left. Whatever the boy thought, it would be foolish to go right where there was just an empty lane with no protection. They'd catch up to her easily that way and she could expect no help at all. Left took her toward people and busy streets. She ran down the lane toward the center of town, then stopped in horror.

The white van was racing toward her.

She stared at it, then back over her shoulder. The two boys were already over the stile. The van thundered closer. She could see the man with the ponytail glaring at her through the windscreen. She looked quickly about her, searching for a way of escape.

There was none.

The van skidded to a halt and the man climbed out. Behind her she heard the boys' heavy breaths as they ran closer. There was nothing she could do. She screamed into the mobile.

"Help me! Help me!"

A hand grabbed her by the arm and shook the phone from her grasp. She stared into the eyes of the man with the ponytail. He glowered at her, then stamped his foot on the mobile and crushed it. The two boys closed in.

"Leave me alone!" she screamed.

None of them answered. They simply picked her up, bundled her into the back of the van and roared off down the lane.

28

SHE CRAWLED to the side of the van, away from the two boys. They didn't move but slumped down opposite her, watching, as the van rocked and bumped along the lane. Neither spoke, and nor did their father, his thick hands tight around the steering wheel, his eyes fixed ahead.

She was shaking. She tried to calm herself, tried not to look scared. There was no telling what these people intended to do but she had no doubt they were capable of anything. She drew her knees into her chest and clasped them.

The inside of the van was a disaster. Nothing was lashed, fastened, or stowed in any order. Sleeping bags, blankets, and kit bags were thrown across one another and everywhere she looked she saw empty takeaway cartons, crisp packets, and apple cores. Beer cans and bottles of mineral water rolled about the floor. In the far corner, wedged under what looked like a tent bag, she saw a battered primus stove and a camping gas heater.

They drove on, climbing now. She could see as she stared through the windscreen that the man was taking them toward the higher ground on the eastern side of the town: away from Beckdale, away from the lake and moor, away from the road home. She felt her muscles tighten. There was little up here but fields and then, as the ground rose further, the start of woodland. Already she could see the first of the trees through the windscreen: gaunt white-tipped conifers, motionless in the frozen light.

Snow was falling again. The man switched on the windscreen wipers and drove on. Trees everywhere now, and still they were climbing, then suddenly they slowed down. The van gave a jolt, and the man changed to a lower gear, then revved up again and turned sharply to the right down a little track. The going was rougher here, but she knew where they were heading and it filled her with fear. There was only one reason she could think of for taking her to such a lonely place.

She looked quickly about her, searching for a weapon. She'd only have one chance. Strike and run. A slender hope and probably a waste of time, but she had to try. She couldn't just let them kill her and dump her. She went on searching with her eyes, trying not to show the boys what she was doing.

She saw a shaft of something in the corner, buried under an old coat. Two shafts, spades possibly, then . . . a gun: a double-barreled shotgun like the one the bearded man had. But both the spades and the gun were on the far side of the van, next to the larger of the two boys.

The van ground to a halt. The man turned off the engine, twisted around in his seat and looked balefully at her, then he glanced at the two boys.

"Get her outside," he ordered.

She made a dive for the corner, grasping for the gun, the spades, anything she could reach. But the larger boy fell on her.

"Don't be stupid," he snarled, pinning her down.

The other boy opened the back doors, grabbed her by the legs, and with his brother now holding her arms, pulled her out of the van. The man was already waiting outside.

"Let her drop," he said.

The next moment she was sprawled in the snow. The three stood over her, staring down.

"Get up," said the man.

She didn't move. She was determined not to. She knew she couldn't stop them doing whatever they wanted, but she wouldn't obey them. Not in this, not in anything. The man looked at the boys.

"Get her on her feet."

They hauled her upright. She let her legs sag, her body droop.

"Oh, that's the game, is it?" The man moved closer and peered into her face. "Stand up properly," he said. "Or this." He cuffed her in the face. "Or this." He cuffed her again. "Or this . . . or this . . ."

She took the blows, wincing each time.

He stopped suddenly and looked into her eyes. She scowled back at him, hating him, hating his sons and hating herself most of all, because in spite of her determination to resist, she had indeed straightened up just as he wished. The man watched her with satisfaction.

"That's better." He glanced at the boys again. "Seth, bring her along. Saul, get the spades."

They marched her down the snowy track. She stared nervously about her. She knew this place well enough. She'd come here many a time with Josh in the days when he'd let her tag along with him. Sometimes, when he went off on his own and no one knew where he was, she'd find him here. He liked to roam the high ground above the town and look down on Beckdale from the opposite side to Raven's Fell. He also seemed to have an affection for the Duke's Folly.

The old ruin was clearly this man's destination too. She could see it now at the end of the track, its round, roofless shell white with snow. She stumbled on, her arm locked in Seth's hand, the man just ahead, the boy called Saul a few paces behind with a spade in each hand. They stopped outside the Folly and Saul threw down the spades. The man looked her over, his black hair glistening as the snow settled upon it.

"Know this place, do you?"

She said nothing.

"Built by an old duke a hundred years ago," he said. "Know what for?"

He didn't wait for an answer.

"He had a big house down in Beckdale. Now converted to the youth hostel. And he had a wife. But he had a mistress too. So he had this little place built for somewhere to bring her in secret. And it worked. His wife never knew about it. But the locals did. And they ended up calling it the Duke's Folly. Because he was crazy for his mistress. And crazy in the head."

Dusty looked coldly back at him.

"A hundred and fifty years," she said. "Not a hundred years. And his wife did know. That's why she left him. Everybody in Beckdale knows about the Duke's Folly."

"Then let's talk about your folly," said the man. "Because you're a bit crazy in the head too." He leaned closer. "Now listen. This is personal. Someone I care about has been badly hurt. And the person who hurt her is the person you seem to want to protect. So for me it's very simple. I need to find that boy."

The man's eyes hardened.

"And I need to find him before those other people get him. They've got their own grievances and that in itself should make you question what you're doing keeping quiet. But I can't be thinking of them." The man paused. "Or you. I must have the boy first—before anyone else. And I won't let you or anyone else stop me doing that."

"I don't know where he is." She glowered at him. "And if I did, I wouldn't tell you."

"Give her one of the spades, Saul."

The boy called Saul bent down.

"You needn't bother," Dusty said to him. "I'm not digging my own grave."

"Pick it up, Saul," said the man.

Saul picked up one of the spades. His father snatched it from him, his eyes still on Dusty's face, then, to her surprise, he started to dig himself. She took a step back. Seth's fingers tightened around her arm.

"Get your hand off me!" she snapped. "I wasn't going to run away!"

It was a lie and Seth clearly wasn't fooled as his grip merely grew stronger. The man went on digging. Dusty stood there, watching. He was soon through the layer of surface snow and turning back the earth. She peered down and saw a hole open, widen, deepen. A few minutes later it was clear what the man wanted her to see.

The two pit bulls lay side by side, snow moistening their fur. Even in death they looked fearsome. Yet this had been no normal death. The animals had been flattened, their faces and necks pummeled. It was hard to imagine what kind of force could do something like this: a hammer blow or some huge, crushing weight, a power so savage and so specific it had blasted every vestige of life from these creatures.

She remembered the engine shed and the blackness that had filled her eyes. Yet something must have stayed the boy's hand and preserved her from such a fate. Something had brought her back. Nothing would bring these animals back.

"The boy killed them," growled the man. "We tracked him up here to the Folly. Found him sitting over there among the trees where he'd lit a fire. Dogs went for him and he just . . . threw something at them. Didn't see what. But they flew back through the air like they were missiles. Never moved again. Stone dead. And the bastard ran off."

The man seized her by the collar.

"If that's what he does to dogs, think what he can do to people. He's already committed rape and God knows what else. How much more damage has he got to do before you give him up?"

"I told you! I don't know where he is!"

"I don't believe you! First we find your tracks together. Then we hear from people in town he's been ringing you on your mobile. Now it turns out you had the guy's ocarina thing in your room. We know the stories going around about you. So don't tell me you don't know where he is."

"I've got nothing more to say to you."

She stared at him with all the malevolence she could muster. There was nothing else she could do now. She couldn't run for it. She couldn't fight them. All she had left was defiance. The man squeezed her collar till she choked.

"Then we'll stick you in the grave with the dogs," he hissed.

She tried to pull back but the man tightened his grip.

"Hold her, Seth!"

Seth held her tight. The man let go of her collar and shouted at the other boy.

"Saul! Help him! Hold her still!"

Dusty writhed in Seth's arms and tried to kick herself free.

"Saul!" yelled the man. "Help your brother!"

"Dad, listen," said the boy. "I don't know if this is—"

"Do it!"

Saul grabbed Dusty by the other arm. She went on kicking and struggling.

"Let me go!" she screamed.

The man raised the spade high above his head.

"Last chance!" he bellowed.

But before Dusty could answer or the spade could fall, something struck the man hard in the face. He howled with pain and dropped the spade to the snow.

"What the—" he muttered, and put a hand to his face.

Blood was trickling down his cheek.

Dusty saw a heavy stone lying in the snow. She kicked wildly out again at the two boys. Both clung tightly to her but now more stones were raining upon them, big, dangerous stones flying from among the trees. One hit Saul, another the man; a third hit Dusty on the shoulder.

"Bloody hell!" shouted Seth.

Dusty kicked out again, wrenched her right hand free and threw a punch at Seth. It hit him in the eye as he lunged forward. He gave a cry and staggered back. She tore herself away from Saul and stumbled over the snow toward the Folly.

More stones came flying out of the trees. The man and his sons raced toward the van, leaving their spades behind. Dusty stopped, breathing hard, and watched them go. She had no idea who her deliverers were—and suddenly she didn't care.

She slumped to the ground, tears flooding her eyes. A few moments later she heard the sound of the van revving up, reversing to the lane, then roaring back toward Beckdale. She heard footsteps in the snow behind her and turned.

It was Denny and Gavin.

They stopped a few feet from the Folly and looked down at her. A moment later Sarah Moon and Vicky Spence appeared at the edge of the trees. They walked down and joined the boys, then all four stepped forward.

Dusty didn't move. She was still crying. Somehow, for all her attempts at defiance toward the man and his sons, she felt no need for bravery in front of these four. Sarah bent down.

"Are you all right?"

Dusty sniffed.

"Yeah."

"Who were those people?"

"It's a long story."

"Is it something to do with that weird boy? The one you're supposed to be . . . I mean . . . don't get me wrong but . . ."

"It's a long story." She wiped her face with her sleeve and stood up. "Thanks. Lucky you were there."

"Lucky they disappeared when they did," said Vicky. "We were running out of stones. You don't get many in the forest. But somebody's used some recently to make a base for a fire, so we took some of those."

Dusty wiped her face again, unsure what to say.

"Aren't you supposed to be in school?" she said eventually.

"Aren't you?" said Denny.

She studied him for a moment. Kamalika and the others were right: there was something of Josh in the face, something in the cheeks and especially the hair. Not so blond, of course, not so silky and beautiful, nor the gorgeous eyes. But there was something.

"I'm sorry I attacked you in the square," she said.

He shrugged.

"It's OK."

"I just thought . . . you know . . . the stone inside the snowball . . ."

"It wasn't meant for you."

"What?"

"It wasn't meant for you. It was meant for that new girl. What's her name?"

"Angelica," said Vicky.

Dusty stared at them.

"But why?" she said. "What's Angelica done to you?"

"She's one of them," said Denny.

"One of who?"

"The travellers. She lives in one of those little caravans. Seen her there with 'em. Right bloody bunch. My estate's just down from that site. Some of them are OK but most of them are nutters. Drive us crazy. We don't want 'em near us. So whenever we get the chance, we let 'em know they're not welcome here. Know what I mean?"

Gavin nudged him.

"We got to get back. We got to tell the police about this."

Dusty walked over to where the two dogs were buried. Their fur was now white with snow. The others joined her.

"Nasty-looking things," said Vicky.

Dusty picked up one of the spades and started to pile the earth back on top of the bodies.

"Leave that," said Sarah. "The boys'll do it."

The boys hesitated, but after a glance from Sarah took the spades and carried on the work. Dusty turned wearily toward the track.

"I'll ring the police," she said. "But not from Beckdale. I'll do it from home. You don't have to get involved."

"But we are involved," said Sarah. "We'll be needed as witnesses. Those people were going to murder you."

"You'll get into trouble for being out of school."

"We'll get into even more trouble if we don't say anything."

Dusty looked dully at her, then shook her head.

"I'm still going home. It's where I need to be."

But home, like everywhere else, seemed a dangerous place now.

29

SHE LEFT THE OTHERS and set off to the lane that led down to Beckdale. The snow had stopped again and the air was still. The brilliant light that had terrified her earlier was gone. In its place was a whiteness tinged with gray. She stared down the hill at the town below.

It nestled there, as dewy as a postcard, smoke rising from innumerable chimneys, the stone buildings glistening with snow. On the far side of the town, clear to the eye from this high vantage point, were the blue-green waters of Mirkwell Lake and the white shoreline stretching around the edge of Kilbury Moor. Rising from this was the majestic form of Raven's Fell.

She went on searching the lane, the slopes, the streets of Beckdale, for signs of danger. All she saw was the little town she knew so well. Yet everything seemed different now, not just the town but the lake, the moor, the fells—and herself.

She didn't know how or why. She stared down, scanning the familiar places, and as she did so, she realized with a start that she was searching not just for people but for some part of herself that she had lost or denied. The feeling of aloneness returned and mingled with the fear that shivered in her heart.

She stepped down the lane, following the tracks the van had made on its descent. There was no sign of it now. She supposed the man could be lying in wait for her farther down, but she doubted it. Something in his frantic retreat suggested otherwise. It wasn't the stones that had frightened him away. It was the thought of being recognized and reported.

She certainly hadn't seen the last of him.

She trudged on, her mind now deeply withdrawn, and as she walked, so her thoughts walked too into hidden parts of herself, as down an undiscovered path. She felt strangely still on this path, as still as the air outside, yet it was a stillness that was new and disconcerting, and she was wary of it.

She walked on, watching, listening. The stillness deepened, and now she felt heat swelling about her again. She looked at the snow. It was glistening, not with that brilliance she had seen before but with a more subtle glow. From far below her came the sound of traffic in Beckdale.

She felt eerily cut off from it, as though it belonged to a world apart from hers, yet this feeling did not last. The more she walked, the more she started to feel the opposite sensation; a sense of inclusion. Yet this unsettled her even more.

It's lonely being everywhere.

She shuddered. The traffic sound seemed to well out of her now, as though she herself were its source. She felt her breathing quicken. All stillness was gone. She stared at the snow, the hillocks, the fields, the stone walls, the shrubs and bushes, the cloud of her breath, and for a few seconds lost all sense of what she and they were.

"You're mad," she murmured to herself.

She gave a start. She'd spoken those very words to the boy and here she was saying them to herself. She gazed around her in this strange nonworld, this strange nonplace, and as she did so, she felt the flames of a deep, white fire stirring inside her, and in everything she saw. She thought of Josh, clung to the image of him. At least he was constant. At least he was real. He might be a memory but he wasn't an illusion like all this other stuff.

"Come back to me," she said to him.

She moved on like a ghost, yet even in this trance-walk down the hill a fragment of her mind was working again. She knew she had to get home, and that she didn't want to get caught by anyone on the way. If she took the footpath around the top of the sheep farm, she could cut across from there to the main road out of Beckdale and avoid the town altogether. She could easily pick up a bus farther along.

She reached the footpath and set off down it: a long circuitous route much favored by ramblers. It would add at least a mile to her journey but she didn't care. She wandered along it, talking to Josh. No words came back in the silence. He was as far away as he had ever been, as near as he had ever been.

"Come back to me," she said.

By the time she reached the main road, it was growing dark.

She climbed over the stile and stood by the side of the road, staring out from beneath the overhanging trees. There was no traffic. All was silent in the dusk. She crossed the road as far as the old stone wall and gazed down past the copper beeches toward the lake. It was now a heavy gray, the surface of the water as still as the air.

She heard the sound of an engine approaching from the town. She kept close to the wall and watched. Two headlights appeared, drawing swiftly closer. She didn't recognize the car and it didn't stop. She waited for the stillness to return, then set off in the direction of home.

Three miles to go and she was already exhausted. She hoped a bus would show up soon. She stumbled on, murmuring to Josh as before. From behind her came the sound of more engines. She stepped back to keep out of sight in case she needed to run. Several cars passed. None stopped.

She pushed on and finally reached the bus stop by the verge. It was growing darker by the minute but there, to her relief, was a bus heading toward her from the direction of Beckdale. She leaned against the side of the shelter and waited. The bus pulled in and the doors opened.

The driver was a morose-looking man she didn't know. She looked down inside the bus, searching for danger, but the only people on board were two elderly women sitting on the backseat. She climbed on, paid the driver and took a seat halfway down. The doors closed and the bus set off again. She sat there, dazed, and tried to make sense of what was happening. But there was no sense anymore. She went on murmuring to Josh, knowing nothing else to do.

The women disembarked at the next stop. No one climbed on. The doors closed again and the bus continued its journey. She sat there, deeply alone. The driver, half hidden behind his partition, seemed so far distant it was hard to believe he was there at all. She felt as though she were sitting in a strange, transparent body gliding through a darkening womb.

The voice in her ear checked these thoughts.

"It's all one," it whispered.

She clutched the edge of the seat. It was the boy's voice, impossibly present. He hadn't climbed on the bus, yet he was just behind her. She made to turn.

"Don't," he said. "You won't see me."

But she could feel him: that powerful, animal heat that both stirred and frightened her. She knew he was close, too close for her to feel comfortable.

"You're right," he said. "I am too close to you."

She felt the heat subside.

"Where have you gone?" she said, still staring forward.

"I'm here. I've just moved back a bit."

The bus roared on into the darkness. She spoke again, her eyes fixed on the beam of the headlights.

"What do you mean—it's all one?"

"One substance, one reality."

"I don't understand."

"Neither did I at first. But I do now."

"I don't know what you're talking about."

"Yes, you do. You've been thinking about this all the way here."

"I've been thinking about Josh."

"You've been thinking about this too."

She felt tears fill her eyes.

"Who are you?" she said. "Please tell me. Who are you?"

"Just someone on a journey, Dusty. Like you."

She wiped her eyes with her sleeve as the bus rumbled on.

"I can't take any more," she said.

"Neither can I."

More tears came. She ignored them. Somehow she knew this was the last time they would ever talk.

"You're right," he said. "We won't talk again. Not properly. Not more than a few words. From this moment on, things will move too fast."

"What's going to happen to you?"

"I thought I could die, Dusty, but I was wrong. So I must find another way to put things right."

The bus thundered on into the deepening night. Yet over to the left, the lake, the moor, the snowy peak of Raven's Fell glowed with a fierce, brilliant light. She stared out at it.

"What does it all mean?" she said.

There was no answer. She turned, in spite of his warning, but all she saw was empty seats. She jumped to her feet, ran to the back of the bus and pressed her hands against the glass.

"Josh," she whispered. "You didn't tell me about Josh."

Standing on the road, fading from view as the bus surged on, was a figure—tall, luminous, like the fiery snow all around—and then it was gone. She slumped into the backseat of the bus and stared vacantly around her.

The light was spreading now. It was not just over to the left but on both sides: a diaphanous blaze, burning within the snow. She could feel it burning within herself too. She saw the bus pull over to the side of the road, and a moment later the doors opened. No one climbed on. The bus waited, the engine ticking over, then the driver looked sullenly around at her.

"This is yours," he muttered. "Least, you said it was when you got on."

She stood up shakily and wandered to the open doorway. The driver was still watching her. She stared around at the glowing landscape.

"What's going on?" she said to him. She gestured toward the shining snow. "All this."

"All what?" he said flatly.

She stared at his expressionless face.

"All what?" he said again.

She swallowed hard.

"All nothing," she mumbled, and stepped off the bus.

The doors closed and the bus rumbled off into the night.

"All nothing," she said.

She looked about her. No wonder she'd almost missed her stop. She hardly recognized this place now. The snow was so bright, so sharp against the darkness, it was like a shadow show, a play of masks and deceptions. Nothing looked familiar. Yet here was the lane before her. She set off in the direction of Thorn Cottage.

All was still again—that same unsettling stillness—yet around it she sensed the storm circling, whirling like a tornado to shatter everything in its path. The boy was right. Things were moving too fast now, and so it felt even as she plodded down the lane.

Her thoughts were racing, her emotions racing. The light was racing, piercing the night with luminescent blades. Other things were racing too, transfigured in the cradle of burning light: the shadows of anger and hate, reaching out from distant places. For even in the solitude of this silent lane, she could feel the looming presence of those who had come to destroy.

She forced herself on, watching the light, the night, the mute spaces around her, waiting for the sounds that would herald danger. Here was the stile just down from the spot where Dad had first glimpsed the figure in the duffel coat. There was no figure now, no sign of people at all, yet she sensed them drawing close, just as she sensed the boy drawing close.

And Josh—somehow he was drawing close too.

She walked on, faster now, as fast as her tired legs could manage, and as she walked, she peered through the night for the first signs of Thorn Cottage. She was desperate to see it, desperate to see Dad and be among familiar surroundings again. There it was at last, the outline of the house, and what was more welcome still, the glow of lights.

Dad was home. She'd been worried that he might have gone out to look for her and she'd come back to an empty house. She started to run. She had to get there as soon as possible, had to warn Dad about the dangers that were approaching. She could feel them more tangibly than ever now.

The lane was still quiet, the night still calm, yet she knew this would not last. She ran on, faster, faster, tearing down the lane, and still the land glowed with glacial fire. Nearer, nearer. She could see the house more clearly now. Both the upstairs and downstairs lights were on. Nearer still. She saw Dad's car outside the house.

And another.

She stopped, staring at it, then walked slowly forward. She couldn't run now. Whatever the dangers that were drawing near, she had to think, had to get her mind right. She reached the two cars and stopped again, looking over them. Dad had turned his around as he usually did so that it was facing the right way to head off down the lane the next time he used it. The other car had been parked just as it arrived. They were close together, bonnet to bonnet.

"Nose to nose," she murmured. "Maybe that's how it's meant to be now."

She stepped up to the front door and felt for her key. But there was no need for it. The door opened at that very moment and she found herself looking at Mum.

30

DUSTY! DUSTY!" Mum pulled her inside and closed the door. Dad appeared seconds later.

"Dusty!" he said.

She found herself embraced by both at once.

"Where have you been?" said Dad. "Are you all right?"

He drew back and looked at her, his hands on her shoulders. Mum still had both arms around her.

"What's happened, Dusty?" she said.

Dusty looked back at them, unsure what to say or feel. Something in their manner told her—even in this briefest of moments—that they had already bonded again.

"I'm all right," she said. "But listen—there's trouble coming."

"What kind of trouble?" said Dad.

"I don't know. I just feel it."

"But what's happened?" said Mum. "We've been worried sick about you. Everybody's been looking for you. Where have you been?"

Dusty listened for sounds down the lane. All was silent but she knew there was no time to waste. Whatever was coming was coming soon.

"I'll tell you what's happened to me," she said, "but you first. And be quick."

"I got your text and came straight here," said Mum.

"I never thought you would."

"I was here by ten in the morning. Found the house empty. I knew you'd be at school but didn't know where your dad was. I had no idea about his new job. So I waited in the car. Got freezing sitting out there. Thought about driving into Beckdale and going to the school but decided against it as I thought it would probably embarrass you. So I went on waiting."

Mum pulled a cigarette out of her pocket and put it in her mouth.

"Is it OK if—"

"Yeah, just go on," said Dusty.

"It's just that I'm a bit overwhelmed. All this stuff happening so fast and—"

"Light it, for God's sake, and get on."

Mum lit the cigarette and took a long drag.

"I started to get really cold in the car, so I went around the back of the house to see if you'd left a window open. Found the back door smashed through from—well, your dad's told me how it happened. So I got in that way." She looked at Dad. "You can go on from there."

"I was at work," he said. "Everything was going fine but I was worrying about you. I didn't really believe your text saying you were OK. I could picture you fighting half the school because I knew some people were bound to mouth off at you."

"They did."

"So around twelve I rang the school to check how things were. Got put straight through to Mrs. Wilkes. She said they were all in a terrible state because you'd gone missing. Told me about your problems with the other kids and her talk with you, and the trouble in Mr. Finch's lesson. Said they were all frantically trying to find you. They'd called the police but no one knew where I was."

Dusty stiffened. She was sure she'd caught the sound of an engine far down the lane.

"What is it?" said Dad.

She went on listening but all was silent again.

"Nothing," she said. "Go on. What happened then?"

"I rang home to see if you'd turned up here and your mother answered."

"In a terrible state," said Mum. "By this time I'd had the school on asking where you were, and I'd hardly put the phone down before it rang again and it's the police asking the same thing, and the next minute it's your dad ringing."

"So you came home?" Dusty said to him.

"Dead right."

"What about the job?"

"They were great about it. They could see it was an emergency and just sent me away. I got back and found your mum here."

"Did the police turn up?"

Dad shook his head.

"DI Sharp's rung several times. But there's been nothing to report on either side. Nobody could find you anywhere. She told us to stay put. She felt it was essential someone was here in case you turned up at the house. So we stayed. I tried your mobile several times but got nothing."

"It's been smashed."

"So what's happened to you?" said Dad.

She told them about school, Bernadette, the incident up at the Duke's Folly.

"Bloody hell!" said Dad. "We must phone the police right away."

"There's more," she said.

They stared at her.

"This boy," she went on. "The one they're all talking about." She looked at Mum. "He was the one who spoke to you at the traffic lights. Called you Mumsligum, remember?"

"'Course I do."

"Dad won't know about that."

"Yes, he does. I've told him." Mum stubbed out her cigarette. "We've talked for hours today while we've been sitting here waiting."

"Go on, Dusty," said Dad. "Tell us about the boy."

"I've met him, I've been keeping this from you. I didn't think you'd believe some of things he does and says. I still don't think you'll believe me."

"He's accused of rape," said Dad. "That's all I know."

"And all I know," said Dusty, "is that he's become part of my life. And that he knows about Josh. And that something terrible's going to happen."

She stiffened again. This time she'd definitely heard something down the lane.

"They're coming," she said.

Mum and Dad listened too, both rigid in the silence.

"I can hear engines," said Dad.

"Maybe it's the police," said Mum.

"It isn't the police," said Dusty. "I just know it."

She listened again. There was clearly more than one vehicle. It sounded like several, some of them large.

"They'll be after me," she said.

"Get upstairs," said Dad. "Go straight into my study and ring the police. Keep yourself out of sight."

"But I can't leave you two to face them."

"You can bloody well do as you're told. And hurry up. We need the police out here quickly."

She tore up the stairs and into Dad's study. The light was already on but the curtains were drawn back. She hurried over to the window and pulled them across, then peered around the edge of them into the lane.

Seven or eight vehicles at least, the beams from their headlights spearing the snow as they drew closer to the house. She reached for the phone but at that very moment it rang. She grabbed it.

"Yes?"

"Dusty, it's Angelica."

"I can't talk now."

"You must!"

"I can't. I've got to ring the police. It's an emergency."

"Dusty, you're in danger. Real danger. Mum's told me she saw you today. She made you some soup. Listen, I've got to warn you. There's a guy with a ponytail. Whatever you do, Dusty, don't—"

"He's just arrived at the house."

She could see the white van through the side of the curtains. It was followed by the van belonging to the bearded man, and then a succession of cars. There was scarcely room for them, even where the lane broadened out.

The man with the ponytail drove on to the entrance to Stone-well Park, turned the van around and pulled up opposite the house. Three of the cars did the same. The others simply stopped. One by one the engines fell silent, then the doors opened.

Fourteen men, four women, five of the men with shotguns. She saw the bearded man with a small group of cronies, most of them familiar from the square. The man with the ponytail stood apart from the group with his two boys.

Angelica spoke again.

"Keep away from him, Dusty. He's my stepfather. Mum split up with him ages ago. He's really violent. I'd have told you about him before but we've only just found out he's in the area with his sons. He's got this thing about avenging what happened to me."

"What?" said Dusty.

"I was raped too. I never told you the whole truth. But I'll have to tell you another time. Ring the police. Do it right now."

From downstairs came a thud on the front door. Dusty rang off and dialed 911.

"Answer," she murmured. "For God's sake answer."

A man answered.

"They're outside the house!" she said. "You've got to help us!"

Somehow she gabbled everything out. There was another thud on the front door.

"I've got to go," she said, and rang off.

She heard the front door open.

"Where is she?" came a voice.

She recognized it well enough now. The bearded man.

"Where's who?" said Dad.

"Don't get clever with me. Your daughter, Dusty."

"She's not here at the moment."

"I don't believe you."

"I don't care whether you believe me or not. She's not here and that's the end of it."

Dusty listened tensely. She'd never heard Dad speak this way, never heard such defiance. Mum spoke too, in a similar, unflinching tone.

"We've called the police," she said. "We rang them the moment we saw you coming. They'll be here any moment. So there's no reason for you to hang around."

There was a murmur from the group out in the lane but Dusty could tell the bearded man was still on the doorstep. He spoke again in the same graceless voice.

"Do you know who Loretta Maguire is?"

"I don't know and I don't care," said Dad.

"Well, you should. She's a girl from Millhaven. She's fifteen and her life's been ruined. Ask me how."

"I don't think I will."

"She was raped by that pervert boy. Not once but several times. How would you like that to happen to your little Dusty? Eh? And how would you like it if the police did nothing and let him get away? Loretta's father's in a wheelchair, so what can he do? Luckily, he and Loretta have got friends. And some of us have decided to put things right."

Dusty frowned. The boy had said something like that.

I must find another way to put things right.

How he could do so now she did not know.

"It's wrong," said Dad. "You're vigilantes and that's against the law."

"If the law doesn't do what it should, then the law has to be broken."

There was a roar from the group outside.

"It's still wrong," said Dad.

"What's wrong," said the man, "is your girl protecting a rapist."

"She's not protecting him. She doesn't even know where he is."

"So how come he's been phoning her? And how come this ocarina turned up in her room?"

Mum answered.

"Doesn't prove anything. She could have found it lying in the street. The only thing that's certain is that you people had the nerve to trash our house and leave that disgusting excrement all over the place."

The man laughed.

"You can't prove anything against us. We could have been given the ocarina by somebody else, who got it from the people who trashed your house." He paused. "But we both know who trashed your house. Just as we both know how Dusty got the ocarina."

"We don't know anything of the kind," said Mum. "So you can clear off and take your bloody . . ."

There was a sound of a scuffle on the step. Dusty listened, torn between the need to stay and the urge to run down. Suddenly the man gave a yell.

"You cow!"

From out in the lane came a shout. Dusty peered through the side of the curtains again. Two of the women were bent over the snow at the far side of the lane. Buried in it was a small, white object. Mum had clearly wrenched the snow-pipe from the man's grasp and thrown it out into the lane. The two women studied it for a few moments, then left it where it was and moved back toward the house.

The voices of the group were growing angrier. It was clear these people had no intention of leaving. She thought of the police. They would be some time yet. Even in normal conditions it took a while to get here from Beckdale. In thick snow it would be much longer.

She moved back from the window, unsure what to do next. Then she heard a new voice at the door.

"Do you know who I am?"

She shuddered. It was Angelica's stepfather.

"I know what you are," said Dad coldly. "You're the man who tried to kill my daughter up at the Duke's Folly. She's told me what you look like and I've given your description to the police. You'll be wise to make yourself scarce."

"And you'll be wise to shut your mouth. I don't give a rat's about you or the police. My name's Haynes. Got that? Jethro Haynes. Write it down if you can't remember it. My stepdaughter was also raped by that blond piece of crap. And your kid knows where we can find him. So you can just trot upstairs and bring her down. Because I happen to have noticed she's in the room above. I saw her looking through the curtains."

From out in the lane came another roar from the group.

"I'll do nothing of the kind," said Dad.

"Damn this," said the bearded man. "Come on!"

Dusty heard a shriek from Mum, a shout from Dad, then a confusion of bellows, grunts and angry yells.

"Don't touch her!" screamed Mum. "Don't you dare bloody touch her!"

Steps in the hall, the sound of a struggle.

"Get out!" roared Dad. "Get out of here!"

A thud, another, a moan from Dad.

"Dad!" she screamed.

"That's her voice!" someone shouted.

More steps in the hall, then on the staircase. Dusty raced out to the landing. Down by the front door she saw Dad sprawled on the floor, struggling to get up. He had blood around his nose. Mum was screaming as she tried to push back the figures crowding in from the lane.

It was no use—all were rushing in—but the immediate danger was closer still. Haynes and the bearded man were halfway up the stairs, followed by two men, three women and Haynes's sons. Haynes caught sight of her as he neared the top.

"Remember me?" he mocked.

"Leave me alone!" she snarled back.

"Tell us where the boy is!"

Mum screamed up the stairs.

"Dusty! Lock yourself in the bathroom!"

Dusty turned and raced toward it. She reached the door and pulled it open. From the other end of the landing came the pounding of feet.

"Bad idea, girlie," said the bearded man.

She slammed the door shut and locked it. At once there was a thud against the outside, then another, and another. She saw the wood tremble, buckle. The next thud shattered it completely. Haynes and the bearded man fell into the room and pinned her beneath the broken door. They stood up and pulled the door aside, then Haynes seized her by the wrist and yanked her to her feet.

"There's no escape for you till you tell us where he is!"

"Dusty!" It was Dad calling from somewhere on the stairs. "Dusty!"

"Dad!"

She saw him suddenly through the gaping doorway of the bathroom. He'd struggled to the top of the stairs, Mum close beside him, and they were trying to barge their way through the angry figures now filling the landing. But there was little chance of getting through. It seemed that the whole mob had forced its way in from the lane. One of the women spoke.

"It's not you we want to hurt, girl. Nor your mum and dad. We just want what we came for. We want to see justice done. Most of us are friends of Loretta. We know the family. She's a good kid. She deserves better than what she got. So you got to help us. You got to do what's right. You got to tell us where the boy is. Then we'll leave you alone."

There was a roar of agreement from the group: a harsh, violent roar. It rose and rose into a passionate crescendo. Dusty stared around at the faces before her, at their raging eyes. The roar died slowly away and in the silence that followed she heard something new.

A soft, clear note rising in the air.

31

IT WAS COMING from the lane. Two of the men rushed over to the window of Dad's study and pulled back the curtain.

"He's out there," said one, "playing that instrument."

"Come on," shouted the bearded man, and without a glance at Dusty, Mum or Dad, the members of the group strode back toward the stairs. Dad squeezed around the side of them, pulling Mum with him.

"Dusty!" he called.

But Mum was there first. She pulled Dusty into her arms. Dad arrived a moment later and flung his arms around them both. But Dusty was already struggling to free herself.

"We've got to stop them," she said. "They'll tear him to pieces."

"No," said Dad, wiping blood from his face with a handkerchief. "It's not our business. We've got to let the police handle it."

"But they're not here!"

"Did you ring them?"

"Yes, but they'll be delayed by the snow. We've got to do something."

"Dusty," said Dad. "You mustn't go out there."

She took no notice and raced down the stairs. The front door was still open and through it she could see the backs of the mob as they faced out into the lane. But her eyes ran swiftly past them to the boy.

He was standing on the far side of the lane, his back to Haynes's van, and he was staring at the mob. The snow-pipe glowed in his hand. His hair and skin were translucent in the night. He was wearing the same duffel coat, the same pale shirt, the same pale trousers, the same scruffy boots. Yet even they seemed to burn with the fire that transfigured him.

Snow was falling in thick, heavy flakes. They floated so slowly they seemed almost motionless in the air. She heard Dad whisper, "Stay here," behind her, felt him catch hold of her arm, but she tugged herself free, ran out into the lane and pushed her way through the crowd.

The snow went on falling. The flakes felt hot on her face. She watched them settle on the ground, hissing as they landed. She stared around at the faces of the crowd. No one else seemed to notice the snow. Their eyes were fixed on the boy.

He said nothing, did nothing. He simply stood there and watched them with unblinking poise. The snow-pipe went on glowing against the darkness. He glanced down at it for a moment, then calmly put it in the pocket of his duffel coat, and looked up again.

No one moved.

Dusty clenched her fists. She could sense the nervousness of the crowd—the boy's serenity clearly fazed them—but she knew it wouldn't last. Sure enough, Haynes soon bristled into action.

"Well, I'm not waiting any longer. I've got my own score to settle."

He strode forward. The boy threw back an arm as if to fling something. The arm touched nothing, yet as it whipped back through the air, the van behind him rocked so violently the two offside wheels lifted clear of the ground, then thumped back down again in the snow. Haynes stopped and the boy lowered his arm to his side.

The crowd drew back, muttering.

"Bloody hell!"

"Ain't natural."

"Keep away from him."

But Haynes stood his ground and was soon joined by the bearded man.

"I'm not scared of you!" He sneered at the boy. "Whatever tricks you play, you won't frighten me off!" He glared around at the mob. "Who's got my shotgun?"

"Here!" One of the men threw it across. The bearded man caught it and brandished it at the boy.

"How about this, then?"

The boy looked at him with the same unblinking eyes.

"Do you really think you can kill me?" he said quietly.

"Bloody right I do," said the man, busy loading the gun.

Dusty pushed forward and gripped the man by the arm.

"Leave him alone," she said. "Whatever you think he's done, it's not worth murder."

"Keep out of it, girl."

"But—"

"I said keep out of it!"

He thrust her away. She fell in the snow but quickly scrambled to her feet again. Mum and Dad tried to hold her back but she broke from them and hurried forward again. She could sense a change both in the boy and in the mob. She stared at his face and saw the answer in his eyes. It made her shudder.

He wasn't going to fight them or run away. He was going to let them take him.

"You mustn't," she whispered to him. "They don't deserve to win."

She could feel the mob gathering strength, confidence, will. They were inching forward. She shot a glance down the lane. Still no sign of the police. She looked frantically back at the boy. He had an almost resigned expression now as he watched his enemies edge toward him. Yet his eyes were still calm. They fastened on the bearded man.

"I'm not guilty," he said in the same quiet voice.

The man glowered back at him.

"That's not what Loretta says. And Loretta wouldn't lie. I've known her since she was a baby. Most of us have. She's a truthful girl."

"She's a fantasist."

"That's a lie!"

"She's obsessed with me. As are so many others. Including you."

"That's a total bloody lie!"

"And since she's never been refused anything she's ever wanted, she's had to invent a fantasy to justify my rejection of her."

"She's not a fantasist!" yelled the man, shaking the gun at him. "She's an honest kid! And you've destroyed her life!"

The boy simply turned to Haynes.

"I've no more destroyed Loretta's life than Angelica's."

"You sick pervert," said Haynes.

"Haven't you realized you're never going to win back your wife and stepdaughter?"

"Shut your mouth!"

"There's nothing you can do that will ever win them back. They simply don't want you in their life anymore."

"I said shut your mouth!"

To Dusty's surprise, the boy suddenly turned to her.

"It's not about rape, Dusty. Remember that. Whatever happens here, it's not about rape."

"It is about rape!" bellowed Haynes. He pulled out a knife. "And I'll show you what we do to rapists."

He strode forward again. Dusty screamed at the boy.

"Knock him back! Do what you do! Do what you do!"

But the boy simply stood there, his back to the van, and watched Haynes draw near. From the Beckdale Road came the blare of police sirens. But it only served to galvanize the mob. The bearded man and five of the others pressed forward. Haynes reached the boy first, thrust an arm across his neck and drove him back against the van. Dusty screamed again.

"Stop them! Don't let them hurt you!"

The boy did nothing, said nothing. The police sirens grew louder and now she could see headlights flashing along the lane. Suddenly the crowd seemed divided. Some rushed forward to join the group around the boy; others pulled back, eyeing the approaching cars.

Dusty raced toward the mob gathered around the boy. They were grunting, growling, baying with anger. She could see the knife moving in Haynes's hand, this way, that way, but bodies blocked her view and she couldn't see what was happening. No sound from the boy, no scream, no groan, then suddenly the men drew back, muttering . . .

"What the . . . " said Haynes.

She pushed her way past them, and as she reached the front, the beam from one of the headlights fell upon the boy, and she saw for the first time what the men had seen.

He was splayed against the van, still standing, still alive. His duffel coat had been torn off him and Haynes's knife had cut away his shirt, trousers, and pants. But only his clothes had been slashed. There were no wounds on his body. His skin was as white and sensuous as the snow.

There were no genitals of any kind.

The bearded man found his voice.

"What the hell are you?" he breathed. "A boy? A girl?"

There was no time for an answer as the police swept in.

Dusty stared about her. The divisions in the crowd were clearer now. Some were running for their cars, others gathering in small groups. Haynes and his sons withdrew to the end of the lane, seeking the shadows by the entrance to Stonewell Park. She felt Mum and Dad pluck at her arms again.

"No." She shook herself free. "Please . . . just . . . "

She turned back to the van. The boy—for so she still thought of him—had not moved at all. He was still splayed against the van, his torn clothes scattered about the snow. Even his boots had been ripped off him.

She glanced over her shoulder again. The police had turned up late but at least they were here in force. Their vehicles blocked whatever exit there might have been down the lane, so there was no escape for the mob that way. She walked slowly toward the boy.

"Dusty," called Dad. "Don't go near him."

She carried on. She had to speak to the boy and it had to be now. She sensed Mum and Dad hurrying after her and looked back.

"Stay there," she said. "Please. I promise he won't hurt me."

They stopped, with obvious unwillingness, but kept their eyes fixed upon her. She walked up to the boy. His duffel coat was lying in the snow. She picked it up and held it out to him. He shook his head and motioned to her to drop it. She let it fall in the snow again.

"Why?" she said. "Why didn't you tell people you're not capable of rape?"

He looked back at her through his snowy eyes.

"I told you, Dusty. It's not about rape. It never was."

She looked over her shoulder again and saw Mum and Dad still standing there, watching. But DI Sharp and DC Brett were approaching. She turned quickly back to the boy.

"What is it about, then?" she said.

"It's about fear," he answered.

He held her eyes a moment longer, then slanted his gaze toward the approaching police.

"This dream has gone on long enough," he said, and without warning he jerked open the door to Haynes's van, jumped in and started the engine. Dusty leaped back, startled. From over her shoulder came a chaos of shouts.

"The van!"

"Quick!"

"The weirdo!"

The boy slammed the driver's door shut and revved up the engine. On an impulse, Dusty tore around to the passenger side. The van was already moving off, its wheels spinning in the snow, but it was still going slowly enough for her to catch it.

She saw Mum and Dad stumbling forward, police officers too. She threw herself at the passenger door and wrenched it open.

"You don't need to run!" she said. "Everyone can see you're innocent now!"

The boy looked grimly around at her.

"I'll never be innocent in this world. Now stand back and let me go."

She jumped in and closed the door.

"Don't try and stop me!" she said.

The boy simply drove on. She had no idea what he intended to do. There was no way out down the lane and practically no room to maneuver here with all these vehicles and people. She saw the boy lock the driver's door.

"Do the same with yours," he snapped.

She locked the door without argument.

"You'll never get out of here," she said.

He took no notice and bent over the wheel. Seven or eight police officers blocked the way forward. To Dusty's relief, Mum and Dad were over to the side, though both were screaming at her to get out of the van. The snow was now falling like white stones.

"Hold tight," said the boy, and he put his foot down. The van picked up speed in spite of the snowy ground. The police officers jumped to the side and the van surged toward the house. Dusty clutched the seat as the front garden loomed closer, then suddenly the boy swerved around the back of Mum's car, shot between two of the police vehicles and headed for the fence that bordered the lane.

"Brace yourself!" he said.

They burst through the fence with a crash and skidded into the field beyond. Somehow the boy kept control as they bumped their way over the slippery ground. The windscreen was almost white now. Dusty reached forward, found the control for the wipers and switched them on.

"You'll never get away," she said.

The boy didn't answer. He was leaning forward, shimmering like a ghost. He seemed barely physical now in his snowy, naked form, even as he wrestled with the wheel and gears. He clearly knew how to drive, but there seemed little point to this. Even if they didn't get bogged down in the field, they'd get caught by the police the moment they joined the road.

The van juddered on, helped by the incline, and after a while she saw the fence at the bottom of the field. Beyond it was the track to Knowle or the Beckdale Road. The boy put his foot down and again drove straight through the fence.

"Turn right and go through Knowle," she said. "You can dump the van by the bridleway and escape onto the moor."

He turned left toward the Beckdale Road.

Her mouth fell open. This was madness. The police would almost certainly be waiting for them at the junction. But the boy drove on, his profile sharply etched against the night. She stared at him.

Even here amid all that was happening she found herself lost in the contradiction of him: the feminine and the masculine, the worldly and the otherworldly; the heat, the passion; the cold, snowy power.

The van rumbled on, snow still falling heavily. Here at last was the junction with the Beckdale Road. No sign of any police cars yet but she knew they'd be here any moment.

"Which way are you going?" she said.

The boy turned right toward Beckdale and drove on. Almost at once they were enveloped by headlights from behind. Dusty checked the wing mirror. Three police cars and probably more following.

"You'll never outpace them," she said. "You'll have to pull over."

The boy simply put on speed and steered out into the middle of the road. The sirens started behind them. She stared at him again. He seemed so ethereal now. She could still feel that animal heat flowing from him, but it was waning. His eyes were on the road, yet on something else too: something she could only sense. She looked down.

"You never told me about Josh."

He didn't answer.

"You said you were getting a picture of him," she said. "What did you see?"

He didn't answer.

"Why won't you tell me?"

"You'll find it out for yourself," he said.

"But how?"

"No time for words now."

"But—"

"No time for words now."

Still the sirens sounded behind them, still the police cars couldn't pass. At last they reached the outskirts of Beckdale. The boy drove on toward the bottom end of town. Dusty stared out of the window.

He was taking her toward the school. She watched it draw closer. There was the front entrance. There to the right was the lane that led down to Mirkwell Lake and the path across the moor to Raven's Fell.

The boy shot around into it. She gripped the dashboard and held on as the van thundered on to the end of the lane. The boy pulled over by the entrance to the car park and turned to face her.

"Get out, Dusty. It's time."

"But—"

"Get out. Do it now, I can't take you any further with me."

From close behind came the glare of lights, the blare of sirens.

"Where are you going?" she said.

He looked at her hard.

"I'm going where you can't follow."

The sirens grew louder, the lights brighter. She stared into his face and knew she was seeing him for the last time. She climbed out of the van and stood there in the falling snow. He leaned across, closed the passenger door and locked it again. Then he pressed his face close to the window and called out to her.

"Don't be angry with me, Dusty."

"Tell me about Josh!"

He smiled at her.

"I'm sorry, little Dusty. Good-bye, little Dusty."

And without another word, he revved up the engine and shot forward. Dusty gasped. She had thought he was going to drive into the car park, abandon the van and run onto the moor, but he was heading for the jetty. A police car flashed past her, its siren scream-ing. Another followed. A third drew up nearby.

She stared at the van. It was racing toward the jetty, the chasing cars close behind. One stopped but the other continued, drawing steadily closer, and then the jetty was upon them and they were careering down it. The police car braked, skidded but somehow ground to a halt before the end. As for the van . . .

The van had ceased to be a van. It had become a cloud, as snowy as the boy himself, a strange, airy form moving in the night; and then it was a bird, a spirit bird flying over water. Dusty watched, willing it to fly on and on and never come down. But then it was a rock, a great white rock, that plunged into the water and vanished from view.

32

MORNING. Cold and still.

Dusty sat in the conservatory, staring out at the pale disk that passed for the sun. Eleven o'clock and it had barely climbed over the rim of the fells. But at least the snow had stopped.

The questions too had stopped. She was glad of that. Since yesterday evening she'd known little else. Answer this, sign that. Nobody seemed to think she might have questions as well. But for the moment the police had left her alone.

Anger boiled inside her. The boy had been innocent of rape and everyone had seen the proof, yet still he'd felt the need to run.

I'll never be innocent in this world.

She frowned. There could be no innocence in a world without justice. He'd been betrayed not just by those who started the accusations but by those who believed them. She understood what he meant now. This was never an issue about rape. It was people's fear that had destroyed him.

She felt nothing but rage toward his enemies.

Mum and Dad came in together and stood by the door. She glanced up at them. They looked like a couple of teenagers waiting for permission to hold hands.

"It's all right," she said quietly.

"What's all right?" said Dad.

"I want you to be together."

He came forward and knelt down.

"And I want you to be OK. So does your mum."

"I am OK."

"No, you're not."

The images from last night floated back into her mind: the van, the lake, the snow.

"He didn't deserve to go like that," she said. "We drove him to it. Well, I didn't. Those people did."

"And the police'll deal with them," said Dad. "I gather from DI Sharp they've made quite a few arrests."

"How do you know?"

"I rang her earlier. She said Mr. Haynes is claiming he'd never actually have hit you with the spade. He was just trying to frighten you into telling him where the boy was."

"Like hell."

"Exactly."

"Is there any news from the lake?"

"Not really," said Dad.

"What does that mean?"

"They've sent divers down but there's nothing to report yet."

Dusty looked at him.

"What are you not telling me?" she said.

Dad glanced around at Mum. She came over and knelt down too.

"Your dad's not lying to you, Dusty, but you're right. There is something he's keeping back." She nudged Dad. "Go on. Tell her."

"Tell me what?" said Dusty.

Dad shrugged.

"I just didn't want to give you false hopes."

"What do you mean?"

"The divers have found the van, DI Sharp said. The water's very deep off the end of the jetty, as you know, but she says they should be able to recover it once they get the necessary equipment in place."

"What about the boy?"

"Well, that's the thing I was . . . sort of . . . keeping from you. I wasn't lying when I said there was no news. That's exactly it. There's no news. No sign of the boy at all. No sign of a body."

Dusty stared out of the window toward the moor and fells. She didn't know whether to feel hope or despair. She remembered the boy's words on the bus.

I thought I could die, Dusty, but I was wrong. So I must find another way to put things right.

She pictured the van swirling, the boy swirling, the waters closing over both. He would never put things right now, wherever he was.

"They checked the van," said Dad. "Obviously they expected to find the boy's body inside. But there was nothing there. And . . ." He hesitated. "This is the weird bit."

"Go on."

"They found the doors of the van locked and all the windows closed. That's got to be the strangest thing. I mean, if he did manage to force his way out of the van, he'd hardly stop to lock the doors after him, would he?"

Dusty thought of the story about the boy and the jail cell. But she said nothing.

"Anyway," said Dad, "that's all I've been told."

He smiled at her and she forced one back. He seemed so much happier now that Mum was home, and Mum seemed happy too. Maybe their marriage had a future after all. As for her . . .

She wasn't sure about happiness or the future.

Dad glanced at his watch.

"I forgot to tell you," he said. "There should be a Mr. Grainger coming this morning to fix the bathroom door and Dusty's window."

"And the back door," said Mum.

The bell rang.

"That's probably him now," said Dad.

He started toward the door.

"Dad?" said Dusty.

He stopped and turned.

"Yes?"

"If it's anybody for me, I don't want to see them. Same if they ring. I don't want to speak to them."

"Apart from Kamalika and Beam, obviously."

"Especially Kamalika and Beam."

"Are you serious?"

"Yes. I don't want to see them. Or speak to them."

The bell rang again.

"Well, they'll be at school today anyway," said Dad, and he disappeared into the hall. A moment later she heard voices by the front door. She and Mum looked at each other but neither spoke. The front door clicked shut and Dad returned.

"I was wrong," he said. "It was Kamalika and Beam. I didn't ask if they'd got permission to be out of school." He frowned. "Are you sure about this, Dusty? They got the bus from Beckdale and walked all the way up the lane."

"Well, they can go straight back again. You haven't left them on the doorstep, have you?"

"No, I sent them away. Said you were asleep."

"I didn't want you to say that. I wanted you to say I don't want to see them."

"Well, I'm not going to. You can fight your own battles. You always do anyway."

The doorbell rang a second time.

"Same again, Dad," said Dusty as he headed for the hall.

But this time it was Mr. Grainger. Dad took him upstairs to see the damage. Mum drew up a chair next to Dusty and they sat in silence for a few minutes.

"Do you want some tea or anything?" said Mum after a while.

"No, thanks."

Dusty stared out of the window at the sky over Raven's Fell. It was gray and heavy and forbidding.

"Wouldn't be surprised if there's more snow coming," said Mum.

"Yes." Dusty squeezed the arms of her chair. She didn't know what to feel anymore. She just knew she wanted to cry.

"Dusty?" said Mum.

"Yes?"

"I'm not leaving this time, OK? I won't walk out again. Not ever."

Dusty looked around at her.

"I'm glad you came back," she said.

"Honestly?"

"Yes. You're good for him."

"Oh."

Dusty forced another smile.

"You're good for me too. And I was lying about the hair. I quite like it."

"Do you? You don't think I should let the old color grow back?"

Dusty half closed her eyes and in the twilight of her mind saw the picture of the boy's face return.

"It's nice either way, Mum," she said.

"You haven't called me Mum for a long time."

"You haven't been here for a long time."

"True." Mum touched her suddenly on the arm. "Nearly forgot. I found something I think you'll want."

"What?"

"Hang on."

Mum hurried through to the hall but was soon back. She was carrying the snow-pipe.

"Guess where I found this."

"In the boy's duffel-coat pocket. I saw him put it there."

Mum shook her head.

"There was no duffel coat in the lane. Someone must have taken it away. This little thing was lying all by itself in the snow. Must have fallen out."

"How come you saw it?"

"Just did. Anyway, I thought you'd want it."

Dusty took the snow-pipe from her and cradled it in her hand.

"It's warm," she murmured. "Like it was last time."

"Is it?" said Mum. "I didn't notice."

"And look—it glows in my hand."

"Can't see it, darling, but I'm sure you're right."

Dad called from the hall.

"Just a minute, Dusty," said Mum.

She stood up and went out. Dusty raised the snow-pipe and stroked it against her cheek. A ripple of energy ran across her skin. Mum reappeared.

"Mr. Grainger says he's going to do the back door first so we can make the house secure. And he'll have your window fixed by the end of the day. But we'll have to make do with no bathroom door for a bit longer. Is that OK?"

Dusty looked up at her but saw only the boy's face.

"OK," she whispered.

Mum disappeared again. Dusty stood up, the snow-pipe tight in her hand. She could feel heat licking over her again. She made her way up to her room and closed the door behind her.

She pulled open the desk drawer and took out the paper face. It too was warm. She held it up next to the snow-pipe. Both were glowing, even in the daylight. She stared at them.

Was this an illusion? Were all the things she saw and felt an illusion? Mum had noticed nothing strange about the snow-pipe. The bus driver yesterday had not seen the burning light. She thought of the boy's words again.

Something not many people can see. But you can see it.

"What?" she whispered. "What am I seeing?"

She put the paper face and snow-pipe down on the desk. Close by, in the open drawer, Josh's photo looked coolly up at her.

The phone rang.

She let it ring. Mum or Dad could get it. She didn't want to speak to anyone today. She heard Dad call up the stairs.

"Dusty! Can you get that? We're helping Mr. Grainger move the fridge-freezer!"

She ignored him.

"Dusty! The phone!"

She walked into Dad's study as slowly as she dared and closed the door behind her, hoping the ringing would stop. It didn't.

"Dusty!" yelled Dad.

She scowled and picked up the phone.

"Hello?"

"Dusty, it's Angelica!"

She said nothing.

"Dusty? Are you there? It's Angelica."

"I heard you the first time. What do you want?"

"Can I come and see you?"

"No."

"Why not?"

"Because I don't want you to."

She heard an intake of breath at the other end of the line, then, "Dusty?"

"What?"

"I'm really sorry about my stepfather. He's a bastard."

"I couldn't agree more."

"I feel terrible about what happened."

"And do you actually know what happened?" said Dusty. "He tried to kill me. He was going to batter me to death with a spade and then bury me. And now the police say he claims he was only pretending he was going to kill me to make me tell him where the boy was. As if I knew."

"He's a bastard."

"We've already agreed on that."

"Dusty—"

"I really don't want to talk to you. If you want to talk to someone, go and find Loretta Maguire."

"But—"

"Two fantasists together. You've got plenty in common."

"You really hate me, don't you?"

Dusty didn't answer. Angelica took a deep breath.

"Dusty, can you at least tell me what happened? All I know is what I'm hearing around Beckdale. They're saying a crowd of people turned up at your house—"

"Including your bloody stepfather."

"Yes, and that the weird boy was there, and he got away and drove into the lake and . . . well, I don't know any more."

Dusty said nothing. The last thing she wanted to do was to talk to Angelica right now. Yet there was no harm in giving the girl a bit of what she wanted, if only to pay back something of what she owed to Bernadette for her kindness.

"A crowd of people turned up at our house," she said. "They burst in and threatened me and my mum and dad."

"Your mum? I thought—"

"She's come back. Anyway, the boy turned up, people threatened him and he drove off in your stepfather's van. I went with him."

"What! I didn't know that!"

"He took me down the lane by the side of the school, then told me to get out and drove into the lake."

Angelica burst into tears. Dusty listened, unconvinced.

"I can't believe it's ended like this," said Angelica. "I don't know if it's what I wanted to happen. The thing is . . . I told you I was raped . . ."

"You might have mentioned it."

"I can hear you don't believe me."

Dusty remained silent.

"I don't blame you," said Angelica. "I'm not very good at lying and I didn't tell you the whole truth before. You probably picked that up."

Dusty thought of the boy again: the beautiful, radiant boy.

"I'm going to tell you anyway," said Angelica. "You can believe what you want. Then I'll leave you alone."

So beautiful, so radiant.

"It was two years ago," said Angelica. "I was thirteen. Mum and my stepfather were on the verge of splitting up. We came to stay in Beckdale. It was summer, really hot, and we went out on the moor. And they were, like, arguing nonstop. I got fed up and wandered off up the fell. Next thing I knew I was grabbed from behind."

"Really?" Dusty wondered what story Loretta Maguire was spinning up in Millhaven right now. No doubt it was every bit as good as this one. "And then he raped you, did he?"

"You sound so harsh. You frighten me."

"Finish your story."

Angelica hesitated, then went on.

"I was terrified. I don't remember much of what happened. I just remember flashes of things. I remember him pushing me facedown among some bushes, and saying if I looked up or ever said anything to anyone, he'd kill me. And then he . . . he put a coat or something over my head and . . . and did it . . . and then . . ." Angelica paused again, breathing hard. "And then he left me."

"Just one tiny question," said Dusty. "One weeny little quibble. If he came from behind and put a coat over your head, how the hell could you describe and accuse a boy you never even saw?"

"I know it sounds stupid, Dusty, but like I said, I remember flashes of things. And the most powerful image I have—and it's stayed in my mind ever since—is the white hair. I just caught a glimpse of it as he grabbed me, but it was really, really white, bright hair. And everyone's gone on and on about this boy's white hair and stuff. That's the thing they talk about most. And it's the picture that's strongest for me."

Dusty thought back to the boy as he stood there splayed against the van, his clothes ripped away. She thought of what he was, what he wasn't, what he couldn't be.

"Your picture doesn't prove anything," she said.

"Maybe not," said Angelica. "But it's still the thing I remember most. It was all I had, all I could remember. But I said nothing about it. I couldn't speak about it. I felt ashamed, dirty, like I was degraded. I didn't even tell Mum. She could tell I wasn't right but I was too shocked to say what had happened. I even tried to deny it to myself. And it's changed me completely. It's made me wary of people. It's made me tell lies. Then, when I started to hear stories about this white-haired boy committing rape, I became obsessed with the thought that it must be him. I became convinced he was the person who raped me. I made up the bit about being one of Loretta Maguire's friends. That was just . . . I don't know . . . me lying again to get your attention. But I was telling the truth when I said he's kept turning up wherever I go."

"And so you told your stepfather and he went on the rampage?"

"No," said Angelica. "I didn't tell anyone except my mum. And that was only a few weeks ago. She found me crying and pushed me to tell her what was wrong. And I poured out the stuff about the rape. I'm glad I did. I needed to talk about it after all this time. Mum asked me if I wanted to tell the police but I said no. I didn't want anyone except her to know. Then she made a big mistake."

Angelica took a deep breath.

"My stepfather's been trying to get back with her and he keeps turning up. He gets really aggressive and he was in this rage because Mum wouldn't go back with him, and he was really scaring me. And Mum told him to calm down because I was going through a bad time. And he pushed her to say why, and she told him about the rape, thinking it would make him ease off a bit. But he went berserk. He went absolutely mad. I suppose it was guilt because the rape happened when he and Mum were arguing on the fell when they were supposed to be looking after me. But since then he's had this thing about finding the boy who did it and taking revenge."

"I still don't believe you," said Dusty. "If you got raped on the fell two years ago, what the hell are you and your mother doing coming to live here? I'd have thought it's the last place you'd want to be."

"It's so I can confront the place where it happened. I told Mum I really wanted to do it. Only it backfired when we went walking on the fell and saw the boy up on the slope."

From down the lane came the sound of an engine.

Dusty tried to think. It was hard to know what to believe. Angelica had already admitted she told lies, and even if she had been raped, it was clear she didn't yet know the reason why the boy could not possibly be the person responsible.

The sound of the engine grew louder. She peered out of the window and saw a police car pull in. DI Sharp and an unfamiliar officer at the wheel. DI Sharp climbed out alone, stepped up to the front door and rang the bell. There was a sound of footsteps in the hall, then the front door opened.

Angelica spoke again.

"Dusty? Are you still there?"

"Yes," she said absently, listening for voices.

"There's something else."

"Oh?"

"Something I haven't told anybody in the world. Not even Mum."

Voices in the hall now: DI Sharp's voice, Mum's, Dad's.

"The boy had a scar," said Angelica.

Dusty stiffened.

"What did you say?"

"A scar. I only remembered it the other day. I don't know why it's come to me after all this time. But . . . when he grabbed me from behind, I caught a glimpse of his left hand and he had this . . . kind of . . . long scar down the palm. Like a knife wound or something. I only saw it for a second."

Dusty found she was shivering. Her mouth was dry. She couldn't breathe. She heard footsteps on the stairs now, and the voices were louder, though she couldn't catch the words.

"Dusty?" said Angelica. "Please tell me. I must know. You saw the boy close up and I didn't. Did you notice . . . if he had a scar like that?"

The footsteps stopped outside the study. Dusty answered as evenly as she could.

"I did see his hands." She paused. "There was no scar on either of them."

"Definitely?"

"Definitely."

There was a long silence at the other end of the phone. Dusty took a slow breath.

"It wasn't this boy who raped you," she said. "It was someone else. It was . . ." She pictured the scar: so clear in her mind, so familiar. "It was someone else."

She heard Angelica crying again.

"I'm sorry, Angelica," she said.

"It's OK."

"I'm really sorry."

"It's OK."

"Angelica?"

"Yes?"

Dusty hesitated.

"I'll . . . I'll see you," she said.

She hung up and stood there, trembling. The door opened and she saw Mum, Dad and DI Sharp looking in. Their faces were dark and grave. Dad walked slowly up to her and took her hands.

"The divers have found a body underneath the van," he said. "But it's not the boy. It's Josh."

33

TIME MOVED like a mist, and the mist was a wordless spell. Yet words there were, and some part of her took them in: body recognizable from identity bracelet; been in water a good couple of years; heavy chains around waist; rocks in pockets; hands not bound; probable suicide.

Now the questions were back: gentler questions, less probing, but back again even so, and that meant more words. She hardly heard them, even when she spoke herself. No, he hadn't left her a note. No, he hadn't talked to her of suicide. No, she couldn't think of a reason why he would take his own life.

She thought of Josh's last words, the same the boy had used before he drove into the lake. *I'm sorry, little Dusty. Good-bye, little Dusty.* Somehow she'd forgotten about the *sorry*. In the last two years she'd only ever thought about the *good-bye*. Now *sorry* had a new range of possibilities and with it a new set of questions. She didn't suppose there'd ever be any answers.

DI Sharp stood up.

"I won't detain you any longer," she said. "I know this is a deeply distressing piece of news for you and I'm really sorry to have had to bring it, especially on top of everything else that's happened."

She hesitated.

"I'm sorry to mention this too, but we'll have to ask one of you at some point to come and officially confirm identification. I don't mean you have to see the body itself. We just want you to check over the things we've found."

"You mean there's some doubt as to who it is?" said Mum.

"No, madam," said DI Sharp. "I'm afraid there's no doubt at all.

We're quite clear that this is Josh's body. But as a formality we must also ask you to confirm that the possessions we've found are his. There's not just the identity bracelet. There's a front-door key, a flick knife and some other small things. I'm sorry to have to ask you."

"It's OK," said Dad. "I'll come with you now."

"It doesn't have to be now, sir. Not if you don't want."

"No, let's get it over with."

"I'll come too," said Mum.

Dusty saw all three look in her direction. She thought of Josh— his face, his hair, his eyes. She thought of the figure at the end of the jetty, forcing the rocks into his pockets, wrapping the chains around his body, then falling, sinking, drowning.

"When?" she murmured.

"When what, Dusty?" said Mum.

"When did he do it? At night when no one could see him? He must have done it at night. Someone might have spotted him during the day."

"You're talking about Josh?" said DI Sharp.

"Of course I'm talking about Josh," she snapped. "Who did you think I was talking about?"

"Easy, Dusty," said Dad.

"It's all right," said DI Sharp. "I know this is a bad time." She looked at Dusty. "We're probably never going to know when Josh did it. Or why. But if it was suicide, then I suspect he'd have done it at night."

Dusty felt a shudder pass through her.

"He'd have drowned before his body reached the bottom. It's so deep there."

"Maybe, Dusty," said Mum. "We're not going to know."

There was an awkward silence.

"Well," said Dad eventually. "Let's go and sort out the identification."

"Are you sure you still want to do this?" said DI Sharp.

"Yes."

"Me too," said Mum.

Again they all looked at Dusty. She shook her head.

"I'm staying here."

"Will you be OK?" said Mum. "You look really pale."

"I'm all right."

"Dusty—"

"I'm all right. Stop worrying about me. Go and sort out the iden-tification. Only can you get rid of Mr. Grainger? He can do all that stuff another time."

"Sure," said Dad. "I was going to ask him to go anyway. But, Dusty, listen—your mum's right. You do look really pale."

"Can you just go?" said Dusty. "I told you. I'm all right."

Dad studied her for a few moments, then slowly stood up.

"Well, if you're absolutely sure." He glanced at DI Sharp. "I'll just go and get my car keys."

"No need, sir," she said. "We'll take you there and bring you back."

"That's very kind of you. Thanks."

Five minutes later Dusty had the house to herself, and the pain she'd been holding inside ripped through her. She didn't make it to the bathroom. She'd barely reached the foot of the stairs before she was vomiting into the wastepaper bin. She moaned with rage, choking and retching, hating Josh, hating herself. As the vomiting stopped, the tears started.

She straightened up, dizzy with anger and a terrifying new kind of loss. She tried to calm herself but it was no good. She was shaking so badly she could hardly stand. She had to do something, had to get a grip. She turned from the messy bin and staggered, still crying, up to her room.

It seemed an alien place, as alien as Josh now was. She slumped down at the desk, thrust her face in her hands and went on crying. It was some time before the tears stopped. When they did, she realized there was something inside her that had never been there before.

A deep, empty space.

She tried to put Josh back into it but he wouldn't go. All that would go was a feeling of disgust. She despised herself now, even more than she despised Josh. Dad was right: she'd been turning into her brother all this time. But she'd been blind. She'd been worshipping an illusion.

She pictured the lake again: the deep, silent water. Perhaps Josh's guilt was worth such a price, perhaps not. She didn't know. She only knew that she felt utterly alone. Josh and the boy were gone and their mysteries had faded with them. All she had left was the biggest mystery of all, and she knew she would never solve that.

She stared down at the desk. The paper face and the snow-pipe were still there. So too was Josh's photograph in the open drawer. She pulled it out, stared at it for a moment, then slowly tore it up and dropped the pieces to the floor. She picked up the snow-pipe, took the paper face and, without knowing why, wrapped it gently around the instrument. The little parcel glowed like a bulb. She rested it against her forehead and felt the warmth seep through her.

"I love you," she whispered.

She didn't know who she was speaking to.

She heard a sound out in the lane and stared toward the window. Something was moving against the gleam of the snow. She could see it through a gap in the boarding. She slipped the parcel into her pocket, stood up and peered out. A figure was standing there, looking up at the house.

Silas.

She hurried out of her room and set off down the stairs, then stopped, trembling. Some words were moving in her head, something the boy had said. *This dream has gone on long enough.* She looked around her.

"Yes," she murmured. "It has."

She walked on, slowly now, taking in everything she saw, everything she felt from these old, familiar things. She could feel heat around her again, and that strange lightness of body she'd felt in Mr. Finch's lesson. She put on her coat and boots, and stepped out of the front door.

Silas was still standing in the lane. He looked more ancient than she had ever seen him, like a creature who had died and come back just to speak to her. She walked out through the snow and stood before him. He looked at her with his squinty eyes.

"What's up, Silas?" she said.

"Ain't right," he muttered.

"What ain't right?"

He eyed her warily.

"You mockin' me?"

"No, Silas. I'm not mocking you. I wouldn't do that. What's not right?"

He went on watching her closely, as though to reassure himself.

"What's not right?" she said.

"Footsteps," he said eventually.

"What footsteps?"

"In the snow. Comin' out the lake."

She felt the warmth against her leg from the snow-pipe wrapped inside the paper face. She reached down and touched the bulge in her pocket.

"Comin' out the lake," he went on. "Ain't natural."

"Where?"

"Eh?"

"Where are the footprints?"

"Down by the old charcoal burner's cottage. Seen 'em myself. They comes straight out the lake and goes on past the tarn and up Raven's Fell."

She frowned. That was some way from where the police had been looking. But then they wouldn't have thought of searching for the boy so far from the spot where the van went down.

She turned and stared over Stonewell Park. Kilbury Moor was a brilliant white but the peak of Raven's Fell glistened with a fierce, radiant light. She turned back to Silas.

"What made you come and tell me this?"

The old man shrugged.

"Don't know. Just thought . . . it's strange, like. And I don't like them police."

"So you thought I could tell them for you? About the footprints?"

"Don't know."

"I'm glad you told me, Silas."

She set off toward Stonewell Park. Silas called after her.

"Where you goin'?"

"Doesn't matter. I'll see you, Silas."

He didn't call out again. She glanced over her shoulder and saw him still standing there, but he was already slipping from her mind. Now at last she understood. There was hope after all. Josh might be gone but the boy was not. Somehow he was still here, and he was calling to her. His mystery was opening up again, and the big mystery—maybe that was opening up too.

She walked on through the snow, her thoughts deep within, her eyes on the burning peak of Raven's Fell. She squeezed through the fence into Stonewell Park, cut across it to the bridleway and on past Silas's hovel toward the distant lake. It was glowing in the afternoon sun. To her right, the moor sprawled away in brilliant light.

She was starting to feel better, even joyous. She'd been turning into Josh but now she would turn into the boy. It was already happening. He'd said as much himself.

You're seeing and feeling what I see and feel.

There's no separation now.

Everything was light; everything was brilliant light. Even she was brilliant light. Her steps barely touched the ground. Sometimes she left prints in the snow, sometimes she didn't. She moved on—walked, floated, she didn't know what—and somehow the moor slipped past, the lake drew near, the fell grew brighter, deeper, hotter.

Snow was falling again in light, glittering flakes that dissolved on her face like warm dust. She touched the little package in her pocket, felt its warmth, its glow. The lake appeared before her. She didn't know how long it had taken her to get here. It should have taken hours. It seemed to have taken only a thought.

Time had stopped again. It was hard to tell if it was day or night. The light was fading and growing, fading and growing. Snow was still falling but she sensed a blizzard hanging in the sky. She ghosted on around the lake, locked in her mind and in her complete abandonment.

Here was the charcoal burner's cottage. Here, as Silas had said, were the footprints issuing from the lake. She bent over them. They were clear to see, though if the blizzard came, they would soon be covered up. There was no time to waste. She had to find the boy. She would find the boy.

She started to climb, her eyes on the prints as they led her away from the lake. They took her past the tarn and on up the path that Mac's dog had taken toward the figure it had seen on the fell. There was no figure there now, only more tracks climbing on toward the peak. She followed them, her hand tight against the warm package in her pocket.

More changes in the light. A darkening of the sky, a brightening of the snow, and now more heat: deep, powerful, throbbing heat rippling through the air, the ground, the snow, and her. She was burning with light now, just as the boy had burned, just as his footsteps in the snow still burned; and on they went, up, up toward the peak.

She thought of Josh again. He too was burning, or the image of him was burning. Tears filled her eyes again. She moved on up the slope, following the prints. Josh was gone but the boy was still here. He had said he couldn't die. He had to be here. He had to be waiting for her just up the slope. He had called to her through Silas and he was waiting up the slope.

She moved on across the smoldering snow, the prints still clear before her, and gradually she drew closer to the summit. Below her, the white expanse of Kilbury Moor stretched like a simmering cloud to the shore of Mirkwell Lake. She stared beyond it to the little town. It too glowed and burned in the pulsing light.

She carried on, her eyes on the footprints, her mind on the boy. She knew he was close. She could sense him in every breath.

"There's no separation," she murmured. "No separation."

And then the footprints stopped.

She stopped too and looked about her. She had reached the summit and there was no more fell to climb—and no boy. She bent down over the ground, trying to deny what she knew to be true. But there was no mistaking this. The prints did what they had done before the gate at Stonewell Park.

They faded into nothing.

She straightened up and looked about her, searching for some sign that they started again somewhere else, but she knew it was fruitless. The hope that had flickered inside her died again. She looked up into the sky.

"No," she whispered. "Please no."

All she saw was snow falling as before, its hot flakes scalding her skin.

"Please no," she said.

She lay down in the snow, turned on her back and stared up at the sky. Somehow she had known it would come to this. She had pretended otherwise, told herself he would be here, but that too was part of the dream. That too had to end.

Now the blizzard came, blinding all thought, all feeling, all self. She welcomed it. There was nothing left now, just the great mystery that she would never solve. She stretched out her arms, opened her mouth, gulped in the snow. Here was the light, the deep, scorching light that burned through her in the blazing snow.

"It's all one," she heard herself say.

She was speaking the boy's words now, as though she had none of her own left. She didn't know what they meant but it didn't seem to matter. She was being erased at last. She was neither a memory nor a vision, for there was neither a past to remember nor a future to imagine. There was only this, and she was all of it.

"One," she murmured.

The snow went on falling, hour after hour, in a bright, endless torrent. She lay back and let it settle upon her, burying her body, burning her dream. Everything was fading now, slipping back into the glistening source—and Dusty was gone, Dusty was no more. Whoever or whatever Dusty had been, she was not there. She had become a world, a universe, a white, lustrous infinity. From somewhere in that infinity came the sound of a voice.

"There!"

And another.

"Hurry!"

Shouts of panic, shouts of pain. Figures stumbling through the snow, panting, gasping, racing across the summit of the fell.

"Dusty!" called one.

Faces peering down, hands reaching out, then a new voice.

"Dad?"

"Dusty! You're alive!"

"Mum?"

"It's me, darling. It's me."

More faces, more voices. Too many, far too many, and all this snow. Why didn't someone bring an umbrella?

"Silas told us where you'd gone," said Dad. "It's going to be all right."

The blizzard was easing but the snow continued to fall. She was so cold now, so terribly, achingly cold, and she was frightened. More words flashed into her mind.

I'm going where you can't follow.

She started to cry.

"It's all right, Dusty," said Mum. "We're going to get you home. There's lots of us here and we've got a stretcher."

She stared up at them: Mum, Dad, Silas, and other faces. She was sure she knew them all but they seemed somehow distorted in the snow. She closed her eyes and let them ease her onto the stretcher. She felt a hand take hers, then heard a voice.

"What's this?"

She opened her eyes and saw Dad holding a crumpled piece of paper.

"You were holding this," he said. "You had it tight inside your fist. Is it important?"

He slowly unwrapped it.

"Just a blank piece of paper," he said. "Shall I throw it away?"

"No!"

She snatched the paper from him and stared at it. She recognized it at once from the creases: the paper on which she'd drawn the face. But no face was there now. The snow had washed it off. It was as blank as the police photo of the boy. She dropped it to the ground and clutched at her pocket.

"It's all right," said Mum. "Here."

She held out the snow-pipe.

"It was lying next to you."

Dusty took it from her and held it tight.

They lifted up the stretcher.

She stared up at the falling snow, then around at the faces peering down at her. Mum's and Dad's seemed so different now after all that had happened. The mystery still weighed upon her and she sensed that it always would. But perhaps . . .

She looked at Mum and Dad.

Perhaps she could be happy again. Dad reached out and touched her face.

"Are you ready now, sweetheart?" he said.

She squeezed the snow-pipe and held it close.

"Yes," she said. "I'm ready to go home."